SUBURBAN LEGEND

Christopher Veltri

I0658450

Ink Smith Publishing
www.ink-smith.com

Formatted by V.J.O. Gardner
Cover Design by Dhiaulhaq Teniro Nikite

Printed in the U.S.A

The final approval for this literary material is granted by the author.

ISBN: 978-1-947578-24-1

Ink Smith Publishing
P.O. Box 391
Lakehurst, NJ 08733

Chapter I

Slumber Party

It was an accident. Things got out of hand and a little fun turned fatal real fast. But every accident starts with a plan. And the plan was this, four young girls dabbling in a little black magic, just some hocus pocus, to see if they could summon a demon for a dark deal.

The girls gathered on the white shag rug under the slow burn of candles held steady in the windless bedroom. The air around them had the sharp stench of industrial strength disinfectant blending with an artificial soapy, rose petal odor.

None of them, Amanda, Shannon, Colleen, or especially the gullible Beth Gardner, had done anything quite like this before. Cold sweat perspired down their soft white skin as three of them knelt on carefully folded beach towels on three sides of the bed. Shannon, seated at the foot, kept making furtive glances at the other two, looking for a reaction or sign that they were freaking out on the inside just as much as she was. Colleen's expression showed her head was empty, as usual, but she seemed ready and willing from her post. Amanda, on the other hand, gazed at Beth like a cat ready to pounce, just waiting for a moment of weakness.

Beth, as intended, wasn't really in on the joke. For her, this was like a higher calling. Three popular girls from school invited her over for a sleepover and then an attempt at a séance? Ohhh, it was just like all those things she thought nice, popular girls do as sleepovers. Things like tell secrets, talk about boys, even try to communicate with the dead while over dramatizing a little fear, but bravely knowing that they would come out with good laughs and memories. Yes, she was eager to participate and had no hesitation with the sudden proposal. Why would she? Could three teenage girls be all that dangerous?

Shannon fixed her attention on Amanda. Her eyes moved slowly up and down, scanning Amanda's body from the thick, curly blonde hair down to the pink fingernails clasped about her kneecaps, back up to her deep sea blue eyes under thick lashes, and back down to the wormed, rotten book in front of her on the floor. Just a few days ago, this all seemed like a good idea. It seemed like an innocent joke to be remembered for years.

****

Earlier that week, the three girls sat in the Wilhelmina High school cafeteria catching up after a summer away from each other. The lunchroom rang with the cheers and laughs of adolescents still on a high from a summer that had just slipped from their fingers.

"Summer camp was mostly the same old schlock," said Shannon Kennedy. She was a tall girl with straight black hair and a pale complexion. The contrast between her skin tone and dark eyes made them appear almost purple if the lighting was right. "I've been going to that lake for years, so it starts to get old. But, I made it exciting when I could."

"Like how?" asked Colleen. "Any fiddling around behind Mikey's back?" Unlike Shannon's practically cold features, Colleen Simpson had tanned skin with wavy blonde hair and a face that was a little rough around the edges, but pretty nonetheless.

"Like sneaking around the camp at night to meet with other counselors for some more grown-up fun and occasionally making some noises out in the woods to scare the kids when spirits were high. Ya know, tradition," said Shannon coolly. "Mikey and I have an open agreement in some ways. Besides, I think I am going to cut things off with him soon...but you didn't hear that from me." She bowed her head down at this and avoided eye contact.

Colleen perked up with interest. "Really? That would just tear his heart to pieces. The way that boy looks at you, you can tell his feelings run deep, so unlike the other guys." She finished with a far-off gaze.

Shannon wanted to change the subject. "How was Germany, Amanda?" she asked.

"Well, I wasn't in Germany the whole summer," started Amanda. "Only about a month." Amanda Klein was beautiful, rich and blonde. Genetic lottery inheritance that she accepted with ease and grace. "I was stuck to that one small mountain town that my family is from which was so boring. The food was great and walking around the town looked like something from a story book, but damn my mother for guilting me at every corner to be at the house with Oma. 'Ohhh, you know you are her favorite, you know she saw so

4

much of herself in you, why can't you just spend a little time with your grandmother and do her a favor for once?'" Amanda mocked her mother's voice and swayed her hand back and forth in front of her face. The other two girls laughed at the show. "Yes, she was dying and yes I was in the will, but this was the first time I went out there. I wanted to explore!"

"So you grandmother did die? I'm sorry," said Shannon.

"Don't be, I am better off for it," said Amanda with nearly no sign of remorse. "And that is what I am getting to. So, after she died, a lot of the family was just going around the house collecting things that they claimed were 'theirs' but they wouldn't let me get any of it! So, I went snooping around in the basement that they were ignoring. Hell, I would too, damn thing was full of old boxes, trunks and wardrobes but I didn't really have anywhere else to look."

"Eww!" said Colleen. "You went in the cobwebs and dust just to look around? Please, I would rather date a slimy trucker!"

"Nah, no way!" said Amanda, honestly pleading. "It was…tidy, not a whole lot of light, but manageable. It was like a big closet or something that just kept going. Anyway, so I see this white dresser behind the furnace, and I mean white white, like alabaster. It was like the light came off the surface and surrounded it, you know like how metal looks when it gets really hot."

"What's abalaster?" said Colleen with her hand raised to halt the story.

"Alabaster," chimed in Shannon, "is a stone, very white. Egyptians used it for sculptures."

Amanda raised her eyebrows, pinched her lips and nodded at Shannon. "Very nice, Miss Kennedy. You've done your homework."

Shannon returned the expression and said, "You expected any less?"

"Where was I?" Amanda continued. "Oh yeah, the dresser. So, I start opening the drawers and let me tell you, good ol' Oma may be dead but her taste lives on. I got these wonderful satin gloves, one of those old timey cigarette holders for refined ladies, and this slick little red dress that squeezes my hips oh so sweet…"

"Reaaallly?" said Colleen all doe eyed, concerned more about the fashion than the rest of the story.

"A dress?" said Shannon skeptically.

"What? You won't say that when I show you later. Anyway, I took a few other hand-me-downs, but I found this wrapped in the dress..." Amanda took a tie-dyed pull string bag out of her genuine leather backpack. She pulled the strings and delicately slid a small brown-red book out onto the cafeteria table. It looked like a big diary. It even had a few old locks that were no more than knotted bindings to keep it from falling open. Colleen squinted at it unimpressed. Shannon put her arms under the table and leaned in until her nose was an inch from the book.

She could smell it, oaky and rough, like a pipe smoking traveler or abandoned saw mill. "Well, what is it?" she said without looking up from the book.

Amanda beamed at her compatriot; this was clearly the part she wanted to get to, the crest of her story. "I have no freakin' idea!" She wore a massive grin as she looked back and forth between Shannon and Colleen. Shannon let out a sigh like she heard the punch line to a juvenile joke so worn out it would cause banishment in some circles. "But just look at the inside!" said Amanda as she moved to open it.

For how old the book appeared to be, it responded in a flexible manner when

Amanda started to open it. The strings on the three locks came undone effortlessly and she opened it at random with ease. Shannon's face was still close to the table when the pages spread and thick air burst from the book right into her nose and down into her lungs. She coughed it back and a flowery, colorful taste coated her throat and tongue. Blood seemed to drain out of her upper body and her vision swam in the brightly lit cafeteria. And just as quickly as it came, it was gone. She blinked her eyes and was back on point.

Holding the book like jewelry on display with a smile, Amanda turned to Shannon. "Did you get that…that thing when you smelled it?"

"I got something," said Shannon as she smacked her tongue and blinked a few more times. "But it's gone now." Shannon moved in closer to look at the book. She saw exquisite handwriting as if the scribe took great care to draw each letter. The words popped sharply off the page. Shannon squinted her eyes at the calligraphy and wrinkled her nose.

"German? Who knows how to read this shit?" said Shannon a little defeated.

"Whoa now, velvet petunia. Don't jump to conclusions. I can read it. Or I will be able to read it...some of it. I have probably a thousand German to English dictionaries at my house. All I have to do is take it step by step and then away we go!"

Shannon slowly turned pages. She found that it looked at times like a cookbook with lists and numbers and other times like a book of poetry with lyrics that took up a tiny space on the page.

"Step by step," Shannon snorted. "Yeah more like baby steps. It's your funeral...oops, I mean...I'm sorry about your Oma." She paused for a moment and then asked, "But why all the fuss? Is it important to your family or something?"

Amanda's eyes were half lidded and she held a drunken smile. She took the book back from Shannon and flipped to a page that she had flagged with a pink post-it note. She spun it around to face Shannon again and slapped her finger on one word that she had underlined in red pencil. She tapped it a few times and then said in a low voice so unlike her usual rude, bubblegum tone. "Anybody wanna put a demon inside Beth Gardner?"

"Get the hell outta here," said Shannon as she finally leaned up from the table shaking her head.

"Do what now to Cabbage Patch?" Colleen asked. She'd quit paying attention when the talk stopped being about the dress. "That girl is pathetic. Oh my god, she tries to be our friend all the time. Doesn't she know that we come from different worlds? We are the chosen few born to be in the sun, she's better off underground."

"That's a 'yes'," declared Amanda.

"How do you know that's what these words mean? And how do you know it will work?" said Shannon. She teased on skepticism but couldn't hold back obvious excitement.

"Ok, one I triple-checked it in different dictionaries. And two, just look at this thing! That alone makes it worth a try."

Shannon couldn't help but smile as she swayed her head slowly at Amanda. "How are we gonna do this?"

Amanda let out a high pitched 'YOW' and slapped the table nearly ecstatic. "Colleen, why don't you go make friends with Beth and see if she wants to come to my house Friday night? No one will be there. My parents are out of town, again."

Colleen looked across the cafeteria with her face squinted in disgust. "Friends?

Come on Amanda, she's so clingy and desperate," she said.

"Look, we need to do this in private. Afterwards we can just ignore her like we usually do. Hell, if we weird her out with this shit, she may just stay away. Come on, it'll be fuu-un!"

"Ok, fine. But if she starts hanging around me I am going to steer her in your direction. Yeah, you're gonna need witness protection or some shit." She got up and fixed her clothes and hair in a rehearsed fashion. "Well, lunch is about over so I will just go on to 7th period. Ladies, wish me luck."

Amanda, Shannon and about half of the guys in the room watched her walk across to the table where Beth sat with a few band member friends.

"Amanda," Shannon said. "This feels so mean."

"Oh, it's bad!"

"Evil!"

"Wicked!"

They covered their laughter and Shannon gazed deeply at Amanda, so happy to see her again. "Oh Amanda," she said. "I just love you sometimes."

"And don't I know it."

****

Amanda opened the book and took out a few sheets of paper. "Wait, I thought you had to read from the book?" said Beth. She was all too ready and willing to participate in this, she didn't even say anything when they tied her hands and legs to the corners of the bed. To her this was a game, child's play.

"That's right Beth, I am going to read from the book. These are just some cheat sheets to help me with the pronunciation, okay?" said Amanda. She turned the pages around to show the other girls. It was dark, but they could just make out that she had written down large words that were separated into groups of two to four letters. Literally baby steps, Shannon thought.

She started to read slowly but in control. With some words she held onto syllables or cut herself off to get ready for the next word, like checking footing while climbing a rock face. Maybe she practiced it, she seems to be really gung-ho about this, Shannon thought. But if she practiced it she would know if it worked, so why are we here? She was beginning to feel foolish about the whole thing. She looked around the room in the firelight and thought that it all seemed too imaginative to be real—

tacky even. Candles and rituals? Even though she couldn't see their faces, Shannon still hoped that her friends did not see her shamefully blushing. And then the flames flickered without any wind and a slow sound started to come out of Beth Gardner.

Beth breathed heavily and it sounded like there was mucus caught in her throat. She coughed a little and said, "Whoa guys, I feel a little funny." She stopped, gulped something down and took deep breaths in and out. Her chest looked to be heaving in large swells like someone was inflating and deflating it with a pump that wasn't Beth. "Ok, stop. I feel sick! I think I am gonna be sick! What are you doing? Stop!"

Amanda kept reading, ignoring Beth. Instead, she raised her left hand over a candle on the nightstand and held her palm down just inches above the flame. If Amanda was continuing, then they all were. Beth, wide eyed and frightened, looked around the bed at each of the girls responsible for her current situation and pulled at the ropes that bound her. "Guys, this isn't funny! I'm..." She was interrupted by vomit that seemed to surprise even her. Colleen burst into loud, callous laughs at Beth's puke covered face. Beth seemed to cough it up rather than heave it. Again, like something other than her body pushed it out.

Shannon felt a little guilt crawl up from deep inside her. She had known it was there when they hatched this plan, but didn't think it would grow, didn't think it would become anything. She looked to Amanda and they locked eyes for only a moment, muted and direct. Shannon knew in her mind that Amanda could not stop reading, or rather, would not stop reading until she finished. Shannon turned to Colleen and said, "Come on, quit laughing and clean her face off."

Colleen choked her laughter and turned to answer, "Are you serious? This is great!" Still no wind, but the flames danced on.

Shannon looked at her and felt something inside her extend out and press itself firmly on Colleen's forehead. "Do it," she said.

Colleen gave a small pout, but did as she was told. She got up, grabbed the towel she was kneeling on and leaned over the bed to wipe Beth's face off. Beth was audibly sobbing and the heavy breathing had not concealed it at all.

14

"Oh, what's the matter Cabbage Patch?" Colleen said as if she were consoling a toddler. "Are we scaring you? Is this what you hoped being friends with us was like? Why don't you...Wow! We've got ourselves a bleeder! Hey girls, I think we scared this one right into her period!" Colleen couldn't stop herself from letting out more vicious laughter. "What's the matter, mommy never taught you how to use a tampon?"

Amanda and Shannon looked at Beth and could see a dark stain quickly spreading through her pants. "What? No! It isn't time! Not yet! What are you doing to me? Please guys...stoooop!" called Beth through confused tears.

Shannon wanted to stop. This was a little too much, felt a little too real and the joke was not funny anymore. But she stayed frozen on her knees at the foot of the bed. It started with a whisper and then growing into hushed words in her mind Shannon heard what she swore was Amanda's voice. No no no, not yet. We must finish. We pull this off and we are set for life!

"Why are you doing this?" cried Beth in a low guttural voice. The firelight danced merrily and then, with a pop, spit larger flames inches above the wick. Amanda's hand held still through the fire and all three girls froze at what they saw next. "I just wanted to be friends!" Beth's voice changed slightly, more stretched out, farther away, through tears slowly trickling. "Is this how you fucking treat people that just want to be friends?"

Her body no longer seemed to be heaving uncontrollably, instead a sound like marbles swirling around a drain issued out of her throat. She pulled at the ropes that bound her to the bedposts and the frame creaked with her movements. For a moment, there were only the sounds of her breathing and then Amanda continued to read from the book. Shannon couldn't tell if she was still reading the same passage or had started a new one.

Beth's body began to flex and stretch as if waking up from a long nap. "Mmmmm, this body is young and strong and oh so delectable." Her voice came out stretched with metallic piping in a reverse flow like she spoke while breathing in. She moved her hips up and down as if grinding an invisible partner slowly, sensually.

Colleen coughed out a choked and strained, "What the hell?"

Amanda stopped reading from the book and looked up directly at Beth. Even amidst this surprise turn of events, her voice was calm. A twinge of reluctance, but bold still. "Do you know why we've called you here?"

"Oh darling," said Beth's body. "You know what you did. And don't worry, you will have your part of the bargain. Now, how about you give me some food before I eat myself!" the girl's body spat. It looked right at Shannon at the foot of the bed and Shannon saw its eyes, cloudy, void of pupils.

Colleen was a statue with her arms held in midair and her hair dangling into her mouth. Shannon aimlessly bobbled her head like it was strung up from above her and losing support. "What did you do?" she could barely force out. "What did we do?"

"Who said that?" growled Beth's body. "What cock-fearing, Jesus-loving virgin said that?" She thrashed her body, still bound, around to stare at each of their faces.

"Virgin?" asked Amanda as she slowly turned to Shannon.

Beth's body laughed with that unsettling inward motion. "I can smell it, even under that soap and perfume cloaked body. Virgin blood! Tell 'em, Shannon. Tell 'em how none of those boys push your buttons like you think they should. How it all looks so easy and thoughtless for the other girls. Always thinking about the other girls!"

Whatever was in Beth was getting violent. The bed groaned, lurching this way and that as the-thing-that-was-Beth-Gardner raged. Beth's left foot broke the post and held it dangling from the rope on her ankle. Colleen, frantic, tried to reach for it but was not fast enough as Beth's leg bent unnaturally at the knee and kicked her flat in the face. She fell back, nose visibly broken, and laid still, blood pouring from her nostrils.

The sounds of bones cracking and moving came from Beth's body. In the shadows of the now crazed firelight, Shannon saw the joints twist and the face stretch. "Do something! Do something now!" Shannon yelled at Amanda. Amanda, almost as if she knew before Shannon shouted at her, flipped to a page in the book marked by a post-it note.

"I'm gonna drink that blood, baby girl. I'm gonna get me some of that virgin blood!" Beth taunted as her eyes started to radiate a low but sickening purple glow.

Shannon felt her body shaking and in an adrenaline fueled focus her vision pulled back to take in the whole scene; Colleen unconsciously bleeding from her face to the right, Amanda running her finger down a page muttering to herself and Beth's body right in front of her breaking free from the pitiful restraints they had giddily tied not an hour before.

Beth let out a war cry and snapped the post on the right foot. "Yeah! It's time!" In a fluid motion, she lifted her two free legs back behind her head and quick as lightning snapped them forward, catapulting her body forward and breaking her hands free. Face to face with Shannon, she spread her lips apart to show rows of jagged fangs, too big for her human mouth. As they elongated, the teeth pierced through skin, ripping Beth's cheeks in the process. Blood and bile drooled out of her mangled face.

"I dare you!" called out Amanda. All of Shannon's insides felt like they slipped out of her body. She could not believe Amanda was egging this creature on.

But she wasn't. Beth eased her body and attention towards Amanda and said, "You dare a demon?"

"Yes." Amanda gulped. "I dare to dare a demon."

"Do you know what it means to dare a demon, child?"

"Uh," she gave a quick glance to Shannon. "Yes, and I still dare you, demon." She sounded unsure and her eyebrows arched up as she finished the sentence as if to ask 'am I doing it right?'.

"Ohhhh," said Beth's body. "Ohhhh, yes, even better." It laid back down on the bed as if to rest. But it did not rest. It laughed in that terrible, inward-rewind laugh and with each unnerving chortle the flames from the candles were pulled from their wicks and circled around her. Both the laughter and fire built in a concentrated area around Beth's body until it went up in a blaze while the body crumbled from within, laughing the whole time. Then, as soon as it started it was over, the fire went out and the laughter stopped. For a moment, Shannon heard her breath in the darkness and nothing else. But the silence was broken by a luminescence just above Beth's body. It was a blue white at first that flickered like a film reel. It sounded like wood splintering and hammering, and the colors changed and filled the room with sinister oranges and purples. Shannon went to scream, but felt her consciousness fade to black.

****

Shannon blinked her eyes open and into focus to the sound of a dog barking. Had she fallen asleep? What time was it? Was that all a dream? Those questions were answered when she breathed in through her nostrils and the smell hit her. That putrid, choking smell. There it was, still on the bed. Beth's body, charred beyond recognition, crumpled in on itself like an expired spider. Despite the fire that had engulfed it, the bed was left untouched. It had ashes and some contact burns, sure, but by and large it looked like the body had burned elsewhere and was then transplanted after the fact.

Amanda was on her nightstand phone with her back to Shannon. The conversation couldn't be heard over the dog barking, so Shannon went to the bedroom door to see the dog. She needed that touch right now to bring her back from pieces. It was all far too unreal and a few wet pooch kisses could help. She opened the door to find Brinley, the Klein family dog, in a tizzy similar to Shannon's nerves. Brinley nosed her hand and let out a sympathetic whimper. To this, Shannon fell down to his level and let him lick her face while she just rubbed his thick Saint Bernard coat anticipating the tears to break through the shock.

"You know he drinks out of the toilet, right?" asked Amanda from behind her.

"I don't care right now," answered Shannon. "Jesus Christ, what happened in here?"

"Spontaneous combustion," said Amanda plainly.

Shannon turned her head from the dog and looked back at her friend. "What?" she said.

"Spontaneous combustion. That's what we'll tell them all. It's a freak accident but it happens here and there and when it does it looks like...well..." Amanda glanced back at the bed and sighed before returning Shannon's stare.

"You're going to lie?" said Shannon.

"Well, which do you think is more believable? At least this way we won't get tossed in the loony bin to boot. Hell, with your family history and all..."

Shannon began to lose her temper. "Shut up! You don't know what you're talking about. Dammit, how can you be so calm right now? She's dead!"

"Prozac. Colleen's got the bottle if you want some," said Amanda. Shannon looked around the room for Colleen but only saw a blood stain on the floor from her broken nose and the light from beneath the bathroom door showed someone was in there. "Look, it will all be alright. It's a tragedy, I get it, but we have to hold ourselves together." She grabbed Shannon's shoulders and held her with magnetic eye contact. "If they think even for a moment that we actually had a hand in this, we're toast. Goners. Murderers locked away for life. I'm sorry, Shannon, I am so sorry. I love ya and I wouldn't do this to you on purpose."

Before Shannon could say anything, Amanda leaned in and kissed her lips softly, confidently. In that moment, everything else seemed to mute for Shannon Kennedy as if time held its breath. Then, Colleen came back into the room and it all washed away as Amanda's arms slid from her sides.

"Hoooo, shit," said Colleen with tissues jammed up her nose. "This is bad. This is really bad." The other two girls

23

looked at her with wide eyes. "My nose! Just look at my nose!"

Amanda rolled her eyes at Shannon before she said, "The police are on their way. They know there was an accident. Daddy always said its best that the police are informed as soon as possible so as not to raise suspicion. Colleen, what happened here?"

"Spontaneous congestion," answered Colleen with a snap of her fingers.

"No," said Amanda flatly.

"Uh, uh, don't tell me," said Colleen with more finger snaps. After a moment or two, a light came to her eyes and she said, "Combustion. Spontaneous combustion. Ha, got it!" She smacked her forehead to mock herself, but then recoiled at the pain in her nose. "Ohhhh, shit, nose."

Shannon would rather be anywhere other than that room and started to make her way out. She rubbed behind Brinley's ears for him to follow, but he didn't move at first. Instead, he shuffled a little where he stood, looked at Shannon in the hallway, then back to the room, then back to Shannon with another whimper. "Come on, boy, let's go downstairs for a while." Still nothing. He looked as if he wanted to herd

24

them all downstairs, but would not step past the bedroom door.

"Go, Brinley, we'll be down soon," ordered Amanda. Brinley let out a low growl like he was thinking, gave a quick, gruff bark and turned to lead Shannon downstairs posthaste. Shannon followed through the halls, past the doors and down the steps to the large family room where Brinley waited for her, panting on one of the large white sofas. She cuddled up next to him and didn't fight it when her mind went blank. The only thing she focused on was petting that dog again and again. The other two didn't join them immediately. It wasn't until right before the police knocked on the door that Amanda and Colleen descended the steps.

The police wasted no time in questioning the girls. Shannon could hear herself talking, but watched the whole thing from behind her shoulder. Words came out with an uncomfortable lack of emotion. "We were there, in the room. She was there, Beth. And then, there was a fire. She was the fire, no, she was on fire, and then she said, I said..." Her voice trembled and the officer closed his notepad.

"Look," he said in a calming tone. "Maybe that's enough for now. We can pick this up later." Shannon looked to the other girls. Colleen used her hands to tell the story and made sure to say 'spontaneous combustion' in between every sentence. Amanda had her back turned to her so she couldn't see or hear her, but, was she playing with her hair? Was the officer laughing?

Before she could figure out more, the bomb dropped. Two men in special one-piece suits carried Beth's body down the stairs and out the front door. "I tell ya, never in my life…" she heard one of them say. The half a dozen or so officers talking to the girls and standing around looked at each other motioning that this might be a good time to go.

"Listen," said Shannon's interviewer. "You girls should get outta here. Some of these guys have a lotta work left to do and you don't want to be around for all of that, especially after what you just went through. Do you have anywhere you can go? We can take you."

"My guest house out back," said Amanda. "There's nothing going on there and we'll be safe with you officers here for the night."

"No, we mean somewhere else, away from here," replied the officer.

"My guest house will be fine," said Amanda.

"No, you don't understand..." began the officer. He was cut off by a short whistle by an older officer in plain clothes leaned against the wall. The older officer motioned for him to come over.

The whole room hushed and watched, so the whispers were ineffective. "You know where we are?" asked the older officer. "That's Klein's kid. Assistant to the D.A., Klein. Why do you think we kept a dead body hush-hush? She'll be fine in the guest house and you get to learn something, capiche?"

The younger officer seemed embarrassed, looked around at the rest of the police and then gave a quick nod to his commanding officer. "That will be fine. Will all of you be staying?" he asked.

"No," said Shannon. "I'm going home. I'll drive." She gathered herself and made her way to the front door.

"One of us will escort you, miss," called out the old cop.

"Fine." Shannon didn't look back to her friends, she just left. In her Volvo sedan, she locked the door behind her and rested her head on the steering wheel. That was when the tears came pouring out. Beth

27

Gardner, a friendly girl with the worst of luck was taken in and then taken over by powers Shannon couldn't even begin to attempt to grasp. Her heart cracked open like an egg.

A police siren interrupted her and made her jump. She wiped her eyes, adjusted the rear-view mirror and saw the red and blue lights behind her. It was time to go home and pray that this was all still just a nightmare.

Chapter II

New Kid

There was an accident. That's always the first thing people say before they deliver the bad news like it's supposed to just soften the blow with reason and logic. Accidents happen, that's a fact, and maybe the only real fact surrounding most of them. Generally speaking, accidents can't be explained so they leave people looking back replaying it again and again to find the exact moment where it went wrong. It's like they're hoping that if they can crack it, they can erase it.

Ralph Marker was a short, sixteen-year-old boy with curly brown hair, freckles and olive tanned skin from years in the desert. That is where it happened, far out in the desert of the American west. He was an intelligent boy, no doubt about that. Constantly curious and inquisitive, but didn't have the smarts enough to know when to quit sometimes.

Out on another dig site with his academically acclaimed professor mother, Ralph would wander the barren trails and search for caves to explore when he wasn't assigned to manual labor or studying the essentials in the makeshift homeschool classroom; which was nothing more than a tent with homework.

Ralph had gone out to a hill with a pair of binoculars to survey the land in search of adventure when a shine caught his eye. The shine moved, and then slithered down behind a large stone. "Only a snake," he said to himself behind the binoculars. The objects were out of focus and the sheen on the rattler's back must have caught the reflection from the sky. He refocused the lenses to get a better look at the large stone. The unnaturally oval-shaped stone stood completely alone in the sand.

Ralph put the binoculars in his bag and made his way in the direction of the stone. After about 30 minutes of walking, he'd reached it and realized that his original perception of the stone was far off point. It wasn't just any stone, it towered over him at twenty, maybe twenty-five feet tall. "Damn," he said impressed. Remembering the snake that caught his attention, he quickly looked around for it before it could sneak up on him. The last thing he wanted was to get bit all the way out here alone.

His mother and her colleagues always told him it was dangerous to go out alone and he didn't want to prove them right. He circled the stone three times and came up with nothing, not even a trail of the snake or any hole it could have sunk into. Satisfied with his safety, his attention turned back to the stone. It was just as round as it seemed, but all around and smoother than anything usually found out in the desert. The base was largest at the bottom and it tapered out to a point at its peak.

He brushed the windblown sand off it and found it to be cool to the touch, almost like there was a block of ice at its core that refused to melt. The surface was smooth, but there were dimples right around the bulbous equator.

His find was interrupted by the buzz of his two-way radio. "bzzzt, Hey kiddo, where are ya? Lunch time soon," his mother's voice cracked out of the plastic speaker. He dropped his backpack and took the radio out of the side holster.

"Hey, Mom, I'm just out exploring again. Be back soon," he said.

"Good, then maybe we can work on your Latin some more. And before you say it, I don't care if it's a dead language, it is the building blocks of modern communication. It's so powerful that it'll make your head spin when you finally get the scope of it," his mother said.

"Yeah, sure. Look, I found something out here, you might want to have a look. I'll tell you about it when I'm back."

He didn't give her time to reply before he switched the radio off and put it back in the holster. She was already lecturing him about Latin, he didn't need a safety course all the way back.

When he reached the encampment 30 minutes later, he called out, "I'm back." His mother walked out of the tent waving her radio at him with an angered slack jaw.

"What did I tell you about turning your radio off, smartass? It's hard to find things living out here because it's easy to die. And what did I tell you about going off alone? I don't care if you have your radio and it's daytime, it's easy to die out here!" It was almost like she rehearsed it.

Ralph held up his hands in surrender. "Before you lose it, I found something that might interest you. It might interest the team. I think I mighta found some handmade work out there."

Her temper cooled almost immediately. "Handmade? Did you touch it? Did you break it?"

"I doubt I could, it was pretty big."

She took his statement into consideration. "Where? Show me."

"I will, but first how about lunch and no Latin, deal?"

She scrunched her face at his ploy and said, "Deal."

Ralph described the stone while they ate beans and franks cooked from a can. She kept asking questions that were too specific for his brief investigation and he kept answering 'I don't know'. With each question, his mother ate faster to get lunch out of the way. Finished with a clang of the spoon in the can, she stood up and asked, "Ready to go?" She quickly gathered her gear before he could answer.

"I'm not done yet," said Ralph.

"Ohhh, eat it on the way, come on!" She was already suited up and heading out of the tent. Ralph obliged and with the spoon still in his mouth, he threw his backpack around his shoulders, grabbed the can from the table, and followed her into the desert's vastness.

They reached the stone with the only words spoken by Dr. Marker. His mother kept asking for navigation cues and hypothesizing to herself out loud what it might be. Her words stopped short once she got close enough to stand in its shadow. "Damn," she said plainly. She looked at Ralph, gave a quick chuckle and started to take tools out of her pack. "How'd you find it?" she asked.

"I went up on that hill back there and just looked around, I sorta caught it out of the corner of my eye."

"This close to the dig and we didn't even know?" She considered the sky for a moment shielding her eyes. "That flight mapping must have missed it. The odd shape probably blended into the surroundings."

Dr. Marker took out a large brush and began to push off the sand collected around the side. "Oh, we've gotta have a look at this," she said once she found the grooves around the middle. "Ho, ho, ho, hooo, is that writing?! Hot dog, look at that!" She pointed to an uncovered symbol. "That must be some native work. I can't think of it right now, but that is not just the Virgin Mary in toast, this is really something!"

"Does it feel cold to you?" asked Ralph. He stood back out of her space, he'd known from experience to stay out of her way while she worked.

"Hell no, we're in the desert."

"No, I mean the stone, touch it."

Dr. Marker took off her glove and rested her bare hand on the stone. "Wow, yeah! It's like an icebox." She gave it a short rap with her knuckles and then turned to Ralph with wide eyes. "I think it might be hollow, something is in there!"

"This seems like a big deal, should we radio the team?" Ralph asked.

"Yeah, yeah, just give me a minute. Damn, would ya look at this?! This could be it, Ralph! This could really be it!"

She went back to her pack to grab a rubber mallet. "I just want to hear what's inside." She walked back to the stone and sized it up, looking for the right place to strike. "Somewhere at the base..." Whack! The stone gave off a strange reverb as the echo inside seemed to go far away and then slingshot back. They looked at each other and with wide smiles laughed at the oddity.

She struck it again, this time at the upper end of the bulb, but this time the sound was different. It didn't give a hollow echo boomerang effect, it started slow and got higher and higher. It wasn't stopping. Dr. Marker put her hands on the stone. "I can feel it vibrating! Christ, what is this thing?" She leaned in and placed her ear against it.

That was when the sound stopped, right after a loud pop like a handgun in a closed space. Ralph was surprised by what he heard first, but then utter terror struck him when he saw what happened. His mother backed away from the stone a few steps holding both sides of her head as blood poured down her face. He could see she was screaming but not hear her over the ringing in his ears.

A gaseous steam shot out of the stone where she had been leaning like the vapor from a boiling teapot. Ralph couldn't breathe, he didn't know what to do. Another moment when by and he could hear her shout, "Cold! I'm so cold, Ralph! Get help!" She fell to the ground and rolled back and forth still holding her face.

Ralph grabbed his radio from his backpack and shouted into it barely hearing himself. "Help! Help! Mom's hurt!" He looked down at the radio and saw that he hadn't turned it back on yet. He turned the switch and shouted louder, "Help Mom! Help us!" Ralph dropped the radio and rummaged in his backpack for the emergency flare gun. He pulled it out, loaded it and shot it in to the air. He looked back to his mother and saw that she stopped rolling. Almost tripping, he ran back to her, fell to his knees beside her, and saw her face. It was blackened. Blackened like frost-bitten dead tissue and lifeless. Ralph couldn't stop from screaming and crying as the trucks from camp raced towards them.

****

It had been two months since his mother died, but Ralph still couldn't shake it. He'd moved out of the desert and back to his birthplace, Wilhelmina, after the funeral and formalities. When his parents got divorced nearly ten years ago, his dad stayed in New England while his mother dedicated all her time and resources to her research and Ralph's education. Whenever he'd asked them why they separated, his mother would say distantly, "We just…we just want different things," while his father would simply say, "Ask your mother."

His return to Wilhelmina was part of the plan as he would normally summer with his father in the New England woodlands. It was important to spend the majority of the time just the two of them without distractions. Ironically, this only applied to time away from home because Ralph's father was all-together too busy with his research and academic functions when they were in Wilhelmina.

"There was an accident," said Ralph seated in the Wilhelmina High cafeteria. Sitting with him at a table tucked away in the back by the brick wall, his childhood friends shifted uneasily at the end of the story. "Plain and simple," said Ralph. "I couldn't have done anything because I couldn't have seen it coming. That's what makes an accident an accident, if it was really my fault, it'd be called something else, right?"

"Right. I mean, they didn't arrest you or anything," said Steven, trying to fit a joke in to lighten the mood. Kyle punched his shoulder and glared him down. Steven Young and Kyle Lauder had been friends ever since they were young children which created an interesting dynamic between them that was simultaneously one-part reliability and one-part irritability. Even their appearances mixed oddly. Steven was a short Asian boy with a slight pudge, but he stood up straight while Kyle was a tall, lanky black kid who slouched just a bit.

Ralph had been there in the beginning and seemed destined to be the third friend, but his parents' split had other plans. They were all still friends, writing back and forth and visiting in the summers, but Ralph had missed everything in between.

"It was an accident, man," said Kyle. "This shit happens and the only thing we can do is live for them out here in the real world, not die on the inside."

"This doesn't feel like the real world," said Ralph with a gesture to the rest of the cafeteria. "Feels more like a zoo with prison guards."

"At least you have a shorter sentence," said Steven. "How did you rig that, by the way, sympathy?" Kyle punched him again in the shoulder with an even stronger glare. "What?" Steven asked this time. "It's just a question!"

"That's ridiculous," said Ralph. "When I came here, they gave me a test to see where I fell academically. Hell, I'm pretty sure they thought I'd be below my age group because of the homeschooling and all, but lo-and-behold I am smarter than the average bear. Why would they just give it to me if I wasn't fit for it? Sympathy? Wouldn't it be more stressful if I wasn't ready and struggled to keep up?"

"Right," said Kyle. Steven just rubbed his shoulder.

"Anyway, I gotta go," said Ralph. "Biology is all the way on the other side of the building and this teacher, Mr. O'Brian, has been really giving it to me about being on time. It's rude if you ask me. I mean, he wastes the first few minutes talking to another teacher anyway so it's not like I'm missing anything."

"Don't worry about him," said Kyle. "He's probably just giving you a hard time because you skipped a grade and his career is a biosphere of children, like this one." He pointed to Steven. Steven said nothing. "Well, you better get going, new-kid."

Ralph gathered his backpack and lunch tray to leave, then Steven said, "Oh hey, shithead, you should come by my house after school, I got something for you. You still remember where my house is?"

"Yeah, Steven, I can figure it out," said Ralph. "It's only down the block or so."

"Cool, I think you're really gonna like this," said Steven.

Ralph walked through the halls and, to his surprise, was in a better mood than he had been lately. 'Shithead'. Why did the insult make Ralph feel closer to these guys again? He couldn't say. He could tell that they were trying to cheer him up in their own ways and that was a good feeling. That good feeling fell away when he heard the bell ring. Damn, still late, he thought.

He arrived at the classroom with no pride in being right; the teacher would not let him slide for being just a couple minutes late. Technically, Ralph was in the classroom before the teacher, but he found out right quick how rules apply to students, yet teachers have amnesty in all affairs.

"I saw you coming in a little behind, Mr. Marker, tsk tsk tsk," said Mr. O'Brian. "That means, anybody? Anybody?" he asked to no one but himself. "Yes, that is correct, Mr. Marker. One more to go until detention. You really are making an impression here at this school in, what, less than a month?" Mr. O'Brian was an obese, pencil mustachioed, pig of a man who, believe it or not, managed to continuously stay single into his 40s.

Ralph didn't reply to any of this. He also learned, within a very short time, that talking back to the mock authority achieved nothing but more trouble for the student. Instead, he just took his seat at an empty lab table in the back in silence.

Disappointed in the lack of a fighting spirit from Ralph, Mr. O'Brian simply continued business as usual. "Hello class, today I will announce the groups for the group project that I know you have all been anticipating. I took the time to select the groups carefully based on your work to better help you all work efficiently…"

He stopped talking when the door opened and a tall girl walked in later than both Ralph and the teacher. "Miss Kennedy, you…mmph…take your seat." He said it more like 'Mzzz' than 'Miss'.

"Yeah, I know," said Shannon Kennedy. Ralph watched her walk to her seat. He'd had his eye on this girl from the first few days at Wilhelmina High. It wasn't a crush, there was just something about this girl that was unusual. Ralph could see its invisible presence on her somehow. That aside, it did piss him off that she got away with being late while he got ridiculed.

"As I was saying," continued Mr. O'Brian. "There will be no working with your friends this time. This is a higher class, I expect higher work from all of you and just like in the real world you do not get to work with your little buddies. I will call out the groups at the end of the class." He gave two short but defined looks at Ralph and Shannon. "I have to make a few adjustments. As for now, I have a nice film to introduce us into the next section dealing with vital chemicals for mammal life!"

No one in the classroom shared Mr. O'Brian's enthusiasm, but there was a communal relief felt all around. Mr. O'Brian put a VHS tape into the VCR and started an obviously dated educational video. Sound and picture warped a little at the beginning, but it fell into place shortly.

"Blood," said the television. "Even the word can cause some discomfort. But, this nutrient, oxygen, hormone high liquid is, first and foremost, one of your closest friends…"

In the dark room, there was an audible groan from several students at this statement. "Quiet," said Mr. O'Brian without looking up from the test papers he was correcting. "Pay attention, you'll learn something."

Ralph only half paid attention. Videos in a dark room were a way to unplug from his current state. Everything moved so fast and nothing felt like it had time to sink in. Here was a place to turn up the static in his mind and sit back in the numbness.

After some time, a couple of the students started to shift in their seats. Their internal clocks nudged them to say that class was almost over. "And did you know," the television droned on. "That the average adult male has about five and a half liters of blood in his body? That's almost twice the recommended daily amount of water to drink. Now think about that!"

Mr. O'Brian looked at his calculator wrist watch and sighed. He jerked his swivel chair to the television set and hit the 'Stop' button on the VCR. "Looks like we must part ways yet again class, so sad. Now, please remember to look at this sheet before you leave so you can see who you are working with. I am being extra nice and letting you go a little before the bell. The smart ones will get to work as soon as possible. The others, will learn."

The class gathered their things and moved towards the front where a large sheet of paper with big letters listed the groups of two or three students to work on the project. Ralph, seated in the back, waited for the group to finally dissipate before checking his group. Before he got up, he heard someone, a girl, call his name. "Ralph? Who's Ralph?" the girl said mildly agitated through the chatter of the students.

The remaining students parted and a few of them made gestures towards his direction. "You?" said Shannon Kennedy. "I am working with you?" A couple kids laughed even though it wasn't a joke.

He didn't reply at first. His face was sort of squinted and crunched as he looked at the faces staring back at him. He coughed, got up and walked toward the front of the room. "Well, I'm Ralph," he answered. "Let's see what it says."

He locked eyes with Mr. O'Brian, happy as a clam, sitting in his over-cushioned chair just to observe. Ralph felt as if he had been put on display in hopes of a slip up for all to see. He squeezed in between the other students to get a look at the sheet. Sure enough, at the bottom written in pen in contrast to all the other names that had been clearly typed out beforehand was his name in the same group as 'Shannon Kennedy' and 'Lisa Meadows'. He traced his eyes up the list and found that his name had been typed out with another group, only it was crossed out with that same pen.

"I got a little last-minute inspiration to spice things up," chirped Mr. O'Brian. "I hope you don't mind."

Ralph turned his attention to Shannon. Her face was stern and cold and she puffed her chest out like she'd never lost a war. "Great, simply amazing," said Shannon. "What are you, 12?"

"No," he said. At first, he couldn't look her in the eyes as it made him a little queasy. He shook it off as nerves and said, "I'm 16. I can go to this school."

"You can go to this school?" Shannon mocked.

"You should count yourself lucky, Miss Kennedy," said Mr. O'Brian from his post. "Mr. Marker here was a homeschooled boy until he joined us. Then, he tested into this class right away, even without my council, just jumped a year ahead! It seems you might have some real brains on your team."

Ralph stretched out his hand and said, "Well then, I guess it's nice to meet you, Shannon."

"You guess?" scoffed Shannon. She let his hand hang in the air, turned around and walked out of the classroom.

"Ohhhh, swing and a miss!" said Mr. O'Brian. He swiveled back and forth in his chair and waited for Ralph to turn around to see his King Candy grin. Ralph could feel O'Brian's gaze burning through the back of his skull sending out toxic messages. Look at me, they said. Turn and look at me you little, nobody punk.

Ralph stood in thought, hand still in the air. It was this type of shit that really got his temper up fast lately. These goddamn people and all their shit. They didn't know what he'd seen, what he'd been through. Before he turned around to say something that might just get him that detention sooner than expected, a small hand grabbed and shook his.

"Lisa Meadows," said the tiny girl in front of him. She smiled and pushed her glasses up the bridge of her nose. "So glad to meet you, Ralph."

"What?" replied Ralph, absent mindedly shaking her hand.

"We're working on the project together," said Lisa. She took her hand back and pointed at the sheet.

"That's right, Mr. Marker. Now, you two should go easy on Miss Kennedy. She just suffered a catastrophic event not too long ago. She was there when young Beth Gardner had her sudden accident. In fact, why don't you two good sports pick up all the slack on this one?"

"Catastrophic event?" started Ralph. His wide eyes and forward gaze caused Lisa to pull back into herself for a moment. He felt he had two options, tell Mr. O'Brian what a catastrophic event really was, or just turn up the static in his head and leave the room. He decided static was the better option; he walked away leaving O'Brian and Lisa behind him.

****

"Damn, took you long enough," said Steven. Ralph stood in the doorway for a few moments to survey the room. There was clutter everywhere. Clothes strewn about the floor, posters with corners folding down the wall, half demolished action figures from a carefree childhood sticking out of drawers. He stepped precariously, almost like he was walking through a den of sleeping lions. Steven sat on the bed in front of the TV playing a video game.

"Nice to see you," said Ralph. "What's this game?" Despite the room itself being a disaster, the aroma was clean, like a carwash. It must have flooded in from the rest of the house. It was almost uncomfortably clean. The sort of clean that makes one feel they need to walk on tip-toes.

"This is a run 'n gun I play, *Alien Attack*. Stupid name. They named it something different in Japan, something cooler like 'Space Beast Ultra Fever', but they gotta dumb it down for us Americans. It's hard as hell but I'm pro so, you know, I'm just trying to beat my best scores." He paused the game and walked to an open drawer at the top of the dresser that the TV sat on. "So," said Steven as he dug through the drawer. "Kyle and I were talking, and we remembered that the one thing that all three of us really like are video games. Do you still game?" he asked over his shoulder.

"Yes," answered Ralph. "There wasn't a whole lot to do in the desert and practically no one my age. Yes, I like video games."

"Check this out," said Steven. He handed Ralph a regular looking cartridge with an unusual, yet vague, cover design. It was ancient temples floating against a purple sky. The game cartridges for the GRX were quite large and rectangular. They fit into the top of the pyramid shaped console like jamming a VHS tape in vertically.

Ralph held it delicately like a jeweler prospecting a precious stone. "*Cuazque*?" Ralph read off the game. "I've never actually seen it in person. Wow!"

"Oh, you say that now," joked Steven. "But just wait until you play it! It is unforgivingly difficult, but the pay off, damn. I had to get that special order from The Shop because it's so rare here in America."

"When I read about it, I thought it was something of a hoax, a myth, a legend," said Ralph. "They say it had...problems."

"Go on," said Steven knowingly.

"People said that their kids would get into trouble and be violent if they played it too long. Nothing serious, I think, just regular kid shit, but you know parents, always looking for an excuse for what their kids do."

"Bingo!" said Steven. "It isn't really cursed or anything, Hell, look at me. I've beaten it probably ten times and I turned out just fine." The smile Steven put on reminded Ralph of a cheap clown off an out dated billboard advertisement for a traveling circus on some forgotten highway.

"Can we play it?" asked Ralph.

"You could, but that would mean me watching you game in my house and that isn't going to happen." He turned off the GRX and ripped out Alien Attack. "I'll lend it to you, but first, there is a test." Steven went back to the drawer to grab a different cartridge. "We must find if you are worthy of *Cuazque*. You must show your skill." He pulled out a game with a Bruce Lee knock-off on the cover.

"Ah yes," said Ralph with relaxed familiarity. "*Blood Revenge!*"

"Oh, you think you know this? Let's see how we do in some co-op. My brother and I used to play this all the time. I'm good, but he was even better. Man, he could land those combos like BAM!"

"Dude, I'm pretty sure I've played this *with* you before."

"We shall see!" said Steven. The GRX switched to life with a pop and fizz. Steven sat back down on the bed and handed Ralph the player-two controller. "Man, homeschooled as an only child, in the desert, in exile. It's like your parents wanted you in solitary confinement from birth, like they thought you were dangerous."

"Maybe I am," Ralph said only half joking.

51

"Bullshit," said Steven missing Ralph's somber tone.

"Well, I'm about to whoop some ass right here, I can tell you that," said Ralph.

"We shall see!" repeated Steven, only this time he raised his finger above his head and then dropped it down on the START button to begin the game.

Just as the game started, they were interrupted by a knock on the door frame. "Hi boys," said Steven's mother cheerfully. She was wearing a colorful Spandex suit with a matching headband. "Stevie, honey, I wanted to put some laundry in before I did my workout. Did you have anything to wash?"

"Yeah, I put it downstairs already," said Steven annoyed.

"Okay," she said with widened eyes. "You know, if you plan on having company over you should really tidy up first." She redirected her attention to Ralph as he watched from the floor. "I know that when I have my friends over I like to make them feel welcome, comfortable...important."

"Yeah, well, this isn't your room, it's *my* room so when I say it's fine, it's fine," said Steven. "Okay?"

"Alright, no need to be sassy," she said. She held the laundry basket against one hip and put her weight on the opposite leg, leaning in the sway. "Ralph, it is so nice to see you again. I just wish it was under better circumstances. When I heard about your mother, well, I broke down. She was such a wonderful woman, it wasn't her time." She held an apologetic, vulnerable face.

"I...thanks. Thank you," said Ralph.

"You're always welcome here, Ralph, even if Steven's not around and you just want someone to talk to, someone to listen. Steven will show that by cleaning his room next time." She turned on one foot and left without waiting for another rebuttal from Steven.

When she was out of earshot, Steven said, "Damn, she can be such a bitch sometimes, always naggin' me. 'Clean your room, do the dishes, why can't you be more like your brother, nyah nyah nyah.'"

"Maybe you should be nicer to her," said Ralph. "You owe her more than you can imagine, maybe she deserves some respect?"

Steven made a sound pushing air between his pursed lips. "She doesn't even

53

work, she just uses the money from my Dad to buy clothes!"

"Maybe so she can spend more time with her kids, you know?"

"Maybe so you can shut up and we can play the game already."

Feeling put off at Steven's bratty behavior, Ralph couldn't help but stab at him a little even if he didn't really mean it. "You know, your mom…"

"Shut up," interrupted Steven.

"I'm just saying…" said Ralph, happy to have found a soft spot.

"Shut the hell up," said Steven jumping into the game to avoid any further discussion. This game was familiar to Ralph, it had been one of his favorites. He wanted to remind Steven that he knew how to play, that he was good. The intro started with the same old message written in blood telling the players how the main character, and in this two-player case his identical clone with the only difference being a yellow tunic instead of a red one, was scorned by an old partner who betrayed him. It was now the players' mission to fight the hordes of assassins that you were once a part of all the way to the head honcho and get back the treasure that was rightfully yours.

54

The game itself was fun for three reasons. One, it was violent. Blood splattered everywhere when you killed opponents and even more when you practically tore the level bosses limb from limb. Two, you were rewarded points when you rescued women who were more and more scantily clad as the game progressed. And most import, three, the gameplay. You felt like you had total control of the character's actions the whole time with tight maneuvering, numerous combo attacks and deadly special moves. Ralph embraced the whole show, feeling more at ease in the pixelated mayhem than he had in months.

As they battled through the first few levels with few words spoken, Ralph noticed that he was often kicking more ass than Steven. Steven would fall in the pits or take on too many enemies at once which meant Ralph had to wait for him to come back or help him when he was surrounded. After a while, he couldn't help but laugh like a drunk after probably the 50th time that Steven was surrounded by heavy hitters giving him a wallop. Watching his character get thrown around as a punching bag and hearing Steven's quick nervous voice calling for help was like being in a cartoon. It was just too funny to hold in the laughter.

According to the in-game map, they were about halfway through when Steven got a game over at the level's boss. "This is bullshit!" he said throwing the controller down on the mattress. Ralph said nothing, only focused on beating the boss. He had played this game enough to know the patterns of the bosses and he could anticipate their moves. This made each boss fight more like a routine than an actual challenge. Once he got into the rhythm, he was on top of it like a master mushing his dogsled team. When the boss took enough damage, his body blew up into more spines than a body could possibly have and enough blood to fill an Olympic sized swimming pool.

"Did you say you were good at games?" said Ralph with a hint of smugness.

"I am, I am just a little off playing in co-op. It's more difficult, there are more enemies and I haven't played this mode in a long time."

Ralph held a blank expression at Steven for a moment. "Sure, buddy," he said. "Don't worry, as long as one of us is still alive, the battle isn't over." At the start of the next level, Steven's character was back sans all the points from the previous booty.

"Yeah, but I lose all my points and power-ups. Lame."

"Coulda been worse, coulda been a game over," said Ralph. "You know what is lame though? Mr. O'Brian paired me up with that Shannon Kennedy girl for some Biology project. I have this strong feeling that I am going to have to do all the work. He totally did it on purpose."

"What?" said Steven. He paused the game. "You are working with Shannon Kennedy? You get an excuse to be around Shannon Kennedy?"

"What? Nah, it's not like that, I mean she is pretty, but she was not excited at all to be grouped with me. It's just a project, not a date. Anyway, that other girl, Lisa I think, she might be helpful. I don't know, I was kinda pissed off, so I just walked out."

"Pretty?" Steven laughed. "Just 'pretty'? I have heard her called a lot of things but not that. You sound like an old man." He continued to laugh. "Dude, she is slammin'! Wait until I tell Kyle, he is going to shit his pants. And who cares if she doesn't even like you, you will be cool just being around her. Wait, her being around you, you being around us? Dude, we could be cool!" Steven had talked himself into a red faced, breathless excitement.

Ralph didn't know what to say, instead he just rocked his head back and forth lightly thinking it over. "I mean, I don't know, I guess?" His watch made a beeping sound and he looked at it. *Five o'clock, should get back to the house and start some homework,* he thought. "Anyway, I should go, I have some work to do."

"But what about the game man, we are making really good progress," said Steven, completely flipping his previous opinion.

"I beat it before, besides, I think I have proved I am worthy of *Cuazque*, eh amigo?" said Ralph holding up the prize.

"Alright, I'll see you, man. Oh, hey, do you want to check out The Shop this weekend?"

"What shop?"

"Ohhhhh man! It's this place that Kyle and I like to hang at. Guy's got all sorts of stuff, I think you will really like it."

"Definitely."

"Cool, let's meet up Saturday and we'll show you the wonders."

"Good deal."

"Later!"

Ralph walked out of the room and down the hall. He examined the front of the Cuazque's cartridge. It looked like Steven wasn't the first owner. The adhesive cover label was foxed at the corners and a few pieces of the plastic shell were chipped off. *Dammit, does this thing even work?*

He let himself out the front door into the sunlight. It might not have been as hot as the desert, but the sun was somehow different. Bigger? He couldn't quite place it. It seemed as if the sky was just smaller here so all the objects were cluttered around it.

Calm suburbia was all around him. Sounds of lawn sprinklers and mowers came through in a harmony that issued peaceful vibes. Bugs buzzed around with that electric hiss and laughter could be heard reaching across yards. The clean, straight lines of the houses in their proud colors, individual yet all the same, gave off a feeling of security. Above all else, Wilhelmina was a town for families.

When Ralph got home, he walked to the side gate into the back yard instead of the front door. It was a large yard with pine trees along the edges and curving around the back. Trees so tall, dense and close that the fence wasn't visible with the exception of the single door. Ralph felt a disconnect at the first step in. The air was different here, more closed in and ignorant to the outside world. An atmosphere all its own drenched in a piney, sappy stench.

In the middle, on the far end of the yard, an old oak stretched firmly towards the sky. Taller than any of the other trees it stood apart, proud and resilient at the crest of the hilly lawn. "How majestic! Like a king's throne," his father said on countless occasions.

The summer after his parent's divorce, Ralph's father thought it was of highest importance that they bond as father and son through something masculine and dignified. To achieve this, he schemed a grand plan of an unparalleled treehouse. Like most plans in their early stages, everything was to be spectacular while of course easily done for a modest budget. Something to be remembered by all who were lucky enough to chance its audience.

Within the first step, they hit a road block. Ralph's father wasn't going to risk damaging the oak 'throne'. Instead, he opted the project stay on the ground rather than up in the branches. Plus, this way the project wouldn't incur any dismantling from his mother by keeping Ralph down on the ground and not welcoming injury swinging from branches.

As the project went from sketches to blue prints to actual building, Ralph's involvement was cut shorter and shorter. Plus, one summer proved to be insufficient timing. A father-son treehouse snowballed into a dad and his buddies slapping together a wooden shack while Ralph, eager to be a part in any way, was designated to tool retrieval, strategic holding down of objects, and observation. "You are helping just like that, pal," his father said on countless occasions.

When it was done, Ralph may well have built it by the looks of it. It had an uneven perimeter that went around the tree that stretched out to a ten or twelve-foot radius depending on the location. The roof was a simple metal top that worked to keep out rainfall and provide shade. At several different sections, pieces could be unlatched and dropped down into the hut to let in sunlight. The only way in and out was a heavy, deep green door repurposed from God knows where. All in all, it was a shack under a tree. But, it was Ralph's shack under a tree.

After completion, electricity was fed into it via power cables dug into the ground from the house as well as a two-way telephone paired with another in the house. The phone was a special model with no dialing capability. It simply rang on the other end when picked up.

Ralph opened the door and stepped into the disarray of old furniture, tables cluttered with intricate models, a bookshelf loaded with paperbacks telling tales of deep-sea monsters and far-flung space princesses. Against the wall was a TV on a stand. This stand, more organized than anything else inside, kept all of his VHS tapes and video games.

With a look around the room and a quick smirk, Ralph said, "I'll get to that homework later." He immediately slammed *Cuazque* into the GRX and let himself fall back into the Lay-Z-Boy chair purchased at a garage sale. The game started up with a slow, creaky melody and a scrolling message overlaying a map.

After the storm,
Your plane has crashed over the lost rainforests
of South America.
You frantically pull yourself from the wreckage
only to find you are the only survivor
of the expedition.

The shock is too much and you faint under the
moonlight.
You awake, still under the starry night sky to
salvage what you can.
But, it has already been ransacked.
The map, radio, food, raft, even the others,
are gone.
All you have is a small knife,
and separate foot prints headed in eight
different directions...

The game's protagonist was a run-of-the-mill forgotten-ruins-explorer type on a quest through the jungle. Ralph had the option to choose his stage and dove right in at the first selection. He could tell instantly this was a different game. The graphics moved in this lava lamp fluidity with characters that seemed to have no definite shape. In a way, it got rid of that choppy look that games usually had: clunky pieces slamming into each other. This was a large billowing flag with each movement connected physically, but visibly separate.

Ten minutes in, things started to turn. It was not that it had a particularly gratuitous amount of blood, it was the nature at which the player slayed the apparently endless number of native tribesmen. When the enemies were defeated, they would not explode in blood or get smooshed and then disappear. Rather, they would bleed out slowly and fall to the ground. Or, their limbs would separate at Ralph's attacks and they might hobble a little bit only to collapse clumsily. What really stuck out were the sounds that they would make dying. Some would scream in pain, but others seemed to embrace it with...pleasure? Ralph couldn't tell at first, but proved to be correct when some of them would rub their own blood over their bodies.

He reached the top of an intricate temple and saw a warrior decorated in feathers and bones standing at a sacrificial altar holding one of the others from your party, laid out and motionless. The warrior raised a blade and ripped it down into the victim's gut. He jerked the blade up the torso with unnerving intent. Through the spray of blood, he ripped out the heart, tilted it and drank from it like a wine glass.

"What the shit?" Ralph squinted at the TV to watch it unfold. He didn't react fast enough to stop the boss from quickly killing his character after drinking the blood of a party member. Ralph's face was contorted with intrigued disgust as level one came to an end.

Without a word, he made another attempt. This attempt was faster, but mostly because he tried to filter out the deaths and just get another whack at the boss. He died a few more times and each time played it better, faster and with more control. Unconsciously, he bit his lip at the fourth fight with the boss. Just when he was about to take too much damage, he made a blitz for the boss and surprised himself when he landed his hit first. Boss defeated. After a deep breath, he watched as the generic adventurer took some of the adornments off the dead warrior and wore them himself. A message came on to the screen.

Your kills have made you stronger.
Continue or Rest?

"Game," said Ralph. "You are just too weird to let go." He was about to select 'Continue' when the two-way phone started to ring and the red light at its base pulsed. He picked up the phone and said, "Yo."

"I made dinner," replied his dad. "Come inside, yo." Ralph hung up the phone and shook his head at his dad's earnest effort. He was amazed at his father's inability to get the hang of the slang Ralph brought home. Even simple things like 'yo' had no actual part of speech to him. In his eyes, they were just trivial attachments to a conversation.

Ralph went back to the game and selected 'Rest' thinking it would save the game. "What? Passwords? That takes a couple points off," he said. The screen presented a three square by three square box with hands holding different gestures. He grabbed a notebook from one of the tables and jotted it down in childish stick figure hands. Then, he flipped all of the switches and walked towards the house.

When Ralph's father had said that he'd made dinner, what he really meant was that he picked up a pizza. Stanley Marker was what many regarded as a solemn man. He was thin framed with wrinkles all around his face after years of thinking and reading texts under weak academic office lighting. He was a kind natured man, and an honest one.

In the years since his reclaimed bachelorhood, Stanley didn't change much of anything within the house. Sure, it was tidy, picked up, but there was a vacancy with settled dust and stale air. He only came home to sleep and occasionally eat. Clothes and necessities had their own space in his college office. With his son back for the foreseeable future, he wanted to be around more often. Ralph appreciated that he tried.

"Ahhh, pizza again," said Ralph with pleasant relief. "I'm worried that one of these days you'll actually cook."

"Well, indirectly I do," said Stanley with short reverie. "I made the money that paid Mentevelli's to buy the ingredients to make the pizza cooked by employees. My money is at the top of it all so, yes, in a matter of speaking, I made the pizza."

Ralph just let this statement pass as he took his first bite. "It's pizza," he said. "Don't make it complicated."

Stanley gave a grunt in agreement. They sat in silence while they ate. Ralph chomped two slices in a hurry and Stanley picked his slice apart first with the toppings, then the cheese and then finally ripped the bread to bite sized segments.

"So, as you know, colleagues of mine live around here," Stanley broke the silence.

"Uhuh."

"They have some chores around their homes, you know daily stuff, that they need taken care of in the event that they are not there. Some, uh, conferences have come up, as they do time to time, that they will be attending. I will be going as well. After that, there are some other matters that need my attention, so I'll be leaving you here for a while. I know you'll do fine."

Ralph stopped eating, brushed his hands off and looked at this father with crossed arms.

"We were talking, and I told them that you, living here now, would be able to help them out."

"You volunteered me?" he asked with disapproval.

"Well, volunteers don't get paid. They said that they would pay you. In cash, half now, half later. They would pay well and it is tiny things like getting the mail and feeding the dog, that sort of stuff."

Ralph had done manual labor and helped out his fair share at research sites while living with his mother. And all for free. She called it character building, but he learned to call it a rip-off. "Money would be nice. There's a lot around here and it all takes money," said Ralph.

"Great," said Stanley. "You start tomorrow. I have drawn up the details for you on the notepad over on the counter. Just grab it before or after school or whenever you're around. Before and after school would probably be easiest. This isn't life or death stuff, but it would be good to show some initiative and, hell, maybe there will be a little bonus at the end." Ralph walked to the notepad on the counter. "Please keep in mind that these aren't just my colleagues, these are my friends. Don't play any games or abuse their offer. Just get in, get the job done and get out."

Ralph saw only three names on the sheet and the work looked minor.

Donald Greenly, Ph.D., 212 Vine Street: Bring in the mail and/or any deliveries that are on the front porch (burglars look for stacks of newspapers and such to see if anyone is home)

Joanna Jackson, Ph.D., 234 Maple Boulevard: Feed dog twice daily with proper scoop found in dog food bag.

Dino Capecci, Ph.D., 153 Ivy Drive: Collect mail, packages, newspapers and feed fish once a day.

"No problem," said Ralph as he dropped the instructions back on the counter. "No problem."

Stanley extended his hands to arm's length, palms facing upward with an unsurprised expression on his face. "You see? I knew you could do it. It's good to keep busy, it helps keep the mind occupied." There was a pause. "It's better than worrying about the past, about what you could have done different."

Ralph said nothing. He wanted to have an answer, but nothing felt good enough, right enough. He was there, she was *right* there. Then in one moment, it was over. Her body remained, but his mother was gone.

"I am going to get some more work done," said his father. Stanley left the room without waiting for a reply or even looking at his son. After Ralph heard the office door shut, he walked into the family room and sat down. Family room. There was nothing in here but a useless, broken gas-fueled fireplace, a sofa and whispers of a family together. His mother hated that fireplace. Ralph let out a short laugh remembering the debates his parents had had about it.

"Safe control of a fire in a house is a marvel of human innovation, really and truly," his father had said. "A height of luxury."

"We don't cook with it, we don't need it to keep the house warm, it's just for show," his mother had said. "Fire belongs outside where it can be wild. The wood crackles as the light and warmth are offered out into the world. It's magic, it's *alive*. The magic makes it live, right Ralph?" She beamed at him and scooped him up in a burst of laughter.

His eyes felt heavy, filling over with water. He held his breath and didn't blink to hold it back. But the memory played over and over in his head. One tear broke over the edge of his eyelid, he let out a hoarse breath and couldn't stop the stream that followed.

Chapter III

Inconveniences

It had been less than two weeks after Beth Gardner's death and things had started to move along as usual for most of Wilhelmina. It was a quiet funeral, closed casket of course. People shared their condolences but then just chalked it up to a freak accident. Normalcy was more desired to most, but for some, it was forever lost. Shannon had started to notice forces creeping in her peripheries, little voices and daydreams that were more than just a distraction.

They nipped at her from dawn to dusk like an irritation just beneath the skin. She'd told no one of this. As far as she was concerned, it was aftershock from the grotesque scene she'd witnessed. In spite of it all, she wanted to believe, *told* herself to believe, that it was an unfortunate spontaneous combustion. But she knew, in the deep of her heart, she knew what she saw.

"Do you guys feel different?" she asked at lunch with the girls. Even on the outside her friends seemed odd to her in a new way. An alien way of shifted impersonation. Amanda, remarkably, had a very calm composure, almost elation.

"Different how?" said Amanda. She paused to bite half of a banana in one mouthful. Through the food, she said, "If you mean different because that god-awful exam is done, then yes, I feel different. I feel like a drill has finally been removed from my brain and I can let free thought flow again. School work just gets in the way of things I want to do, such an inconvenience. Colleen, any words?"

Colleen, on the other hand, seemed to be suffering headaches. More than a few times, Shannon caught her rubbing her temples in a slow circular pattern with her eyes closed, almost like singing herself to sleep. It seemed like a twitch she couldn't help. "My head feels like it is shrinking and has been since…I don't know, that night?" she said in a dry voice.

"Speaking of that, your nose looks great by the way, what's your secret?" asked Amanda.

Colleen gingerly touched the bandage on her nose to test for pain. It did look great considering it was broken and bleeding not very long ago. Hell, it barely looked like it needed a bandage any more.

"Nothing. I don't get it. It just kinda sorta fixed itself," said Colleen. "You know what *is* weird? Do you know that test we just took, Amanda? I totally, honest to god, forgot about it because we were out for a few days after Beth, and also…well…you know. But when I sat down and read the questions, I had a sort of cloud lift and I didn't feel nervous. Seriously, I think I did pretty well. It was like, this is going to sound funny, but it was like I could hear the answers right after I read the questions."

Shannon watched her, not touching her food, with narrowed eyes and hunched towards her voice which had been quieting to a whisper to avoid eavesdroppers. Amanda was not so concerned. Finished with the banana, she moved on to a sloppy sandwich that slipped out more than she fit into her mouth. "Was it like you were remembering from class? Like your memory was just really sharp?" Shannon asked. Even she could hear the doubt in her words. Colleen was never the brightest bulb and some sort of sudden clairvoyance seemed too coincidental, too out of the blue.

"No. I mean, well maybe. But what it was really like, was like I heard the answers from somewhere in my head. You know like a big radio antenna slapped on my forehead picking up signals. I didn't know the answers anyway, so I just went with what I had in my brain. But you know, it was strange how…correct it felt, how natural the answers came each time. It was like all I had to do was ask the question and this voice answered, this singing voice faraway, sweet, a woman's voice, it was dreamy."

The two listening girls pulled back at this. Amanda even stopped eating for a moment to give her full attention. If the situation didn't feel so heavy, Shannon could have laughed at the look and food smeared on Amanda's face. Never had she seen her so unguarded to leave a smudge on her face, but dammit she was still adorable.

"I gotta tell you, it was a little freaky," continued Colleen. She looked down and forked through her salad without eating much. "I, like, never complete a whole test with all the answers filled in, but this time I just nailed it."

Amanda had regained her composure. "Yeah, well, we'll see," she said. "I studied for that test for hours and even I had some issues with it."

"No, this was different," said Colleen. "This wasn't like studying, this was like *knowing*."

There was a stop in the conversation that was nearly tangible. Shannon broke through it saying, "I am still so mixed up about what happened, I mean, Jesus! She died right in front of us! And that book. Amanda, something is really wrong about all this, we need to see someone about…"

"Keep your voice down," commanded Amanda. "And don't talk about that book here. Nothing we did caused what happened as far as anyone else can prove. Nothing that we could have changed, and definitely not something we were responsible for. It's sad and it's scary, but we were just in the wrong place at the wrong time. Look at me." She locked eyes with Shannon. "Don't worry about what happened. We are all safe now and we will get through it together."

Shannon felt those words push against her forehead like a printing press. Never before had Amanda taken such a tone with her. It felt real. It felt like truth in that moment. "Now, we all have gym class next, so I suggest we get a move on," said Amanda. She picked up her trash and walked towards the exit without waiting for the other two. Shannon looked at Colleen for a response, but Colleen simply rolled her eyes, sighed, gathered her things and got up to leave. Shannon followed them.

In the girl's locker room, Shannon and Colleen changed for class while Amanda sat on the bench in between lockers and drank a soda. "Aren't you going to change?" asked Shannon.

"No," said Amanda. "Today's a fat day. No gym for me." Amanda usually was excited for gym class. As a high energy girl, she always took the opportunity to get physical.

"Coach isn't gonna like that," said Colleen lacing up her sneakers.

Amanda tossed the empty can to a nearby trash can and missed. "Well, I don't like coach so that makes us square." She left the room without waiting and without picking up the can on the floor. Colleen chuckled and again followed. Shannon picked up the can, dropped it in the trash and left the locker room.

All the girls lined up for roll call in the gymnasium waiting for coach to arrive. On the other side of a large curtain that split the gym in half, the boy's gym class could be heard. Loud laughter, name calling and sneaker squeaks made the girls giggle and whisper to each other. There were times when the curtains would swing apart and the classes could see each other or a boy would crash through in an attempt to catch whatever ball was in play. Those short teases energized each class. The attempt was to help the students focus and feel less self-conscious, but putting up boundaries and rules only increased the value of the opposite sex. The curiosity and temptation boosted the hormones and had a reverse effect. It wasn't rare to find students flirting and scurrying away together after class. Why did they try to restrict it? Because it had power. Only the restriction made it more powerful.

Coach walked in and even though the girls were already lined up, she announced, "Alright ladies, line up," out of habit. She was a short woman with even shorter hair. She moved down the line and called out the name of whoever she stood in front of. The game was simple. The girl in line would say 'present' or coach would start counting until they did. However high the count, that girl owed that many push-ups. Complaints doubled it. Needless to say, the girls played ball without hesitation.

Amanda was the only girl not dressed for class. If you weren't dressed, you couldn't do gym. If you couldn't do gym, that docked a letter grade. Shannon stood next to her in alphabetical order and kept giving her looks as coach moved down the line.

"Kennedy," said coach.

"Present," said Shannon.

"Klein," said coach. Amanda said nothing. She gazed toward the curtain, twirled her hair a little and smiled. "Klein!" coach shouted in Amanda's face. Again, Amanda was just lost in imagination. "One, two, three, four," coach began. "Five, six, seven, eight, nine, ten." Several of the girls made noises of disbelief. "Eleven, twelve, thirteen, fourteen, fifteen." Coach lost her patience. "Thirty!" The girls made more noises of shock. "Klein!" coach shouted again.

Amanda looked around and then faced coach. "Who, me?" she said in a bright tone. "Present." She smiled at coach and stayed put.

"Klein, you know the rules, I want thirty, on the ground, now!" said coach. "And don't think you get to slide because you aren't dressed. That's thirty push-ups and you lose this class. And that's thirty for, Kennedy, too, let's see if you have any heart mixed in with all that dumb. Do you understand me?"

Amanda took a deep breath, looked to Shannon and winked. She turned her full attention to coach and said, "Look Mister Ma'am, I'm not doing shit. Look at me, I'm tight like a tiger, I don't need this stupid gym class. And for those push-ups, you do 'em! Show Shannon how it's done."

The line of girls hooted, whistled and clapped. Coach was frozen. The girls calmed down to see what would happen next. Coach shook her head and blinked her eyes. She let out a "Pssshh" and a growling "Hmmmmmm." But still, nothing. Shannon's mouth and eyes were wide open. Amanda looked at her out of the corner of her eye and raised her eyebrows in a quick jerk.

"Fine," said coach. "The rest of you girls, laps, now, go!"

The girls let out an almost unison "What?" as they slapped their thighs at this bullshit. They wanted a fight, but instead the air got let out.

"Laps!" repeated coach. The girls slowly started to move away from the line and jog around the room. "Not you, Kennedy, not yet. You're with me." Shannon walked to the middle of the sectioned room and looked back at Amanda in disbelief. "Face to face, follow my speed," instructed coach. Shannon mirrored coach's pose and started to do push-ups with her. She glared at Amanda who sat in the bleachers as the rest of the class sweat it out with laps and she had one-on-one with coach.

****

Shannon was pissed. Both at Amanda and at herself for agreeing to meet after school. Something was up. Something was wrong. She didn't feel like she was in danger, but this was all certainly uncharted territory. She paced by the window in her house as she waited for Amanda and Colleen to pull up. While she waited, she thought of the things she'd say to Amanda. She wanted to tell her off, but she didn't want to make her angry. She wanted to understand what was going on, but she didn't want to get left out.

Shannon walked to the window to look for any sign and saw nothing. She only saw the large, clustered houses with all their front lights on from one end of the block to the other to ensure it stayed a proper neighborhood. Shannon knew she should like the well-trimmed lawns, aesthetic trees and well-to-do manner of the whole thing. But she could barely gag it down. It was too much presentation without any body to it. All that 'well-to-do' and what did they do with it? The same as everyone else without a moment's hesitation. It made her feel guilty, unworthy. Before she could think more on it, she heard a car horn from outside, ran to the window and saw they'd arrived.

She checked herself in the mirror and then walked out the front door. At the bottom of the stone walkway that led from her house to the street, a tight, boxy white Mercedes Benz idled lightly. Shannon slid into the back seat, and said, "This isn't your car, how did you talk your mom into letting you drive it, threaten to feed her cats to the dog?"

"I have power," answered Amanda. She was wearing a school uniform that wasn't affiliated with any academic institution Shannon was familiar with.

Shannon shivered a little and wondered, *Amanda, what happened to you this summer?*

Colleen twisted around the front passenger seat and said, "Psssh, what are you talking about? Her mother is just out of town, no magic here." She turned back to Amanda. "But seriously, sunglasses at night? What are you, some kind of beatnik?" Amanda said nothing and drove out of the neighborhood.

Emerald-green lawns turned to row houses along the street as they drove out of the more respectable area and into the main commercial district in the downtown area. To call it downtown made it sound much grander than it actually was. Being in the suburbs of New England, nearly everything was old by American standards and this metropolitan set up was nothing compared to the larger cities. Instead of sky-scraper buildings and blocks upon blocks of commerce, they had narrow one-way streets that were filled with buildings practically standing on top of each other. And to make it even more bland was that they could find themselves out of town and in the woods all too quick driving in any direction.

"What are you listening to?" asked Shannon indicating the choice in background accompaniment.

"Do you like it?" said Amanda as she turned the volume up. The ignorant rap lyrics pumped out of the stereo speakers in comical juxtaposition describing the high life of drug dealers out smarting the cops.

"Ugh, I know right?" Colleen chimed in. "It just sounds like it's trying way too hard, but still missing the target."

"Oh, please," said Amanda. "Music is all about love and sharing. Musicians make this stuff, put it out into the world and then it is anyone's to have and hold sacred. The rest is inertia. Once you make something and send it out, you cannot control the spread." There was a calm lull when no one answered and there was only the jumpy beat of the music and the athletic hum of the Benz. "If you don't like it, just go on to the next one and leave it be. But I like this." Amanda turned up the volume a little more.

Shannon leaned over the back of the driver's seat and said to Amanda, "It doesn't sound like love to me."

"Love means different things to different people," said Amanda. She reached down into her purse between her legs and pulled out a pack of Virginia Slims, her mother's brand. She stuck one cigarette in her mouth, and prepped the car's lighter. When it was ready, she lit the cigarette and passed it to Colleen.

"Will your mom notice if we smoke in her car?" Colleen asked, only half concerned.

"She smokes in the car, genius," Amanda answered while she lit another cigarette. She reached back to hand it to Shannon without looking. "Here, honey, this will help keep your figure."

Shannon was hesitant, but only for a moment. It wasn't the first time Amanda had offered her a smoke, but it was the first time she accepted it. Shannon took the cigarette, placed it gently between her lips and took a long, deep drag like they did in all the movies; so cool, so collected. Of course she breathed too deep her first time and coughed it back. The other two girls laughed at her, but she wasn't going to let that dissuade her. Once her lungs recovered from the rookie mistake, she made a cautionary second attempt. "So," she said, starting to get the hang of it and breathing out smoke without looking like a chump. "What are we doing tonight?"

Amanda pulled into the lot of an all-night convenience store and parked the car on the far side of the lot on the fringe of the glowing neon lights. "I want to try something," she said. Through the windshield, the shop was clearly visible in front of them. It was a typical corner store with aisles of snacks, a bank of beverage refrigerators along the back, coffee pots with the same sludge since that morning, dirty magazines behind the counter, and an ATM on the side opposite the entrance. At 17, none of them had their own bank card, but it wasn't unusual for Amanda to slip into her mother's purse and snag a few hundred dollars, or even a credit card, when necessary.

With the car parked and turned off, Amanda turned to face the two other girls. "Look, that shit from the other week was crazy and I think we can all say that that book was for real. Beth did not just happen to catch fire when we were reading that. Plus, there have been other things."

"Other things?" said Shannon.

"Yeah, other things," said Amanda. A long pull from her cigarette filled a pause. "Didn't you see what happened in gym class today, pretty girl?"

"Oh my god!" said Colleen. "I could not believe it. The way you just told her off like, 'Why don't you do 'em, bitch?' And then she did! She actually did it!"

"*I* actually did it," said Shannon. A twinge of her anger at Amanda came back. But, just a twinge, more like an annoyance really. "What was your secret, did you just pay her off?"

"Nope," said Amanda. "Truth be told, I made it up as I went. Sorry about that, Shannon, I sorta got caught in the moment, you know?"

Shannon glared at her friend for a moment and held her breath. She wanted to be angry. She *should* be angry. It was bullshit. But she just got angry that she couldn't get angry. And then she let the air out. "No shit?" she asked.

"No shit," Amanda agreed. "Listen, I think that when that thing with Beth and the book, well, happened, I think something got into me, got into *us*, from the other side. That book gave us something, but I don't really know what it is." No one said anything. They knew what she was talking about, but nobody had really put it into words yet. It was like a fragment of a dream that leaves an inky gauze over your psyche muddying your thoughts all day, but you can't remember a damn thing.

"Colleen, didn't you say something about a test that you didn't study for?" asked Amanda.

"Yeah! And I totally aced it! I think. Either I'm a genius or..." She trailed off noticeably to connect the dots. "Hey, do you think I can like, read minds or something? Like some James Bond shit?"

"I don't think anyone reads minds in James Bond," said Shannon. She felt anxious. She didn't want it to be real. She wanted it to be a freak accident and nothing more. If it was real, then it suggested something worse, something terrifying. She didn't want to believe that there could be anybody, or any*thing*, pulling strings behind the curtain.

"Whatever, you know what I mean."

Shannon said nothing.

"Listen, let's just take it easy and one step at a time," said Amanda. "Colleen, remember last year's Christmas party at the country club my mom hangs around where you tried to steal as much from drunk people as you could?"

"How could I forget? I still have all that stuff, well, most of it, hidden in my room. I wear some of the necklaces and rings. Look, see?" She held out her right hand and showed a loose-fitting ring that was probably only a fraction or so away from pure silver. "This was from that short, old dork who kept breathing in my face with his fishy breath and telling me how much I reminded him of his ex-wife. Look, it's got some Latin written on it." She slid the ring off and tried to read the message inscribed on the inside. "Car...Pah...Car...screw it, it's a dead language for a reason."

"Great," said Amanda. "I want you to try to take something from a guy that goes in this store. Do you think you could get his ATM card and PIN?"

"I think I could steal a card, but how am I supposed to get the PIN?"

"Ask it."

"Ask him? That's ridiculous."

"Ask it! The card, ask the card."

Colleen squinted her eyes at Amanda as she tried to figure it out.

"Like the test. Like how you got the answers on the test. We just went over this!"

"Ohhhhhhhh," said Colleen. She still wore some confusion on her face.

"Look, can you do it?"

Colleen stubbed out her cigarette, stepped out of the car and bent down to the window. "Girl," she said confidently. "I know it." She laughed and walked away into the shop with overly accentuated sways and frills in her stride.

"I swear to Christ, this girl sometimes…" Amanda sighed.

Shannon and Amanda waited in the car; finishing their cigarettes and watching Colleen roam aimlessly around the shop. The attendant at the counter was reading some gearhead magazine and trying to not pay too much attention to the jailbait.

After maybe ten minutes and another cigarette for Amanda, a car pulled up near them and a man in his early thirties stepped out towards the store. Colleen looked from him to the girls in the car, lifted her hand to give the 'OK' signal and gave a quick wink.

The guy went right to the counter as the whole scene played out in silence from the view of the Mercedes. Amanda watched, still wearing the sunglasses and smoking, while Shannon almost ripped the fabric from the driver's seat squeezing it so hard from behind. They watched as the guy pulled out a thick looking wallet, slapped it on the counter and pointed to a few packs of cigarettes and a lottery ticket. Colleen was on him like a cat, twisting her hair and batting her eyelashes. From the view of the car they only saw what looked like a quick flirt lasting a couple moments. The guy, wrapped up in Colleen's show, tried to pay for his purchase with a bank card, but the store clerk said something and motioned to the beaten ATM on the far side of the store. The guy took one card from his wallet and walked over to it, leaving the wallet on the counter. He took out some money and paid for the smokes and lotto in cash. Colleen motioned a phone up next to her ear, the guy laughed, and then he asked the clerk for a pen and bent down to write something.

He left the shop looking pleased and accomplished despite his early '70s used pickup and gut peeking out just above the belt. Colleen waited for him to leave the parking lot and then walked gingerly back to the car.

"Cha-ching!" said Colleen holding up a green American Express card. "That fool didn't even see it coming, Jesus, right on the counter. I think a man's brain is directly linked to his penis."

"Nah, the pecker does all the thinking," said a yet-to-be impressed Amanda. "Did you get the money?"

"No, but the PIN is," she touched the card to the side of her head and bunched her face into forced concentration. "The pin is 4796! Whoa, I can actually hear it. It's still that singing voice, oh it's so sweet." She swayed back and forth humming to a melody neither Amanda or Shannon recognized. She repeated it again and again in a daze.

"Well, get the money," said Amanda.

Colleen jerked her body out of the dance. "What, now?"

"Yes, now! I need to see if it works. This is why we're here!"

"Ok, jeez, how about a little, 'Cool job stealing that guy's shit' every once in a while?" said Colleen. She didn't wait for a reply before she walked back into the store. At the ATM, she slid the card in and started pushing buttons. A piece of paper came out, she looked at it, crumpled it into her pocket and started the whole thing again. This time she looked like she got it right when some money came out. She folded it and walked back to the car. The attendant just shook his head and said nothing.

"Son of a bitch," she said. "That low-life is broke as hell." She handed over two twenties and a ten, fifty dollars. "I got it right on the first try, but then the machine said," she reached into her pocket, pulled out a receipt and read in a mocking high tone, "We are sorry, but we cannot complete your request at this time due to insufficient funds. Anyway, boom! Do you see that? I make the money!"

Amanda spread the money out in front of her and did a slow, polite society clap. She turned around in her seat, lowered he glasses to look at Shannon in the eyes and said, "Now, what can you do?"

"Nothing," said Shannon without hesitation. She broke eye contact, looked down at the floor and bit her lip for a second. She shuffled her feet a little.

"Oh, I doubt it's nothing," said Amanda. "Come on, show me some magic, baby!"

"Don't be a chicken shit!" chirped Colleen. "What is it? What are you scared of?"

"Nothing," Shannon repeated.

"Fine, whatever you say," Amanda said as she stubbed out a half-finished cigarette. "I've got a plan and I am going in there, but when I come back out, you better have more than 'nothing'." She stepped out of the car and closed the door. Shannon waited a beat and then stepped out as well and slammed the door behind her.

"What's this now?"

"I'm going in there with you," said Shannon. "I'll figure something out as we go. That seems more our style anyway." Amanda said nothing but only grinned with one side of her mouth, showing a row of sharp, surgically aligned white teeth.

They went into the store and split up. Shannon wandered in the back near the refrigerators and Amanda headed straight for the counter. The pimpled guy behind the register lowered his magazine and focused his attention on the adolescent aphrodisiac that graced him with her presence. "And what can I do for you?" he said.

Amanda reached into her pocket and pulled out the pack of cigarettes she had lifted from her mother' carton. Still wearing the sunglasses, she lit the cigarette and pushed both of her hands into the pockets of her skirt, bulging out from below the fabric.

"Sorry, sweetheart, but no one can smoke in here, rules is rules."

"Yes. But *I* can smoke in here," she said. She blew smoke up to the ceiling from her lower jaw.

"Oh, yeah, sure. *You* can smoke in here." At first, Shannon thought he was being sarcastic by the reflecting answer, but he didn't say any more about it. He only stood there and rocked a little bit like a person would bob along with the waves.

"Now," said Amanda. "I want you to empty the register and give me all the money." At this, she pulled out her right hand and pinched the cigarette between her two fingers to form a gun with her hand. "Or I will blow your brains all up and down that wall, you hear me, boy?"

Almost on cue, the clerk started to sweat and breathe in heavy, short pulls. "Oh, come on missus," he said in a higher, frantic voice. "You don't have to do that! Look, I am getting the money right now."

Shannon watched with her mouth ajar as he actually reached into the register and started to pull out the measly takings of an all-night convenience store at the outstretches of town. She walked from the back of the store to just a couple feet behind Amanda. The clerk didn't seem to even notice her or look in her direction at all for help. He was fixed on those gaudy

95

glasses. Shannon peered directly into his eyes; a film like the glaze milk leaves on the glass after a healthy swig washed over his eyes.

What the hell are you thinking? she asked herself and then, like someone had been listening, she got the answer.

In a moment, it was as if all her thoughts and any other sort of distraction in her brain were wiped away and she could see in her mind's eye just what was going through his head. Just as an old photograph can push away the present and bring back old images so clear and precise, she saw into his thoughts as if she were looking through his eyes. From that window, Amanda was not holding a cigarette in a mock gun pose. Instead, he looked down the barrel of a smoking, black .9mm semi-automatic pistol. Behind the counter, just within reach of the clerk but still concealed from the view of any customers, was a small, old and dirty, but still loaded, snub-nosed revolver. She could feel his fear and his wish to grab the gun, but something wasn't letting him, like a dog wanting to fight only to be pulled back by a taut leash.

Shannon, afraid of the possible consequence, shouted, "He's got a gun!"

"What?" Amanda shrieked. She turned and broke her connection with the boy and that was all it took. In that instant, he reached below the counter and ripped up the snub-nosed, single action revolver. He pulled the trigger, but the first chamber was intentionally left empty to avoid accident. Nothing happened. He swore, stumbled with it and finally pulled the hammer back to rotate to the next shot.

Amanda heard the first 'click' of the gun and whipped around. She put both of her hands up in the air with her palms facing the clerk and simply said, "No." It wasn't a shout in fear, it was a command to him. She had watched it unfold and just didn't like what was coming. She chose for this not to happen.

He stopped, shook with the gun in his hand and bunched his eyebrows together in pain. "No," she said again. "You just fucked up. Why would you try to hold up your own store?" The clerk made a small whimper and then put the gun in his mouth and, without as much as a goodbye, pulled the trigger.

The store was small and enclosed. The first thing Shannon registered was the noise. Or better yet, the lack of it after one huge pop. She closed her eyes to try to force the high pitched electric scream out of her brain and unclog her ears. After it didn't go away for a few moments, she opened her eyes to what had caused it. The clerk's body had been forced back by the shot onto the short counter behind the front desk. He slumped for a second or two against it and then fell to the floor. The blood and bits of flesh contrasted darkly with the white walls, flashing in the bright florescent lights. If you didn't know better, it looked like someone had splashed a pitcher of sangria against the wall in a drunken joke. But the globs of spatter on the wall were slices of membrane, gray matter and shards of bone.

Shannon looked at Amanda who stood in the same spot with her hands on the side of her head. She was frozen there just staring at the unforeseen future that was now a messy past. It was too messy. Too messy to deal with and they had to leave now. Shannon acted first and started to push Amanda out of the store. With her ears still ringing and vision slightly blurred in shock, an image was brought to her attention as if from an outside informant. And again, like the gun, she got a flash of a VCR behind the counter wired into two tiny closed circuit black and white TVs.

Repeating over and over like a nagging child pulling at her dress, she made the connection between the image and what might happen to them if anyone found that tape. *No cover ups this time. No reason for cover ups this time,* she thought to herself.

She bent over the uncollected money, pushed the 'Eject' button and pulled the tape out of the machine. Her force had ripped the video tape at one point and made a trail waving behind her as she rushed out of the store.

She put Amanda into the back of the car, went around to the passenger's side and proceeded to push Colleen into the driver's seat with her body. Ears still ringing, she shouted, "Drive! Drive!"

Colleen's terrified face told Shannon she saw the whole horrible event and she nervously started the car. They pulled out of the lot and drove away, back into the night and further out of town into empty streets surrounded by thick woods on either side.

Shannon let the tape fall to the floor, put her face in her hands and started to cry. Still quite deaf from the close-range gunshot, she focused on the heaving of her chest. Far away and nowhere near the seat right next to her, she heard, "…your face!"

"What?" She felt the words come out. "What about my face?"

"I said you have blood on your face!" said Colleen.

Shannon looked down at her hands and saw red patches from where she had swiped away her tears. It wasn't a lot, but it was enough that anyone would know what it was and enough to make Shannon's stomach roll. She pulled the mirror down and looked at her face. Sure enough, coming down the sides of her cheeks in smeared lines broken apart by tears was blood. In a trick of the light, it seemed as if the blood poured directly from her eyes.

Chapter IV

Shop Talk

Even though there was money in it, Ralph would have preferred to just go home to his video games rather than visit the different esteemed professors' houses and do what Kyle and Steven had dubbed, 'bitch work'. He felt nervous not because it was hard work, far from it, but because he would be just going into people's houses when no one was home. Welcomed or not, Ralph felt a little sense of trespassing that was both exciting and unnerving.

When he walked up to Donald Greenly's house, the first thing he noticed was the well-kempt lawn and thick shrubbery surrounding it. Hell, the front door was not even visible until he walked the short, winding concrete walkway that led up to it. Once inside, Ralph could tell immediately that it was empty and, like his father's house, was empty most of the time.

Donald Greenly's house wasn't just tidy. It was professionally clean. The furniture, carpets, and walls had a fresh, spotless gleam to them as if they had only just been taken out of the wrapping. This enhanced the edges of the minimalist design that carried from room to room. With the door shut behind him, Ralph felt he was tainting the space simply by breathing the air.

He walked delicately into the kitchen so as not to disturb the essence of purity bottled in this house. On the table, he found a note with his name on it and dropped the mail down on the tabletop to pick it up.

Ralph, thanks for helping out! Take this as an advance and spend it wisely.
     -Dr. Donald Greenly.

Ralph counted the money that was attached and found that it was more than the rate his dad quoted. "Not bad at all," said Ralph as he pocketed the cash. Now that that was done, he looked around the kitchen. Immaculate sheen reflected from all surfaces. Something was off. Something made this house seem like it was trying its damnedest to convince Ralph it was a house and nothing more. He decided to poke around a little more.

Rooms down the hallway all followed suit with a lemon-scented newness that would be insulted at Ralph's intrusion could those walls speak. The bathroom made him chuckle to himself. For a man living on his own, Dr. Greenly had a decidedly, purposefully pink bathroom. The floor tiles, shower, sink, towels, lights, even the damn towels and soap in the shower. Pink. The look of it influenced a hyper-hygienic smell that made him feel filthy in contrast.

Ralph went to wash his hands and face to combat the insecurity, but saw no soap on the sink counter. Without thinking much of it, he grabbed the unused bar from the shower and made do.

He made sure the front door was locked tight and then checked the list of addresses written up by his father. All three houses were somewhat evenly spaced, but still not far from each other or Ralph's house. This would make it quite easy to hit them on his way to and from school, provided it didn't start to get too cold too soon.

He reflected on the terror of winter he had heard from his father, friends, and general folk around town. He was too young to really remember it in detail, but he did remember the cold, dark sensation well enough. The winter here, from what he gathered, was an annual tax comparable to biblical forces demanding sacrifice and placing a dark, lasting depression over the land. The worst weather Ralph had seen in recent memory was a thunderstorm while visiting for the summer. Peanuts compared to the frigid clutches of winter.

The next house had that common suburban charm of being practically the same as every other house around it, but just different enough it could be picked from a line-up. Ralph's father said that Dr. Joanna Jackson wanted to be home the first time Ralph got there in order to show him how she'd wanted things done. And when she answered the door, Ralph was instantly happy that she was.

Joanna was a large, middle-aged African-American woman who wore bright colors with her graying hair pushed up and a posture that been imitated by statues around the world. As a full-figured, achieved woman, she was proud of who she was and eager to talk to anyone.

"Well look at you!" said Joanna. "I could have picked you out of a classroom of 300 you look so much like your dad! Well, a little cuter but you get that from your mother, right?" Joanna laughed at her own joke. "Come in, come in!"

Ralph walked into the house and noticed how it was the complete opposite from the Greenly house. This place was warm and alive with pictures all over the walls of a sizable family at different locations around the globe. Ralph saw a younger Joanna with two small children and a dark gentleman at the Grand Canyon. Then, an older, but still much younger than now, Joanna with four teenagers and the same dark gentleman wearing that same suit at the Eiffel Tower.

Joanna noticed where his attention was. "Those are my babies," she said touching the picture with her callused, work-worn hand. "They are older now and moved away, but they are still here, you know?" She gazed deep into the picture. "Well, not all of my babies have left me. This one keeps me on my feet. Arty!" she called into the house.

She led Ralph down the hallway into the kitchen and in less than a moment Ralph heard claws scuffling against the wood floor as a furry dog scuttled in to meet them. Breathing heaving under a shaggy, yellowing coat was Arty.

"He's an English Sheepdog. They are known for their friendliness. Do you like dogs?" asked Joanna. She pet the dog vigorously which caused him to wag his tail and stretch his neck out. Ralph reached down to the dog and let it smell him. Arty took a few sniffs, licked his nose and then pressed his head against Ralph's hand for him to pet it.

"I love 'em, but I never had my own. Is that okay?" Ralph regretted asking the question. Now that he'd said it, he wondered if Joanna would deem him unsuitable for the job.

Joanna just laughed. "No worries. He's very well trained and he can get in and out easy enough through his door. The only thing I need from you is to bring him food twice a day. You understand that if I just left it all out he'd eat himself sick." She turned her attention to Arty and talked in that baby-talk that dogs love so much regardless of the words spoken. "Because then he'd get sick and fat, wouldn't you? Wouldn't you?" This was too much for the poor animal. Arty could barely contain himself as he made short circles with his head, whimpered a second and then flopped onto his side to reveal his tender tummy for Joanna to rub.

"I'm tellin' you, you spoil that dog, Joanna," said a gruff voice. Ralph turned to see the dark gentleman from the photographs looking down at them on the kitchen floor. "Name's Rufus Jackson, you must be Ralph Marker." Rufus reached his hand out and Ralph shook it. "So, think you can take care of this mutt for the doctor?"

"It doesn't sound too hard," said Ralph. "It'll probably be fun."

"He'll be fine," said Joanna. She stood up from petting Arty. "And you don't have to refer to me as 'the doctor'. We are home. There is no need to be so formal, Rufus."

"Just speaking the truth," said Rufus. "Now I know it doesn't sound hard, but this here mutt has been my wife's surrogate grandchild for eight years now and we still don't have any grandchildren, so you can guess how important that damn dog is!" Rufus widened his eyes and nodded his head to add emphasis.

"Surrogate grandchild?" asked the doctor.

"Just speaking the truth, baby," Rufus winked at her and she smiled back.

Joanna proceeded to show Ralph where in the mudroom he could find the sack of dog food and how much to pour into the bowl labeled 'Arty' with an old, chipped measuring cup. Arty followed them around, watching to make sure Joanna didn't forget any details, but Ralph suspected it was more for the chance opportunity he'd get a treat.

"And that's all there is to it," said Joanna after she'd repeated the whole routine about three times. "I have the lists of numbers we can be reached at on the fridge. I'm bound to pick-up at one of them so just start at the top and work your way down if you need to call. Now, we are just about ready to go, just a few last things. Here's the key." She dropped a single, gold key into Ralph's palm. "Arty has already been fed for the day so you don't have to do anything until tomorrow. Any questions, Ralph?"

Ralph had been taken over by a heavy feeling when he came into the house and found that the Jacksons exuded a welcoming sensation unlike any other he he'd felt. For a moment, Ralph was envious of this family. He pushed those bad feelings aside and just said, "Nope, I got it."

"Glad to hear it!" said Joanna. She walked him to the front door out of the kitchen where Rufus had begun to tease the dog just to rile it up a bit. "If you started from your house over there, then Dino's house is probably next, right?"

"Yeah, last one."

Joanna paused in the doorway with her hand on the knob. "Dino...he's a little strange, but he's a good guy. I bet he'll have some sort of out of the way communication set up for you. After his wife died in that car accident it's like he lost a big chunk of himself with her, even if it was years ago." She looked at Ralph and saw the distant look in his eyes. "Ralph, my heart bled for you and your father when I heard. Marie, your mother, she was electric. You could feel her before she even stepped in the room. All that passion, and lord could that woman talk!" She laughed and wiped a tear from her eye. "I don't know if she told you, but we kept in touch, after the divorce. Letters, mostly. She was a good woman, and a great friend." Joanna wiped another tear. "I know what she and I had doesn't compare. She was, is, your mother for Pete's sake."

Ralph listened patiently. "I want you to know that you aren't alone missing her. I hope that makes it easier."

"I," started Ralph. "I could have stopped her. I could have saved her if I did something."

"No," Joanna interrupted. "Don't even think that, don't *ever* think that, honey." She grabbed his shoulder. "What happened was tragic, no doubt about it, but it happened and there is nothing you did wrong, okay?"

"Okay." Ralph thought it sounded like a lie, but let it sit a moment. "I gotta go. It was great to meet you." He turned and left without waiting for a reply. Again, those bad feelings crept their fingers around his torso, his neck. He took a deep breath, coughed and walked on down the road.

Dino Capecci's house broke the rhythm of the suburban, cookie-cutter roadshow. It had a boxy design with large windows, bare surfaces and metal borders all along the edges. The front lawn had no foliage and was cut in a precise diamond pattern. The mailbox was housed in a brick fortress. And the front door was heavy, metal and held a rectangular peephole that would slide open from the inside. It looked like a fashionable cage.

When he entered the house, the motif continued with bleach white carpeting and soft greens, blues, and reds painting the walls. The furniture was sleek with clean, crisp leather on stainless steel support. On an end table in the living area, a phone base of imitation wood blinked a single red light. Next to it was a note that said, "Ralph, push button." Ralph obeyed and the tape recording machine rewound and then played one message.

Cloaked in traffic ambiance, the hushed voice of a fugitive on the run came out of the machine, "Hello, Ralph? This is Dr. Dino. If you are getting this message, then you found the house and got in alright. Like the other professors, I am currently in route to our, ah, conferences and would very much appreciate it if you could gather my mail, sort it and just, you know check on the house. I would like the mail separated into three categories. One, regular mail addressed to me. Two, any mail addressed to my daughter, Tuesday. She is on some sort of 'soul searching' expedition, basically a fancy way to say that she is hunting for exotic ways to spend money. Three, any mail from Tuesday. I might not like her current habits, but she is still my daughter and I look forward to hearing from her. One other thing I would like you to do is feed the fish. Just a pinch of the fish food near the tank will do. No special treatment or cleaning necessary, once every other day or so. Now, as for your fee, I would like to wire the money directly in portioned payments. I don't like leaving money around, so I didn't. Cash and check can be commandeered without a trace. Please call me at my message service number, ah, 725-891-9966, and give me your banking info. If you don't have an appropriate account set up for me to send to, leave a message explaining that and then tell your dad to just go ahead and pay you for what we discussed. I will then wire him the portioned payments. Check this machine regularly and take notes on the messages. When you have taken accurate notes, delete the message. Also, place the key you let yourself in with next to the mail on the table. I wouldn't want that to get misplaced. From now on, use the garage to let yourself in and out. The keypad code to open the door is '9281'. Don't do anything to the car. I will keep you updated only if I need to. I think I've made these instructions clear. I'm trusting you with a lot, but your father vouches for you. Do a good job. Thanks." *Click, Beeeeeep.*

"Weirdo," said Ralph. He looked at the mail he grabbed on the way in and started to separate it on the coffee table. It was all just mail for Dino except for one card that simply said, 'Dad' as the recipient. He placed this one aside and stacked the others in a pile.

The fish tank was very tranquil. Large, sinewy fish glided through the water peacefully against a mock cove environment. Bubbles periodically rose from a treasure chest at the bottom that opened at timed intervals. Ralph brought his face close to the tank to watch the fish. For a moment, he wanted to tap on the glass, but then felt it would only be out of an immature drive to mess with the lunatic he was now working for.

He fed the fish, gave the place a once over and left through the garage. As expected, it was a bare space with one vehicle. A tight, seafoam green convertible with the top down sat polished and screaming for attention in the garage. Ralph whistled at it, and then pressed the button to open the single large garage door. As the door went up, Ralph caught a large note on the inside of the door that said, 'Remember, 9281' before climbing above. He walked outside and shook his head as he entered the code into the outdoor panel.

That was easy. Unusual, but easy, he thought to himself. I don't have a bank account, so I have to get the money from Dad. This guy is so paranoid. This is

Wilhelmina, what could happen in an empty, locked house?

Finished with the first rotation, Ralph walked home in the early evening with a little more money in his pocket and a better picture of what his dad had volunteered him for. Now, his mind wandered to *Cuazque*. Despite the violence and initial uneasiness he'd felt with the game, it had become relaxing. A way to unplug and push all of that other stuff, all that shit, to the sides out of sight and focus on one thing. Focus on being someone else, somewhere else with clear goals, clear dangers and an earned victory against difficulty. The battle fueled a sense of serenity.

****

On Saturday, Ralph left his house, took care of his 'clients' with a little extra attention for Arty, and then headed to meet Kyle and Steven. He was eager to start the day. He, personally, was requested to be places. It was loose, but for the first time since he moved back to Wilhelmina he felt like he belonged.

Steven told him to meet at Lester Park, situated on top of a hill that overlooked much of the downtown area. Ralph remembered it from his childhood and decided to test his memory to see if it could get him back. With one or two wrong turn corrections, he found the winding path up to the park. One thing in particular he remembered was the 'rainbow'. The 'rainbow' was an arched ladder, bent at the middle touching the ground on both sides. Children would climb across starting from one side, going either above or below the colorful bars, and attempt to work their way to the other side. His mother forbid him from playing on it, but summer visits were a different story so long as she didn't find out.

It was the first thing that came into view and Ralph knew he was at the right place. It looked faded and chipped now, nothing like the bright tower he'd remembered, but nostalgia still brought a smile to his face. Just behind it at a bench, he made out the shape of a hunched boy with another tall, lanky one leaned over his shoulder.

Once he got closer, Ralph saw Steven consumed in a handheld game as Kyle gave advice, or more likely jeered him, from behind. Ralph raised his hand and was about to call out to them when Steven squeezed the game white-knuckled to let out a fraction of his frustration and yelled, "Shut up! Just shut up, will ya!"

Kyle put his hands up in surrender and laughed. "Hey man," he said with a smile. "Don't hate me 'cuz you suck!"

Steven's back heaved as Ralph approached. Steven snapped his head up and scowled at Kyle before bending back to his game. Kyle slowed his laughter when he saw Ralph. "Awwww yeah, look who decided to show up!" he said. "See, I told you he'd come."

"Damn, you're slow!" Steven growled. He pushed his glasses up the bridge of his nose, beads of sweat peppered his forehead. "Finally, we can get outta here, this game is giving me cancer!"

"What are you playing, *Tetris*?" asked Ralph.

"What? No," answered Steven. "It's *Bubble Jump 2*, but it's crazy hard and this asshat keeps talking to me while I play!"

"Ehhh, what is that, a platformer? I only like puzzle games on the handhelds like," Ralph weighed some options. "*Tetris*. I can just jump in and play however long I want, then get up and go, right?"

"Why would I want to play puzzle games? You can't beat puzzle games."

116

"No, but I don't always want to beat the game. I like playing the game for the game. Beating it is sometimes the worst part because there's no more game then. Besides, puzzles are always changing which makes *Tetris* infinite in game."

Kyle gave Ralph an admiring gaze and said, "Man, that was beautiful. It's like, you looked into the game's soul or something."

For a moment, Ralph was impressed with himself, until Steven burst his bubble. "Yeah, bullshit. Puzzle games are for crazy people. All you do is the same thing over and over again. That is the definition of crazy, you idiots, doing the same thing again and again and again and again!"

"Nah, man," said Ralph. "I don't see it that way."

"Don't listen to this basket case," said Kyle. "His relationship with games borders on domestic abuse. Psssh, did you see his gutted controllers?" He shook his head at Steven. "This kid right here has broken enough controllers to build a Vee Dub Bug. Damn Steven, don't you know there are kids in Africa who never even *heard* of video games?"

"It's not my fault they break so easy," said Steven. "If the builders would test some of the games, I bet they would make better controllers, but as of now, I consider it wear and tear of a dedicated practice. Like an athlete's equipment or knight's armor. The way I see it, my no longer functioning controllers are an achievement." He lifted his hand palm up to accentuate how he was trying to make an elegant statement, then turned and started to lead the others out of the park towards town.

"Yeah, an achievement like those pictures of your mom in my sock drawer," said Kyle, scratching his nose to cover his mouth. Ralph didn't see it coming and let out a burst of laughter. Kyle joined in and after no return fire from Steven, they laughed even harder.

Kyle wiped tears from his eyes and asked, "So you found this place just fine then, huh?"

"Yeah," said Ralph. "I remembered it from when I was a kid. Once I saw the rainbow, I knew I was in the right place."

"Ahhh, that rainbow," said Kyle. "Did you ever hear what happened to Steven on the rainbow?"

Steven spun around. "Shut up. That was a long time ago."

"Exactly," said Kyle. "It was a long time ago. And besides, he's probably gonna hear it sometime. Why not from us so he gets the true story and not one of the dozen versions where you sound dumber and dumber? Come on, man, consider it therapy."

"Fine," said Steven. He turned back around and walked ahead of the other two. "Just tell it right," he said over his shoulder.

"Good, I like the grown-up attitude. And don't worry, it's simple so it would be hard to mess up." Kyle turned his attention to Ralph. "Way back when, when we were in like first or second grade, Steven called Amanda Klein a stupid, stuck-up, rich, white bitch. She wasn't gonna stand for that, but she's smart, she's patient. She waited for opportunity, and when Steven was hanging down from the middle of the rainbow, she found it. She pulled his pants down, drawers and all, in front of everyone!" He laughed at his own story before continuing. "Well, not *everyone* everyone, it was only like fifty kids under the age of ten and maybe four teachers old enough that even the apocalypse wouldn't surprise them."

119

After Ralph laughed and clapped, he weighed the story for a moment. "You're right, it isn't *that* bad. Do people still bring it up?"

"You told it wrong!" said Steven. "She pantsed me before I called her the rich, stuck-up bitch she is. You said what I did before you said what she did. It makes me look like the villain. She ruined me from that day forward."

"Ahhh, hush, I told it like it happened. You don't screw with rich girls, more money means more crazy. Besides, she didn't *ruin* you, drama queen, it was just kid shit that got bunched up with all the other lunacy."

"She deserved it."

"Maybe. But you did too."

"No. If she slapped me on the face, I could live with it, but that was unforgivable. I will never talk to her again."

"Good outlook, she probably wouldn't give you the time of day anyway."

"Just, shut up," Steven snapped.

"Amanda Klein," said Ralph. "Where did I hear that name? Oh yeah, she was there when that girl died, right? Jesus, she just caught fire."

"Yeah, man," said Kyle. "Beth, Beth Gardner. Damn, I knew her, well, sorta. I think we all sorta knew her. I couldn't believe it when my mom told me. She works at the hospital, a nurse, and she said she was long gone by the time she got there. Some sort of freak accident."

"No accident, those idiot girls were probably playing with fire and whoops, Beth's up in flames," Steven added, happy to pivot the conversation.

"Nah, man, something's weird about this," said Kyle. "Everyone's left those girls alone because they don't want to bother them after what they saw, but I think they're hiding something. I couldn't believe how fast they came back to school. And why would Beth be at Amanda's house with the other two in the first place? Nah, something stinks."

"Like what?" pressed Steven. "They invited her over to, to, to, torture her? Yeah, those mean bitches probably would do that to sweet Beth."

"Stop it, now you're just looking for an angle to hate."

"Maybe."

"Ah, shit," said Ralph. "I have to work with that girl, Shannon Kennedy, on my project which I still didn't start."

"Maybe the teacher will have pity on her and give you all an A," Kyle offered.

"No. No way. O'Brian told me himself that I should just take the weight off her and do it all by myself. Well, by myself and with that other girl, Liza? Lisa?"

"Lisa Meadows?" asked Steven.

"Here we go," said Kyle.

"Yeah, that was her name. Wait, is there something wrong with her, too?"

"No, not at all," Steven said in a dreamy voice. "Lisa Meadows packs a brainy punch. You think you bad just 'cuz you skipped a grade? Lisa skipped two. I can't believe you got grouped with those two right out of the gate. Lucky bastard."

Kyle rolled his eyes and said, "He has a point. Hell, Lisa would probably do it all herself just to prove she could. I say you're sitting pretty on this one, Ralph. You could probably just sit back, play video games and let the girls do all the work."

"I wouldn't learn anything and besides, that's just shitty. I should use it as a chance to burn O'Brian and really make an impression on him," said Ralph. "I couldn't do that."

"Won't know until you try," said Kyle.

Conversation quieted down as the boys walked a steep decline into the busy streets of downtown Wilhelmina. The sidewalks had even concrete and the streets were smooth without potholes or cracks. People could be seen through storefront windows shopping or sitting outside of restaurants enjoying the last leg of summer with a good bite.

Steven stopped the group in front of a slim brick building with the curtains pulled in the windows and no signage out front to signify any sort of business. "Alright, here's the deal," said Steven with imitated showmanship. "This the spot, but I want to give you a little prep before we go in. This place has like, everything, and if it doesn't, Phil has a knack for obtaining rarities." Ralph looked across the street and all around for the usual bright neon lights game shops had. It couldn't just be some guy's house, right?

"Got it? Good. Let's do it." They walked in a straight line through the alley between the brick house and a hair salon next door. Dolled up middle-aged women looked up through the big window for a moment at them, and then returned to page lazily through monthly advice on how their lives needed to be fixed.

Through the alley and in the back, Ralph found a pebble-covered parking lot with a few cars and a ramp leading into a basement door. On the back of the brick house a sign read, 'The Shop'.

"You know, I thought you guys just called it that like a nickname. I didn't actually think, well..." Ralph didn't finish the sentence, but instead gestured to this sign.

Kyle stared at it and said in a glossy tone, "Yeah, dig it." Kyle and Steven walked down the ramp. Ralph let out a sigh and followed. Through the door, his eyes needed a few seconds to adjust to the dim, underground light, but the smell in the windowless dungeon assaulted his nose. A mixture of pizza, mildew and a hint of pot made him cough. After adjusting, Ralph saw rows of shelves filled with games for a range of consoles, a corner full of comic books with two pale twenty-somethings in the clutches of debate, and miscellaneous other stuff in a corner labeled, 'Garage'.

Gibby Haynes's voice streamed out of the speakers singing about lost youth with morbid tendencies.

Steven and Kyle walked off in different directions. His reservations before entering quickly subsided in place of a familiar, connected feeling. He recognized the items on the shelves and the feeling The Shop gave off. Comfort came easily.

Ralph walked through the aisles, looked thought the games piled on top of each other with no semblance of order. When he reached the end of an aisle near the 'Garage' section, he started to browse the games closely. From the other side of the shelf, he overhead two people talk ardently.

"Back from the dead like how?" asked one of them. "Do they become mindless zombies? Or are they, you know, with it?"

"They aren't zombies, not really, they are as much of themselves as they can be, but they are under your control," explained the other.

"I like where this is going."

"Shut up, get your head out of the gutter. They're the undead, don't be gross."

"I didn't say anything."

"You said enough." There was an audible sigh. "Okay so bring people back from the dead. Or, you cannot die. Better, you have super healing. You are extra, extra hard to kill. But it can be done."

"I can only have one power?"

"Yeah, *only* one. Greedy son of a bitch."

"Hmmmmm, it would be cool to be a one-man army and just walk through the opposition, but I don't like getting by hands dirty. I want a legion of the undead."

"Nice!"

"Yeah, we could infiltrate anywhere with pure numbers, and then if they go down, all I gotta do is say, 'Rise from Your Grave', and we're back in the fight. Then, I bring back the enemies they took out to fight their own team! Now I'm thinking!"

"Keep going, keep going."

"Just think about it, being locked in a room with one of them, you blow 'em away and they get back up, you take 'em down again, and they get back up! And, and, and the pieces that you just blew apart start movin' again, independent of the body!"

A low, grounded voice broke up the banter with clear words saying, "Look, you two have been fantasizing together all day and not bought a damn thing. If you don't, I am gonna have to ask you to leave. This isn't a knitting circle. Get it?"

Ralph laughed a little, but turned it into a cough to stay on the sidelines for

126

what might happen next. "Don't act like that, Phil," said one of them. "You know you like this game. Play with us."

"If I do, will you take it outside?" asked Phil.

"Fine, we'll go, but first?"

"Easy. That super healing ability. Corralling the undead would be such a chore, so slow and messy. I'll do what I need myself, get it done right. Besides, you can't trust anyone these days."

"That's boring."

"Whoops, don't care, bye."

Ralph listened to the two guys walk out of the store and felt the energy they built go with them. It sounded like fun to spitball like that, even if it was nonsense. For a moment, he juggled the two options in his mind to see how he felt about it. *It would be cool to never lose a fight, no one could stop me. But, on the other hand...*

"Yo," interrupted Phil. "You cool, man?" Phil was a short man, about 5'6" in shoes and weighed 140 pounds with a full stomach. There was a clear attempt at compensation with his hair, both facial and cranial. Under glasses that even a senior citizen would call large was a lush, full beard, trimmed and shaped professionally. Above the glasses, a shiny, cascade of gloriously vibrant blonde hair. A short, thin, lumberjack princess.

Ralph's reaction to the question was to just stare wide-eyed and blink. He couldn't believe that such a stern, confident voice came from this substitute teacher-looking short stack. At a momentary loss for words, he let out one, 'ha', and then said, "Yeah."

Phil squinted his eyes, looked Ralph up and down once and shrugged. "I've never seen you here before, so I hope I didn't give off the wrong impression how I handled those two. They had it coming and it doesn't mean they won't be back in a day or two to play that same damn game and end up asking me for a job. Trust me, they had it coming." His arms were full of games that he shelved wherever they fit. "They buy stuff, occasionally, they just need to be reminded." Once his hands were empty, he reached out to Ralph and said, "Anyway, name's Phil and this is my shop, pretty cool, right?"

Ralph shook his hand and repeated, "Yeah." He noticed Phil squint his eyes at him again as if there was small print he was trying to read on Ralph's face. He didn't like that look so much, it was too piercing.

"Yeah, I'm Ralph. My friends, Steven and Kyle brought me here, do you know them?"

"But of course," Phil said as he let go of Ralph's hand. He arched his body back to lob his words over the shelves. "Kyle, your game's in and your bill's late!" There had been dragging steps, but they stopped in attempt to remain undetected. It was bad timing as the songs changed and there was a silence that only made it more obvious he was found out. Loud bass guitar wails followed by a heavy groove opened up a man's aggressive talk of authoritarian hypocrisy.

"Steven and Kyle said that this was *the* spot for games and stuff. I can see why. It's got spunk," said Ralph.

"You game? What have you been playing lately?" asked Phil.

"I've really been getting into *Cuazque* lately. I've wanted to get my hands on it for a while, but there's not a lot of them around. Steven lent me a copy."

"*Cuazque*, huh? Yeah, I think Steven bought that one from me, right Stevie?"

Steven walked into the aisle with a new, still in the plastic wrap game, in his hands. "Yeah, I did," he said. "But when I asked you about it for tips and tricks, you had nothing. In fact, you acted like you didn't even want to play it. And you call yourself a game nerd, tsk tsk tsk."

"What, you think I'm not nerd enough for this?" said Phil. "I tell you what, why don't you bring in some regular, run of the mill big-wig to open up a game store with his studied business models and investors and market studies and then compare that shtick against my place. They'll flop like a fish out of water. Desperate, futile effort. I got the juice in this joint."

"What juice?" Steven pressed. "You're hidden away, you kick out customers and you don't even organize your merchandise. Seems like you're the one running out of air."

Phil smiled and said, "Do you know why I don't organize the merchandise? Because when you don't know where to look, you don't know what you'll find. Looking for one game, three or four might catch your eye along the way. And do you know why I am hidden away? Because all you squashy little bums can't stand the rest of the world and you need to hop from one sanctuary to the next. You want it to be secret, special. And do you know why I kick out certain customers? It's a ruse, a game I play just to make them feel like they have an actual presence here, an identity. Keeps them coming back to this treasure lair again and again."

"That's darkly manipulative," said Ralph.

"What business model isn't?" Phil simply put. "I just know what you all want. Something unusual, something with a slight glimmer of the beyond you start to believe in after hours in front of the TV. That's why I have the most successful game store, not just around the lake, but in the valley."

The gravity of what Phil just spelled out began to make an impression in the basement's atmosphere, but it fell apart when Kyle said, "It's also the *only* game store in the valley." Steven looked to his friend and let out a triumphant cheer of laughter.

"Maybe...but you're still indebted to this store."

"Don't worry, I got dough for the Man," said Kyle. He walked over to the front desk, reached in his pocket and pulled out a crumbled fold of bills. With a lick of his thumb and pointer finger, he said, "How much?"

"I'm not the Man," scorned Phil. "I just know how to punk the punks. You want to pay for the new game too? Be right back." He pushed through a sleazy bead screen doorway into a backroom and came out a few moments later. In his hand, he stretched out a plain cartridge out of the box towards Kyle, and then pulled it back before it got too close. "That's twenty bucks, including late charges, on that tab you had, plus this…let's make it an even sixty dollars and we're square."

"Psssshhhh," said Kyle, breaking his cool composure. "Man, that's bullshit. I know you only paid like twenty dollars for that game at a flea market, why can't we do an honest forty?"

"You're right, I did get it at a flea market," said Phil. "For fifteen dollars, but I had to go to five different markets in five different places and deal with all those circus animals for the better part of a weekend to get it for fifteen dollars. Now, if you want to do that yourself in a car I know you don't have, with needed patience that would probably cause your under-developed teenage brain to travel time out of frustration, be my guest. Until then, I'll cut you a deal. Fifty."

"Screw it, fine," said Kyle. He put forth exaggerated effort to count out the money loud and slow on the counter with most of the bills being ones and fives. Around thirty dollars, Kyle's voice had raised into a mock job of an old, biddy teacher counting numbers for toddlers, Steven ripped the bills from his hands and quickly counted out the remaining twenty.

"Jesus, what is wrong with you?!" said Steven.

"No man, I was making him work for it and you ruined it," said Kyle. "You can't just give it out like that. Now, this shit better work, or I want my money back *with* late charges, feel me?"

"Don't worry, Kyle. The game works just fine. It sucks, but it works. I mean, the graphics were nice, but it played so clunky. Was like…foreign construction equipment. Come to think of it, why this game and not something newer? Ya like 'em aged?"

"I heard that if you beat it under twenty hours in one sitting, no saves and no deaths, then the next time you play it the girl is naked the whole game."

"What girl?"

"The girl in the game, man, look." Kyle put the cartridge down on the counter and pointed to the anonymous, space-suited protagonist on the front. "This girl."

"Whelp, I thought that was a robot."

"Really? That's a big investment for a rumor. Besides, are the pixels enough to get you hard?" asked Ralph.

"Yeah, yeah," added Steven. "Why don't you just swipe a Playboy from your dad? Five minutes. Bang! Done."

"Five minutes?" Ralph asked Steven.

"It's not like that," said Kyle. He weighed the game in his hand a little and peered, not at it, but through it. "I am not trying to get a nut off with this game, it's just, when do you get to play a game as a naked girl where you jump around blowing up aliens? I see the pixels on the screen, but in my head, it all looks different...it all makes more sense." He trailed off at the end and stared down at the game.

"Whatever works for you," said Phil. He threw his arms up in a surrender gesture. "As long as your pervy tendencies rely on games or comics, you know where to find me."

Kyle rolled his eyes in silent agreement and moved over to sit in a beanbag in the comic section to study the cover more. Phil, returning the agreement, pulled out a bookmarked catalogue from behind the counter and opened it with a red pen in hand. Ralph watched him scan a page and then slowly turn to the next page. "Why did you stop playing *Cuazque*?" asked Ralph.

Phil slowly turned his attention up from the spread catalogue. "Ahhh, that game gave me a headache? No, it wasn't that. It was like," Phil flicked the red pen against his face, harder with each strike. "My jaw was clenched tight and I ground my teeth, like I was on…you kids wouldn't understand that. Uh, that and uncomfortable muscle tension, my whole body was ready for action, to jump. Somewhere in there and I just didn't enjoy it. Plus, I've heard some campfire stories about that game that helped me stay away from it."

"Campfire stories?" asked Ralph. "I've read some odd things about it in magazines, but I thought that it was all a joke. You know the drill, unreasonable kids in some nowhere town breaking stuff, starting fights, hurting animals, and they wanted to blame it on the game. Some even said these kids lost it and killed their whole family. Jesus, it really built a legend around it."

"Well, I was talking to a buddy of mine that I meet at a bunch of different

135

sales and shops, he does sorta what I do, going around and looking for rare games to resell. He collects more than he sells, though, there's a true-blue nerd for ya. He told me that *Cuazque* was made by just a handful of people. Most of it was by these two guys, Jacobi and Fritz or some shit. They ran the show, and after the game came out, their office space burned down. They couldn't tell the source of the fire, some freak accident, I guess, but the insurance still paid out and big." Phil saw he had the full attention of the three boys. He paused, straightened himself and continued.

"So, those two guys, Jacobi and Fritz, bailed to South America for *some* reason. Maybe they were looking for something, maybe they were running from something, but the story goes that they went to develop a new game, a sequel, down there, in those lost rainforests."

"Sounds like you remember a lot," said Ralph.

"Eh, it's coming back little by little."

"I hate that shit. 'People said, I heard'," Steven mocked. "It's the cycle of bullshit urban legend formula. It always happened to someone's friend's uncle or another person's girlfriend's cousin. It's a shit story with ingrained distance set up so no evidence can actually be called upon. Plus, there are plot holes and mistakes; really dumb characters, bad decisions, spooky circumstances and in the end, there is no explanation. It's a lame-o tactic for people to scare children, *children*, into staying in line and doing what they're told."

"Maybe, maybe not. Those stories are harmless fun, something to imagine but not think too deeply about," said Ralph. "Think of it this way; someone told Phil, someone told that person. More than one person makes people. People told Phil the story."

"Don't dress it up like that," said Steven. "You know what I mean."

Ralph ignored Steven and turned back to Phil. "When you said 'campfire stories', I thought you meant about the game itself. I haven't beaten it yet, but *Cuazque* is noticeably unusual. It gives me a sick, sorta guilty feeling in my gut. The way it looks and moves is real screwy too, but I can't *not* watch it. I anticipate, expect, even look forward to the violence, but when I get it, I feel bad, man. But I keep playing." Ralph shook his head and laughed a little in spite of himself.

Phil nodded. "Yeah, I hear ya. There was something special about the blood, that was important, I remember that."

Steven saw an opportunity and jumped right in with attitude. "Awwww, a little bloody fuss and muss frightens you?" he said in a tone reserved for teasing little children. "Get real, that's every game out there. *Fatal Fighting*? You rip out a dude's spine through his body." To really drive it home, Steven mimicked it by putting his hand on his chest, grimacing and then pulling the same hand forward clutching an invisible spine with a shaking arm and pained expression. "See?" he cut the act. "No big deal."

"This works differently," said Ralph. "When I got to the first boss and he drank the blood for power, it, well, touched me, outta the TV."

"Now I remember," said Phil. "It wasn't that there was blood and violence, it was *how* there was blood and violence. Jeez, yeah, that drink of blood, right out of the heart like that. I think he killed me and that's when I stopped playing. Another bud told me how it ends, and it was all just batshit weird so I didn't feel the need to invest myself."

"What do you mean weird?" asked Steven. "You conquer the land and become their ruler. A little dark, but you climb to the top. What's wrong with that?"

"What? That's not how it ends," said Phil. "That's not how it ends at all. Nah, nah, this is way more gruesome and unsettling. I think I blacked it out it was so nasty. I can't remember too much, but I know that you are off, Steven. Are you sure you beat this game?"

Steven scrunched his face and swayed side to side thinking. "Uhhhh, I think?"

Phil lowered his chin to his neck and looked at Steven over the rim of this glasses. "You think?" he said. "You know what I think? I think you are making it up. Come to think of it, it's too hard for you, Steven. You talk a big game, but I've seen you in action, it ain't pretty."

"Ohhhhhhhh!" said Kyle. The Shop filled with laughter from everyone but Steven.

"Shut up," said Steven, quick on the defense. "Shut up, you, you, you and your pixel porn just shut up!" This only worsened the blow and amplified the laughter. Steven glared at each of them deliberately until the laughter finally calmed down. "Screw this, I'm hungry. I'm going for a slice." He left the store without waiting for a reply and slammed the door behind him. Ralph felt bad for a moment, but only for a moment.

Kyle caught his momentary victory said, "Don't worry about him, Ralph. He's a little soft sometimes, but he'll be fine if we meet up with him and just leave this talk here. A slice or two is always a good idea. Phil? Wanna join?"

Phil considered the option, but decided against it. "Nah," he said. "I better stay here and be responsible, you know, practice my business model."

"Got it. Let's go, man, I know exactly where he went." Kyle reached over the counter, grabbed a plastic shopping bag for his game, and lead Ralph out of The Shop. The two boys walked in silence for the three blocks to Mentevelli's. Out front, the sign hung above the glass door entrance and Ralph recognized the same image from the pizza box of the grinning chef. Under the name Mentevelli's, the slogan told patrons, "Remember to Eat Your Pizza!"

Inside, they saw Steven's back to them sitting in one of the cheap, particle-board bench booths. "I got this, go ahead and sit down," said Kyle. He walked up to the counter with different pizzas on display behind glass to talk to one of cooks working. Ralph sat down across from Steven, tried to make eye contact, but was met with Steven's head turned down and held down.

"Ralph," said Steven.

"Steven," he replied.

Kyle slid into the bench next to Steven. He gave Ralph a smirk, and then nudged Steven with his elbow. No reaction. He did it again. "Stop it," said Steven.

Kyle clicked his lips. "Come on man, I just bought you some pizza, relax," he said.

"Pizza first, then I *might* relax."

"Fine."

Six slices of mushroom, pepperoni and olive pizza slid onto the table steaming after a quick warm up. It was the day's special and even though it had been sitting out for hours, a few minutes back in the brick oven rejuvenated its glory and the boys entered pizza nirvana bite by bite.

"Mmm!" said Kyle with a clap of his hands. "This shits the best. I could eat it on a full stomach, no issue. You know, Ralph, this pizza is gonna spoil you. How was it in the desert?"

"They didn't really have pizza out there," said Ralph. "I mean, they called it pizza, but it sucked so we never really ate it. It was thin, potato chip crunchy and boring. Like a cooked saltine cracker topped with ketchup." Even Steven chuckled at this. Enamored by the delectable pie, it was hard to stay bitter. Aggressions and annoyances that were present only minutes ago wafted away at the arrival of rich, baked pleasure. Consuming the saucy, cheesy, crispy bread provided a serene atmosphere that replaced sharp words with welcomed complacency.

"So, got any more stories I should know about?" asked Ralph.

Kyle and Steven gave each other a look in silent commune. "There is something of a local legend in Wilhelmina," started Kyle. "They call it, 'The Witch's House'. It's a broken down old shack tucked away near the lake. The story goes that a woman lived there a hundred years ago, alone. Some say her husband and kids left her when she proclaimed her love for Lucifer, some say she killed 'em all and hid the bodies. There was no investigation, no trial. See, this old bat had money, she was protected, and Wilhelmina was growing back then, so a

142

gruesome family murder wasn't exactly something they wanted to advertise." Steven laughed, Ralph narrowed his eyes and kept a cold composure listening. "They just left her alone in that house. When she'd come to town, dressed all in black, people avoided her like the plague, children threw stones, but she just kept to herself. Years went by and let me tell you, people didn't live too long back then so it was a huge surprise that she reached 70, 80 years old. But, after all that time, her mind started to get a mind of its own. One day, a man, some banker, saw opportunity in the property and after countless letters left unanswered, decided to muster up the strength to go into the woods after her."

"Here it comes," interrupted Steven.

Kyle waved his hand in Steven's face and continued telling Ralph the story. "Do you know what he found?" he asked rhetorically. "Past the front walk where the mail collected in a ruined pile, down through the trees, he noticed birds circling above and flies all over with a rotten stench that grew the deeper he walked. Determined to make a profit, he marched on, until he found the source of the putrid smell. Propped up on crucifixes, the

143

remains of cats and rabbits and rats and toads had been splayed and bled out. Scores of sacrifices filled the yard right in front of the house. But he didn't run yet. Not until he went in the house, not until he found the old crone sitting in a chair, dead, with a purring cat in her lap."

"Ooooohhhh," mocked Steven. As Kyle told the story, he had been folding his paper plate into a small, thick triangle. He waved it in the air to enhance his joke.

Ralph let out a forceful breath. "Is that it?" he asked.

Steven grinned and turned to Kyle. "Not even the best part," said Kyle. "You see, when that banker found her, it was her alright, but she was young. She was an 80-year-old woman that looked no older than 25. They say she had tears running down her face when the townsfolk went to collect her. Youth restored to a horror-stricken, sad, lonely old bat."

Ralph thought about it a second. "Killing all those animals made her young but still killed her?" he asked.

"Some would say," answered Kyle. "The way the black magic works is that you have to get the attention of the dark powers that be with dark acts. More than 50 animal carcasses musta done the trick. I think she was running from something. I think she killed her family for her rejuvenation. That sounds like one hell of a way to get the attention of evil powers. But they wanted more, so she kept killing the animals as payment."

Ralph didn't like where his mind went, but he had a question. "If she'd already killed her family, she must not have thought much about human lives. Why did she kill all those animals instead of people? I mean, you said terrible acts attract demonic attention, right? What's a bunch of rodents worth in black magic?"

Kyle pointed at Ralph and poked his finger at him in agreement. "Now you're thinking," he said. "Because maybe she didn't kill her family. Maybe, she was trying to bring them back. A lot is uncertain. But one thing that is true, is that that house is still here. Nobody touched it after what happened."

"Yeah," said Steven. "And all the old folks say that the land is cursed. Cursed I say! So that any person who dare wander to the Old Witch's House will lose their pets in an awful accident."

"What if you don't have any pets?" asked Ralph.

"Pfft, I don't know," said Steven. He was clearly not a fan of this ghost story. "Probably something just as bullshitty. It's just some old Wilhelmina legend made to scare kids into staying away from the house because it is ancient and broken. Kids are dumb. Kids fall through loose floor boards or cut themselves or some shit. Plain-old scare tactics."

Ralph sat back in the plywood booth, drummed a few fingers on his now pizza-filled stomach, burped and said, "Have either of you gone in?"

At the same time, Kyle said, "No" and Steven said "Yes". Kyle turned to look at Steven with raised eyebrows and a stiff upper lip.

"No," Steven admitted.

"Lying sack of shit," said Kyle.

"Lame," said Ralph.

"Eh," said Kyle. "It isn't that exciting. In the end, I never heard of the curse affecting anybody and it's just an old, busted house."

"Then why don't wreck it or something?"

"Because someone owns it. Someone crazy."

"Yeah? Who?"

146

Steven gave a forced chuckle, turned to the side and darted the folded paper plate into a nearby garbage can. "Shannon Kennedy's mom," he said after it hit the inside of the can with a thud.

"Ha! For real?" asked Ralph.

"There's more to it than that. Some sort of second cousin removed inheritance that only worked under the full-moon. People say that that crazy lived on through the house and whoever owned it was both cursed to keep it and lose their minds."

"No shit?" said Ralph. "Why do I not feel surprised?"

"You wanna see it?" asked Kyle.

"Can we? How far is it?"

"It's a ways to hoof it, but I think we can see it from a lookout point, cool?"

Ralph stared at Kyle for a second and then gathered up the rest of the plates and napkins. He dumped them in the garbage, turned to look at the other boys and said, "Let's go!" Kyle and Steven followed him out of the pizza shop.

Kyle led them down a few blocks perpendicular to their original course towards a large concrete wall against a hill with a staircase cut into it that zigzagged to the top. Ralph felt the stairs were getting taller and taller as they approached and when they arrived he stopped to measure the height.

"Come on man, we gotta get high for this," said Kyle.

"That's gotta be more than fifteen stories!" said Ralph.

"This was your idea," said Steven. He and Kyle laughed and started up the steps without waiting for Ralph. Ralph took a deep breath and went after them. *This damn northeastern landscape,* he thought to himself. *I'd rather the heat and the flatness.*

After twenty minutes of staircase switch-backs and embarrassing panting, Ralph reached the top of the hill. Another, smaller park sat atop with benches and old, bent trees. Ralph could see all of Wilhelmina unfold around him with the town to the south and the clustered neighborhoods to the north. From here, the quaint town with its old American architecture seemed noble and proud. In the opposite direction, organized, aesthetically pleasing neighborhoods held bigger and bigger houses on bigger and bigger lots until the green of the encompassing woods swallowed them up. From this point, taking in the wide stretch on a surface level, Wilhelmina was a pocket all unto itself, far away from worries, dangers, and dark histories of the rest of the world.

"You see that bald spot out there?" asked Kyle. He pointed to a field out beyond the neighborhoods, alone in that dense wood, where corn or wheat had once grown but now it was a barren wasteland. A grouping of tall, skinny trees sat in the center looking like they had a jump on fall with branches bare of leaves. The grouping waved back and forth in the breeze as a unit and cloaked a boxy shape within.

"That's it? I can barely see it," Ralph complained. "I wanted to get a better look."

"You can knock yourself out getting over there. Me? I'm ready to test this baby out," Kyle tapped the game purchased from The Shop.

Ralph looked to Steven. "I think I'm in the same boat," said Steven.

Ralph wasn't ready to go alone. "Hmph," he said. "Fine. Maybe another time." Ralph looked back over the town and noticed police activity at a small store on the far side.

"What's that? Did something happen?" he asked pointing to the store.

"That place?" asked Steven. "They get robbed all the time, I guess this time something serious must have gone down for the police to section it off like that. Eh, it's all the way over there, that's not our problem. Just forget it, man, it's happened before and it will happen again."

The boys walked down through the park and headed towards their houses. Although exciting in the moment, the Witch's House fell from Ralph's mind as *Cuazque* in the treehouse crept closer and closer. For the rest of the weekend, alone with the TV, Ralph plugged away at his newly budding dark obsession.

Chapter V

Check-Out Girl

The neighbor chore circuit Monday afternoon was familiarly repetitive for Ralph. As he approached his home, he went over the objectives just to be sure he didn't forget anything. *Greenly house; mail, newspaper, check,* he thought. *Jackson house; mail, Arty was shy, didn't want to come near me, still fed him, check. Capecci house, mail, fish, used the pretty pink bathroom, check. Now let's get lost in the jungle.*

He opened the metal door to his treehouse with excited energy, but lost momentum at the sight of a tall, dark-haired girl snooping around with her arms on her hips and her back to him.

"Who the hell are you?" he asked.

The girl turned around quickly in surprise and looked down on him with wide, deep, dark eyes. After a moment, her expression changed to a more stern, serious look. "Hi, Ralph," she said in a friendly tone. "I thought I'd find you here."

"Cool," said Ralph sarcastically. "What do you want?"

"I'm Shannon, from class." She brushed one side of her long hair behind an ear. "We have to work on that assignment for bio, remember?" She was aggravated at his cluelessness.

"Oh, right," said Ralph. "Look O'Brian already tried to get me to do the work alone, so if you're here to try to convince me too, just cut the crap and tell me, I'm a busy person."

"What?" Shannon was taken aback for a breath. "No, I don't want to do that. Actually, I want to contribute as best as I can. Things have been a little *unusual* for me and I'm hoping this will bring some boring normalcy to help calm things down."

Ralph felt uneasy but he didn't know why. "How did you find me here? Better yet, how did you *think* you'd find me here?" He dropped his backpack onto the ground, leaned against the doorframe and crossed his arms.

"Your friend, Kyle, told me. He said you'd be here after school so, here I am." She eased herself into swivel chair and spun it around all in one fluid movement. She was lying, of course, they had not talked. She saw the image and location of this place the first time she met Ralph, but thought nothing of it at the time. After the convenience store, she wanted more practice so there would be less mistakes down the road. For the days leading up to this meeting, she thought he might live in a treehouse.

"I like the nerd-dungeon by the way. I imagine it's a pretty cool hideout."

"It can be," said Ralph, still in the doorframe, still skeptical.

Shannon rocked back and forth in the swivel chair and threw up one hand in an, 'I don't know' gesture. "Well, here I am," she said. "Got any ideas for the project?"

It wasn't an attraction Ralph felt. Yes, she was attractive, very pretty indeed, but he wasn't getting butterflies in his stomach. A slight danger beyond the horizon, a hint of pointed fangs. He shook it off by taking a deep breath, stretching out his arms and slapping his legs. "I've been kicking some ideas around, but haven't really decided yet. To be honest, I thought you would just weasel your way out on account of what happened."

"What happened?" asked Shannon with pointed interest.

"Well, with Beth Gardner," said Ralph. He couldn't tell if she was glaring at him or trying to look through him somehow. "I heard you were there when she, well, had her accident," he continued. "I can only imagine. Hell, you don't have to tell me about seeing some weird freak shit like that, I've...well, I can guess how strange it must all be."

"Strange doesn't even scratch the surface." She decided he didn't know anything after all. "Did you know Beth?"

"No, I'm kind of the new guy around here so I only found out about her afterwards." After what he saw happen to his mother, he couldn't help but feel bad for this girl in front of him. A small part of him regretted cursing her for what O'Brian suggested. "I think some boring normalcy can help after shit like that."

"Right, the project," said Shannon. She gave him a warm smile, turned her head to the ceiling and tapped her foot in thought for a few moments. "What about something to deal with the power of influence over people?"

Ralph weighed the idea. "Sounds cool, but there are a lot of chemicals rushing through the brain, sounds like a lot to take on."

"Yeah."

"Besides, this is Biology, not Psychology."

"Yeah."

"But I like the idea, let's keep it human like that."

"Yeah?"

"Yeah," Ralph dragged out. He looked around the room in hopes of inspiration. Nothing was clicking. He closed his eyes, and thought to himself, *what do humans need?* "Blood," he answered out loud.

"What? Where?" asked Shannon.

"No, no, no, no, no," Ralph moved around the tree in the center of the shack to the other side of Shannon. "O'Brian gave us the answer the other day, it's all about the blood. What about the effect of digesting blood and human flesh?" he asked with a sick twist.

Shannon looked at him quizzically, narrowed her eyes and held them on him. She bit her lip unconsciously. "Like, cannibalism?"

As if he hadn't thought of it that way and had to connect the dots, Ralph turned his head to the side and questioned, "Yes? What do you think?"

Shannon jerked her head back and let out a forced breath. "I think it's great! It's nasty, but it's like a *real* thing, you know? People don't want to talk about it, but it's all throughout history, all over the world." She gave Ralph a look. "They condemn it, but taboo topics aren't short on an audience."

That initial uneasiness was quickly forgotten for a relieved connection. Macabre, but they agreed it was a good idea. "You know, Ralph," said Shannon with a shake of her long, white index finger. "You're alright. I gotta go now, but I liked the brainstorm. I talked to Lisa today and told her to meet in the library after school Wednesday. Can you make it?"

"Sure."

Shannon sighed, stood up straight and said, "Great." She walked out the door, through the yard and was gone.

Ralph watched her go and closed the door after her. "Well," he said in the empty treehouse. "That went nicely." He flipped on the TV and GRX. "Care to dance?" That slow, music box melody welcomed him to the travesties of the hapless explorer and Ralph eased into the electronic gaming sensations with a crazed, almost lecherous, smile.

****

The ratio of books to open space in the library made it feel less like an actual library and more like a room with a bunch of bookshelves because they didn't fit anywhere else. It wasn't small necessarily, but it was sure a wasted opportunity of space. The deep green carpet and faux mahogany finish on the wood paneling really brought on a classic 'study' feel to it. Along with the large windows flooding in the setting sunlight, it became a used, but productive room to work in.

Lisa Meadows, a short Japanese-Caucasian girl in thick, aged glasses walked the aisles peering through the gaps in the books. Under jet black hair, she had a tiny figure and soft voice to match. She stood out to Ralph after their first meeting in O'Brian's class, but not for the reasons most high school girls stand out to most high school boys. She wasn't overly girly or showy. She was visibly younger than her peers. Still, his eyes drifted her way time and again without his control. And, unknown to him, hers behaved the same.

She narrowed her eyes at Ralph as he sat at a table paging through a book, jotting down a note or two and then repeating the process with another book in the small pile he sat with. Lisa looked around the library, saw that that Shannon Kennedy girl wasn't here yet and decided to make her way over to him. As she turned the corner at the end of the aisle, she stopped, ducked back in and straightened out her black dress. It looked like it nearly choked her with how tight it was at her neck and the long, starched sleeves kept her arms straight and pointed.

After a deep breath, she again walked out of the aisle towards his table. With his face bent down into a book, he didn't hear her light footsteps approach. Hands clasped around the shoulders of the chair directly across from him, she said, "Whoa, is that blood?"

Slowly, Ralph looked from the book with half-lidded eyes. Once he recognized her, his expression widened in slight nervousness and then he calmed down a few notches. "What?" he asked.

Lisa smirked at the change. "Blood," she repeated. "Is that blood you're reading about?" She gestured to the open book. "You know, it's pretty messy once the body starts to split open. Humans are a lot more fragile than we think. Takes only one tiny cut in the right place and everything just spills out." She accented this by pushing her hands forward in a wavy, viscous manner. "May I sit?" She didn't wait for permission.

He blinked a few times, caught himself staring at her and coughed to break the moment. "Yeah, it's blood, for O'Brian's project. He actually seemed a little excited when I told him the plan, so, might be bad news for us."

"What do you mean?"

"It feels like a game for him to see how I'll react. Like the other day, when he asked that question about genotypes and phenotypes? He didn't even give it room to breathe before he called on me. I didn't have my hand up or anything."

Lisa smiled and let her gaze relax a little. "But you knew the answer."

Ralph sighed and leaned back in his chair. "Didn't mean shit to him, he said 'No' just as fast as he called my name and then asked someone else. They said what I said, he said 'Right' and then glared at me."

She laughed and then said plainly, "Ralph Marker." There was a pause in the conversation. "You've never had a group project before, have you?"

"Not really, no. I haven't had a group, much less a whole class, to project with, I guess."

"So then where did you learn about genotypes and phenotypes? Was it a trick? You a psychic?"

"No tricks, no magic, just homeschool in the middle of nowhere." He barely finished the sentence before a short fit of coughs took over him. After he coughed on the table, books and then the inside of his elbow, he took a deep breath and slowly let it out. "Sorry, that's kind of nasty. I've had that for a little bit, must be the weather up here."

"Don't worry about it, it's good for you, probably good for me too."

"Ha, ha," he mocked. "Now *that's* nasty."

"No, I'm serious. All that bacteria and phlegm you just expelled into the air is what makes people's immunities strong. They fight the little battles, so the big battles aren't that bad." She leaned in closer. "You see, all those weirdos with their constant sanitations and hyper cleanliness are the weak ones. They won't be able to weather the plague. As for me, I have protection against the danger."

"Because I'm probably sick?"

160

Lisa gave a short shrug. "Among other things."

Ralph tilted his head in thought. "Maybe you have something there, you know, allowing some of the filth in to build up against it later."

"You gotta break yourself if you want to get stronger."

Ralph had to chuckle. This girl was being so odd, but it didn't *feel* odd to him. It felt like dancing to a song you haven't heard before but keeping up with footwork, moving to the groove just fine. "You're a very different person, Lisa Meadows."

Treating it like a compliment, she said, "You are a very different person too, Ralph, and don't let people make you feel bad for it. The same is boring, the same has been done. We need different and new especially here where nothing is new. No, this place is just an old town with a slight hint of a reputation that they maximize in order to make the citizens feel honored and lucky to live here. Don't let 'em fool you, it's just like any other New England suburb. Cold winters, lame traditions and old money…speak of the devil."

Lisa and Ralph turned their heads to find Amanda Klein walking into the library and looking out of place in an instant. She walked up to a librarian behind the counter, asked a few questions and was led towards the aisles of shelves without making eye contact with anyone.

"If you ask me, that girl needs a good ass whoopin'" said Lisa, both joking and not joking.

"I've heard some things about her from Kyle and Steven. Just sounds like she is nothing more than a really popular, really bratty rich kid." Ralph didn't want to talk about Amanda.

"They told you that, did they?" she asked in a suggestive tone. "Did they tell you what she did to the younger Steven Young?"

He rocked his head back, smiled at the ceiling in memory and said with a one-sided smirk, "With the pants? That was hilarious!"

"Yeah, it is pretty hilarious," said Lisa in that same tone. "But it ain't even half of the shit she's pulled in her day. She's wrecked at least two cars. A few years back, she bit some girl for spreading a rumor that she had gotten a whole laundry list of STD's from the basketball team and *she* got expelled. Some even say that she brings water bottles of vodka to give to younger students so they get drunk and cause trouble, just for the hell of it! If she was any other student, she would have been kicked out of this school long ago. Instead, teachers get fired for trying to punish her and other kids change schools after standing up to her. Honest, hard-working federal employees are out of a job because one shitty little girl is *way* too used to getting her own way. Believe you me, that girl is going to grow into a real monster one day."

Ralph felt a little out of breath listening to her. "Yeah, you're probably right," he said with a laugh. "Skipping two grades, huh? So, you must have some demons, then."

"What do you mean?" she asked.

"Something my mother would say, you know, when someone is really driven, it's like they got demons." He checked his wrist watch.

"Doesn't seem like our lab partner is showing up. Big surprise," said Lisa.

"That's fine, I have enough notes to get me started on the research."

"Don't down play it, she's in cahoots with Klein back there. She'll probably just try to get us two to do all the work." She didn't say it like she thought it was a bad thing.

163

"Eh, she's not that bad," he said. Lisa stared wide eyed at him in hopes he'd change his answer.

Her dagger-eyes lost their bite when the loud speaker said, "The library will be closing in ten minutes. Ten minutes."

Ralph gathered the books, crammed his notebook into his backpack and stood up from the table. "I have to go. I have these chores I do for my neighbors...that sounds funky. It's like a job."

"Sure. Fine," said Lisa. "How about you give me half those books and I'll get started on the research too. No need to be a hero, Ralph."

"You sure? I mean, I already know where I need to look in these, so I have a head start."

"I'll figure it out." She took the books from him.

Ralph narrowed his eyes in skepticism. "Careful now, you might make the group project easy and fun, O'Brian wouldn't like that."

"Let's take our chances," she said.

Ralph gave her a quick raise of his eyebrows and then walked out of the quiet, open room. Lisa decided to hang back to help the librarian tidy up and sort books after closing, something she usually did when she could.

The library had emptied of everyone but Lisa, the librarians and Amana Klein cradling half a dozen books in her arms to the main desk for check-out. She looked around the room and then locked eyes with Lisa. The two girls stared at each other until the librarian behind the desk called to Amanda and handed her the books. Amanda collected them and left without looking back.

I stay out of your world, what are you doing in mine? thought Lisa.

Chapter VI

Camp-Out

    Shannon, Amanda and Colleen met in Wilhelmina's business district after school Friday. Cheery people walked the streets going to dinner, window shopping and using any excuse to be out and social. Fall crept in more each day as summer's warmth seemed to flow out an open window and away.

    The other girls had been doing what Amanda called 'Extra Credit'. Colleen had been acing all her classes, even French which came as a massive surprise to Madame Price who would chastise her verbally in class on a near daily basis. Amanda...Amanda had been going around late, skipping school and not telling them what she was up to. But it was all gravy because nothing had stopped them and people just left them alone when it came to Beth's burning. They didn't want to trouble them with bringing up that traumatic event and why ruin a perfectly good reputation with some spot of sickness?

"Well, thank you all for coming," said Amanda to the two girls sitting on a bench in front of her on the busy sidewalk. This was her idea, again. "I think by now we can say that there is no question of the power we hold. I feel like we are close to a breakthrough, a new level. I've been reading in the book and I think I've found a way to help us better control these gifts so that way we don't end up with repeating what happened last time." Even though she spoke to both Shannon and Colleen, this was clearly directed at Shannon.

"That was out of control. It wasn't my fault," said Shannon with crossed arms.

"It was out of control, but you did get your hands dirty and we don't want to put that to waste." Amanda's calm tone countered Shannon's rising temper and she kept the momentum before Shannon could interrupt again. "Nevertheless, we haven't had any trouble afterwards. So today, for the good of the group, I would ask that you trust me and, without hurting anybody, get these items."

Amanda held out a folded piece of paper that Colleen snatched up quickly. "Groceries, a car and an empty house?"

read Colleen. "What, you want us to pull these things out of our asses? Better yet, why don't we just go to your place, you have all these things at home."

"No, that won't do," Amanda corrected. "I want you two to think out of the box and find a way for someone to give them to you. I can handle the groceries, you can handle the rest."

"Oh, sure, a car and an empty house are just as easy to get as groceries which are, you know, sold is a store!" said Shannon.

"I'm not paying for the groceries. *That's* the test. Come on, this will be fun. Have fun with it, always. You're smart, work together and find a way for them to want to do it. Convince them it's in their best interest to let you have, let you borrow, some stuff. What do you think?" She directed the question at Colleen.

Colleen stared at the paper a little longer before a slow smile curved its way across her face. "It isn't illegal to just ask people for things. Come on, this'll be fun." She nudged Shannon a little and gave her a short nod.

Shannon looked back and forth between them. "No mistakes this time? No mess?" she asked.

"Absolutely not," answered Amanda. "And when it's done everything will be in order."

"It better be."

"Great! Meet me at the grocery store down the road when you've completed your mission, ladies." Amanda pulled the straps on her genuine leather backpack, turned and crossed the street through moving cars without a scratch and without waiting for another word on the matter. Shannon watched her with multiple emotions tugging her nervous system in different directions. Somedays she'd wake up feeling like her old self, but then she'd remember the terrors she witnessed, terrors *she* helped create. Divided, torn, confused forces plagued her when she was alone. The only way out was to keep moving forward.

"Why do I keep letting her talk me into this shit?" she asked to no one in particular.

"Probably because you love her," replied Colleen in a flat tone.

"What?"

"Well, if you don't know why you do something you know you don't want to do but you do it anyway that's the only reason, right? Look at my parents over in their dumpy house. All they do is argue and

169

look for ways to sabotage each other, but they stay together. They have their moments. In their own fucked up way that's their love."

Shannon was impressed. "Colleen, that's probably the most insightful thing I've ever heard you say."

Colleen beamed and the air around her felt warmer immediately. "Well, you girls give me a lot of help, I think some of the smarts are finally rubbing off on me. Speaking of, I think I have an idea!"

Shannon laughed a little. "Speaking of what, the smarts or rubbing off?"

Colleen held her hands in the air, waved them for a moment in thought and then pointed at Shannon with both of them. "Both!" With a pep in her step, Colleen led the way to her calculated solution. They walked to a building with stained and faded paneling, blacked out windows with neon beer signs glowing from the inside, and a sign that read 'Smitty's'.

"The bar?" asked Shannon with disappointment.

"Yeah, they never card me in here and there are all these mountain men all the time. I think we could squeeze something out of 'em."

Shannon considered the option and decided she didn't have any better suggestions. "Okay, but let's make a quick plan before we go in. I'll look around with my, whatever this extra vision thing is for guys that have what we need. How's your sleight of hand?"

"Sharper than ever," Colleen said in an eager tone.

They both giggled a little. "Good, then you need to grab the keys when we I give you the signal, got it?"

"Got it."

Colleen opened the door for Shannon and they walked in. The smoky air made them cough at first. Twangy music played just loud enough to keep conversations private. And large figures huddled around pool tables intimated Shannon. Colleen pinched her arm affectionately and led her deeper in to the lowly lit bar.

Smitty's was not too crowded, but people were comfortably getting their licks in. People who had just gotten out of work on a payday and felt it was about damn time for the weekend to start. Other people who hung around there day in and day out that never seemed to have a job but always had money for one more beer.

The local folk glanced over at the girls sensing the strange breed instinctually and made a judgement in half a second. Older women worn by years of the drink, tobacco and long nights twitched their mouths a hair, turned away and took a large gulp of their drinks. Men pushed their chests out, sat straighter and told their tall tales louder and with a higher measure of bullshit.

Static sounds entered Shannon's mind like the roar of a stadium as the home team nails the winning run. She couldn't make out anything. She pulled it back, breathed slowly and resorted to using her ears to get her bearings. Chats about sports, chats about cars, but then one stood out. "...up to the cabin soon. Weather is perfect and it's always hunting season out there, ain't it boys?"

The speaker was a tall, beefy, bearded man with dirt on his face under a John Deere cap. He stood at a table where two other men sat looking vaguely interested. They were against a wall behind a pool table. Hearing them with her ears wasn't what Shannon would call 'Super Human'.

"Them," she said to Colleen. "Follow my lead." Shannon walked over to the table and the two listening men took notice immediately. She looked at them purposefully and they held her eyes with an appetite. One wore a plaid shirt with the sleeves rolled up, the other had a t-shirt that shamelessly let his gut spill out.

At the table, all conversation stopped. "Hi," said Shannon. "I'm Katie and this is Sally, buy us a drink?" The plaid shirted man licked his lips while the other let out low and slow chuckles from his sizable gut. *They must be more than twice our age, but still less than half our wit,* thought Shannon.

"Oh, sure, sure, I got it," said the one in plaid.

"Oh, yeah," said beer gut. They were energized tenfold compared to moments earlier and their breathing carried short laughter. With sweaty hunger, they eyed each of the girls invasively, stood up and walked to the bar competitively.

Without missing a beat, Shannon took one of the empty chairs and Colleen slid into the other. The storyteller took a sip of his beer, smacked his lips and grinned at the sight of his sudden jackpot. Shannon let him have a moment of reflection. "Do you like to hunt?" she asked in an intentional tone. It was over dramatic, and Colleen almost lost her cool. She had to kick her chair under the table to let off some steam.

"I live for it," slurred the main the John Deere hat. "I plan to go this weekend so long as I can make it out of this bar. How are you girls with a bit of blood?"

"Oh," said Shannon in that same phone sex voice. "It doesn't bother us one bit." She couldn't believe the words coming out of her mouth were hers. She *never* talked like this before. She leaned in closer and quieted her voice. "I even think it's exciting at times. Somehow, it makes me feel more alive, you know?" Her hand reached out and touched his with a circular motion of her fingers.

Without even trying, images flooded her mind and she saw exactly what was on his mind. Tucked away in a dark room, the shapes of their bodies flexed together in sweaty embraces pumping and groaning. The short, rhythmic breaths made her stomach heave and she had to pull herself back.

When she let go, his expression turned dark and wolfish. Without hearing, she knew what he was saying in his mind, *What do you think, little girl, does that make you feel more alive?* He conveyed this with a burp and wobble in his stance.

Colleen picked up the que and said, "Where do you go to hunt? Some place special?"

The man held his attention on Shannon a moment longer and then turned to Colleen. "Damn right I do," he said. He reached into his pocket, pulled out a ring with four keys on it and swung them in front of her. "My little home away from home."

Colleen took the keys and his beer out of his hands. He didn't put up much of a struggle. "Do you like magic, woodsman?" she asked. Before he could answer, she dropped the keys to the bottom of the glass and began to chug the beer. Gulp after gulp she kept eye contact with him. Finished with the beer, she slammed the empty glass on the table, held her empty hands in the air and smiled. The woodsman clapped and laughed.

Shannon wasn't sure where Colleen put those keys, but she knew she had them and after seeing the two other goons start to make their way back from the bar she decided it was time to go. "We got more where that came from, woodsman. We just have to use the bathroom and we'll be right back." She hooked her arm around Colleen's and pulled her towards the exit.

Smiling at his random fortune, the woodsman didn't even notice they walked in the opposite direction of the ladies' room.

Out the door, down the street and around a corner the girl's ran. Once in cover, Shannon shivered and said, "Disgusting! Did you get them?"

Colleen screwed up her face, leaned forward and retched the drenched keys into her hand.

"I take it back. *That* was fucking disgusting," said Shannon.

Colleen rolled her eyes and wiped the keys off on the leg of her jeans. "Now we play the guessing game." She held each key one at a time for a moment and then repeated the process.

"What are you doing?"

"Shhhh, do you hear that?"

"What?"

"Shhhhh," Colleen closed her eyes, took a deep breath and hummed out one note. "That. Do you hear that sound?"

"I hear you."

"It's singing to me." Colleen hummed again, louder this time. She turned her head to wait for a reply only she heard. Shannon saw her perk up and head down the road to a parking lot in between two

176

buildings that was about three-quarters full. Shannon caught up with her at the entrance to find her humming again. This time, her mouth was open a little so the hum was a ghostly moan into the parking lot.

"Ohhhh, there you are," said Colleen with relief. She walked up to an old and battered blue Jeep that was probably the biggest wreck of shit in the lot. Then again, judging from the owner, it was a fitting match. Colleen opened the driver's door and reached over to unlock the passenger side.

Shannon looked around to make sure the coast was clear and then climbed in the Jeep. Colleen gave her a sideways glance and then turned the key to start the engine. With a loud growl and heavy rattling of the insides it came to life. She was beside herself and slapped her hands against the roof in amazement at her own skill.

"Way to go, girl!" said Shannon. "Now, let's get outta here before they've figured it out." Colleen laughed uproariously for a moment and then drove the Jeep down the street towards the grocery store.

"What was that, like, ten minutes?" Colleen asked. "Not even! In, out, bang,

177

brand new car!" She cackled and smacked the dashboard. "We improvise so good, don't we?"

Shannon did feel triumphant escaping that pit of garbage. "You say that now," she joked.

"Now what did that chump say about a cabin?"

"Here, let me see the keys." Shannon grasped the keys dangling from the ignition and held them in closed-eye contemplation. Slowly a cabin hideaway in the woods came into view. At first, the cabin was splotchy and faint, but other details in the surroundings gathered around like liquid coalescing. It sharpened and an aura popped around. Then, with great speed it flew away from her as her vision travelled backwards trailing through switchbacks and side roads back to town until her sight fell back into her head in the rumbling Jeep. When she opened her eyes, there was a subtle glowing path laid out before her. She didn't know where to go, but she could sure see it plotted out ahead. "And I got it," she said.

"Roger, that," said Colleen. No questions, just affirmation. "And is that Amanda right there?" She drove into the grocery store parking lot and Amanda met them at the entrance with a stocked cart.

"Ladies," said Amanda. "Let's load up and ship out." She walked around to the back of the Jeep and put tall, filled paper bags into the trunk. Shannon moved to the backseat, Amanda say in the front and they were on their way.

After, Shannon directed them out of town, into the woods and clear from those buffoons in the bar, Amanda had some questions. "So, how did you do it? By force? Did you screw someone?"

"Well..." started Colleen. "Shannon and I were able to meet a man who was all too eager to share with us. Would you call it charm?"

"Simple feminine wiles," said Shannon. She felt a creeping sensation of pride at their success, but then the images pulled from his head came up too. She'd never thought it was hard to get a guy aroused, but that was unsettlingly excessive. She wanted to drop it. "That and the sloppiest, grossest magic trick I've ever seen." Colleen heaved up a laugh and gave her a wink. "What about you, Amanda, how did you get such rare commodities as groceries, another one of your mom's credit cards?"

"Oh, you're gonna love this one," said Amanda. "I walked in to the store and found a cute clerk stocking milk. He had these rosy cheeks and fluffy, dirty blonde hair." She smacked her lips. "So, I tell him, 'I'd like some help. I need a big salad, potato chips, rotisserie chicken, candy, mineral water, soda, strawberries, angel food cake, whipped cream, cookies, rum and vodka.' It took him a moment to take it all in. Then, he dropped the carton of milk in his hand and said, 'This way'. It was spilling all over the floor and he just left it! That's when I knew I had him. So, then I say, 'We'll need a cart', thinking he'd get a free one in the front. Nope! He saw one that already had stuff in it so he took it."

"He just took someone else's cart? What was in it?" asked Colleen.

"Oh, not much, eggs, milk, vegetables, some shit. Who's ever it was wasn't around to stop us, musta been in the bathroom or something. Anyway, he started to collect everything and pack it in the cart, you know, doing his damn job like he's supposed to. We come back around to the front, through an empty check-out aisle and, get this, he asks, 'Paper or plastic?'"

The three girls laughed and Amanda slapped their shoulders playfully.

"I know, I know, I know. I couldn't take it myself, so I kissed him on the cheek and said, 'Paper, sugar'. He bagged it all up, even the stuff in the cart already, walked me out the store then I told him to beat it."

Colleen slapped her leg. "Hot damn," she said. "This is more like it. No fuss, no muss, just us girls having fun!"

"Bingo, babe," said Amanda. "I want us to relax, let our hair down, stretch our legs, and these gifts are the key. I just wanna have fun, girls!"

"Well, that's reassuring. I am honestly surprised that we were able to do this so easily and without hurting anyone this time." It pained Shannon with a quick shot to mention, even vaguely, what had happened the last few times, but less now. She wanted to put it out there and compare it. To make it known they were getting better. Maybe Amanda was right. Maybe they could control it.

"Honey, we are barely into the woods. This mission is still active. Just keep that positive attitude and we'll be just fine," said Amanda. Her voice was reaffirming, stabilizing. She had a plan and it was all going to be okay.

She reached down to the Jeep's radio and turned it on, leaving the tuning to the station it was last at. "This is Monica, your music maven, and thank you for listening to 97.9, The Needle, Wilhelmina's *only* correct choice for sounds to fit any and all activities. Let's get into a deep groove with this classic to guide you into the night," said a thick, creamy voice through the speakers. With the discombobulated keyboard intro leading into the seductive jam, 'In-A-Gadda-Da-Vida' gave them a beat to march in to the woods. Shannon navigated Colleen like she had been to this cabin before and there was no question if she knew where they were going. She felt energy, positive energy. This was a good place to be and she trusted her friends.

****

The newly acquired yet severely used Jeep made coughs as it finally hit the top of the last hill. Right at the crest, Colleen stalled it on purpose and the engine cut. "What was that? Is that normal?" asked Shannon. She stiffened up and held tight to back of the headrests at the sudden change.

"Relax," said Colleen. "I got this." She hunched over the steering wheel to control the windy descent through trees towards a well-manicured cabin in the forested hills. Wearing sunglasses she found in the Jeep, she wrangled the controls as if she were wrestling a mechanical bull. Shannon breathed in short, tight breaths when she felt the wheels below her sliding against Colleen's doings.

After one last bump that jolted the three girls into the air, Colleen ripped at the parking brake and the Jeep stopped dead. "Pow! Piece of cake!" said Colleen. She opened the door and slipped out like a snake along the edge of the battered old heap. Amanda opened her passenger side door and stepped out slowly. Shannon, meanwhile, needed a moment to catch her breath in the backseat.

"I tell ya, it's not just people with this hearing thing going on in my head," said Colleen. "This baby talks to me, well maybe not *talks* to me talks to me, but I can feel what it is gonna do next like a river tide."

"Very poetic, Colleen," said Amanda. "How about you, girl scout? Couldn't you tell that we weren't gonna crash?"

Shannon climbed out of the Jeep, legs shaking, and brushed off her jeans. "I guess it was just nerves, but I lost focus. I couldn't think of anything, I just waited for it to happen to me. Hell, this is really heavy shit to wrap my head around."

"Don't worry, Mzzz Kennedy, just give it time and direction."

They were on the outskirts of the Wilhelmina valley. Dragging that piece of shit up the switch backs for what felt like hours did afford some remarkable view. Shannon centered herself and gazed deeply at the cabin. Her sight followed the edges and looked for a point where the structure stopped and the ground began, but couldn't tell the difference. Compared to her first vision of it, the cabin looked lifeless and empty in person. *Ok, what can you tell me?* she asked herself. She tried to encompass all of the lot in one view; the dark wood cabin with red shutters and roofing, the tall intricately branched maple tree that had lost nearly all of its leaves and the dirt lot that held it all.

Eyes scrunched in concentration, her vision started to skew in front of her. Instead of sharp lines of reality, it started to blur and bend as if she were looking through a soaked lens. Colors and borders stretched and pulled and burning crimson pushed through the seams in little cracks that gave way to large, pulsating bulges and then…it was gone.

"Hey, beautiful," Colleen shouted from behind the Jeep. "You just stand there and look pretty, 'kay? Don't worry about us carry all this shit in. What? No, it's fine, we got it. That good, just stand right there."

"I'm coming, I'm coming"

Amanda lit a cigarette as she walked towards the back of the Jeep. When she passed her, Shannon heard her say, "I know exactly what you were doing...what did you see?"

"Couldn't tell you. Nothing, probably." Shannon just kept walking by her. She grabbed two grocery bags in a bear hug. With only a little strain, she carried the 'donated' food and booze into the cabin following Colleen. Amanda shut the trunk, empty handed, and walked in after them.

"Would you look at these digs? Daaaaamn!" said Colleen with her arms on her hips. "I'm actually impressed with that knuckle-dragger."

Mounts of various animal heads adorned the walls. Smooth, stained-wood surfaces were free of cluttered and full of rich grain. A fireplace, framed in rounded stones, screamed for attention in the center. The furniture looked old and handmade, but tough enough to last a storm. Without a second thought, Colleen dropped her armful of groceries on the table and let herself fall into the squashy looking sofa. The only ling that they had was the dying twilight sipping itself through the windows. "Next question," she said, craning her neck towards the ceiling from her regal lounging. "Does it have electricity?"

"There's a generator in the basement," said Shannon. The answer came out quickly and, to her surprise, without much thought. She set her things on a long counter and say in one of the chairs surrounding the coffee table in front of the fireplace. The floor rug was a well-cut blending of different animal furs making for an oddly attractive bit of barbarity.

"Look at the big brain on beauty! Bet ya five dollars you're wrong," said Colleen.

"Bet you ten you won't turn it on," countered Amanda.

Colleen was upright on her feet in a heartbeat and walked around in search of the basement door. "Where's the money, bitch?" she said when she found it and started down the stairs.

Once she was out of earshot, Amanda took a seat opposite Shannon, stubbed out the cigarette directly on the table and pulled the book out of her bag.

"...Amanda," Shannon whined.

"Hush, sweetie. This book is a godsend from beyond the stars."

"From beyond is right."

"This magic is everything. It is the key to the invisible door. It is the gateway to infinity. There is nothing we can't do with it and no one will ever know our secret."

Across the cabin the girls heard a spring door swing open and then swish back shut. Claws on the floor clicked into the room and a hefty, spotty orange and red cat rubbed itself along the corner of the wall. Its green eyes took them in without fear. It stretched out and wandered indirectly towards Shannon. It sat down at her feet and fixated those eyes not straight at her, but in the area around, in front of, behind and through her. The cat purred, clawed at her jeans and then rolled into a ball at her ankles.

"Shitty kitty," said Amanda. She wore a scorn on her face and dug her eyes into the cat. It looked at her and hissed. Then, unsatisfied with its threat, it stood up on all fours, arched its back and hissed with enough force to spit out a spray of saliva.

"Hmph," said Amanda with a sly grin. "Get out of here." The cat called off the attack immediately and ran out of the room. They hear the swish of the spring door and it was gone. "What was I saying? Right…the book…"

Just then, there was a loud crank and then a low rumble as electricity flowed through the veins of the cabin. Lights cracked on and a few of them dimmed down after the initial spark. "Whoa-ly shit! You girls gotta come see this! Get down here!" Colleen shouted from the basement. Shannon and Amanda glanced at each other for a moment and then Shannon got up to find her friend.

In the basement, the light was nearly blinding at first. Commercial grade bulbs flooded the room to show a finely brushed dirt floor disturbed only by Colleen's searching footsteps in the dark. It was practically empty except for the generator, a large wash basin with a hose attached to a faucet in the corner, an assortment of tools and cutlery cleaned and nearly organized by size on the wall. Below that was a thick, wooden, blood-stained work table.

Colleen let out a whistle. "Lord have mercy, look at this shit! What. A. Psycho."

"He's a hunter," said Shannon matter-of-factly. "This is his hobby, his

188

way of unwinding...his calling, if you will."

Colleen snickered a little as she made her way to the tools on the wall. Amanda walked up behind Shannon, placed a hand on her should and whispered, "What do you see?"

Images flowed through her mind like memories of yesterday. She could see years of labor in this basement of a man peacefully, methodically bringing his bagged game down here in a large tarp and working like a surgeon to gut, skin, dismember, clean and hide the animals. It wasn't out of sick desire or malevolence, it was out of a passion for the craft. It was a religion. "It is almost...almost wonderful to watch him work. It is so precise and careful. Years of practice and honing." She turned herself around to get a full view of the room and then faced downward to look at the floor, how there were now multiple sets of footprints where there were none. "We shouldn't be down here like this."

"Ohhh, get over yourself. We are in this middle of fuck all and, and, and you're worried about getting caught by a drunk who couldn't see us steal his keys right under his nose?" said Colleen. "Fuck that! Check it out, I have never even used one of

189

these things before in my life, but ZAP, one try, no questions, let there be light!" She let out a loud HA. "I'm tellin' you, this brain-game we play is really getting into the mechanics, ladies!" She nodded to Amanda and put out her hand. "Pay up, baby!"

"Later, but for now," said Amanda. "I've got a better idea." She turned on her heel, jerked her head for the two girls to follow her and started upstairs.

The three girls started a fire, poured some drinks, ate, laughed and gossiped about younger times. For a while, Shannon felt that this was exactly where she wanted to be. In the alcohol cloud, she smiled and loved her friends. All the previous hexing dissipated. The sun had gone down and the moon had come up and their fun was broken by a loud knock at the door. Shannon and Colleen whipped around and stared, startled. Amanda finished her drink, set down the empty glass, pulled a wide grin and said, "It's time."

"Time for what?" said Shannon, now mildly drunk. There was more heavy rapping on the door. She tried to reach out with her mind, but came back with a simple *thump, thump, thumping* like a drum. Amanda stood up and crossed the room to open door.

In the doorway, a large-framed young man held a Mentevelli's pizza box. He wore a red jacket and hat with matching insignia. "Did you ladies order a pizza?" he said in a deep, distant, cold voice. His stare was far-off on his pale, blue face. He looked as though someone had locked him in the walk-in freezer.

Amanda moved out of the doorway to let the pizza boy enter the cabin. His movements were lifeless in the way a sleepwalker gets around the house afterhours. He placed the pizza box on the counter, turned around and locked his gaze at the space above the girls' heads. Colleen gawked at him and giggled a little. Shannon squinted her eyes as she approached slowly. Amanda strode up to him with long steps and exaggerated arm swings.

"Well, golly, you sneaky bitch!" said Colleen. "Your work, I assume?"

"What did you do to him?" Shannon asked concerned.

"I only gave him my phone number," answered Amanda. She leaned on his shoulder and cracked a wide-eyed smile like a girl out on a sweet date. "Well, one of my numbers." She laughed, stood up on her tiptoes and kissed his cold cheek. There was no reaction, not even a blink, from the

191

pizza boy. Only a small sway when Amanda leaned her weight on him.

Shannon walked up to him, stood with her feet at shoulder length, and reached up into the hair under his hat with both hands. With closed eyes, she watched the events from his point of view in a mirrored reverse show. First, she saw the long ride up the mountain away from town trace backwards down to Mentevelli's. Then, a steady watch on the pizza cooking from ready to raw in the brick over. The pizza had been made expertly, carefully with ingredients placed over the pie with special attention. Customers buzzed by in blurry dances. Then, with a great flash and refocus of his vision, everything slowed and played out in saturated colors and watery lines. One object glowed with intensity. A shining piece of paper with a lipstick kiss pushed on to it and a phone number written on it. The paper dropped from sight for an even greater presence. Amanda. Light emitted from her soft edges like a celestial body. The paper slid back across the orange laminate countertop into her hands and she walked backwards. And, as if she were floating, she drifted out and away from the shop. Her vision cut at that moment.

Shannon pulled her hands back and looked into the pizza boy's eyes, glazed over like an old dog's cataracts. *It's amazing he made it here at all in that state,* she thought. "But what is he doing here?" she asked.

"You like what I did there?" asked Amanda. She walked over to the center of the living room, grabbed her bag and took it to the bathroom. She left the door open, inviting Shannon to join her.

Shannon followed her and stopped at the bathroom doorway. "Did you really kiss that paper?" she asked.

"Believe it, honey," said Amanda.

"Okay, so, how'd you do it?"

"Get this," Amanda started to undress. "I wrote all the instructions down on a piece of paper and then at the bottom, I wrote the number, kissed it, and ripped off that bit. That's all I gave him and violá!"

Shannon watched Amanda's reflection take off her blouse and jeans to show a slim, firm and still soft and healthy young body. Amanda caught her staring and waited until Shannon's eyes made contact with hers in the mirror. She smiled and winked at her before stepping into a sleek red dress. She pulled the dress up, put her arms through it and holding up her hair asked, "Mind zipping me up?"

Shannon stepped into the bathroom to stand behind Amanda. With her hand on her shoulder, Shannon's breathing got heavier and her heartrate quickened. The zip on the dress was smooth from small of Amanda's back to the base of her neck. Once zipped, Amanda turned around to face Shannon just inches apart. "That wasn't all I did," she said. "I figured it needed a little zest to get the job done, so I bit my lip, hard, until the blood came out, before I kissed it, just as an extra measure." In the close quarters, Shannon felt a great tension as if she stood on the shore of a beach on the brink of a tsunami wave crash. She placed her hands against the edge of the sink on either side of Amanda in hopes to steady the feeling, but it only grew. Amanda didn't resist her. Instead, she moved her hands up Shannon's back and brought her closer.

"You don't think I've forgotten our little game, have you?" asked Amanda. "You know, that's all I thought about all summer. That one hot afternoon in May when we were just lazing on my bed reading magazines in shorts and t-shirts, just us"

194

"I couldn't focus on one word on the page," said Shannon. She moved her head next to Amanda's and smelled her in through her nose. "Maybe it was just the heat, but I had to touch you, my mind was screaming."

"Mmmmmm," Amanda leaned her head back with her eyes closed, exposing her delicate neck. "Your touch was nervous, tender and...electric! You opened me up so easily, Shannon."

"Amanda, sometimes around you I lose control...I am under *your* control..."

Amanda smiled and gave a short chuckle. "You know, for a virgin, you do the dance pretty well, almost natural." Shannon kissed her neck softly and squeezed her waist. Amanda held her close and rubbed the backs of her shoulders firmly.

Then, Amanda pushed Shannon back from her. "Easy," she said. "We've still got work to do." Shannon breathed heavily, she was shaking with nerves. The fire inside her boiled her blood and made her want to ignore Amanda, but she obeyed. She backed away and let the air in the room cool ever so slightly. Amanda kept her eyes on her as she reached into her genuine-leather backpack and pulled out a

195

dark colored lipstick. She put it on, slipped on a pair of red heels and walked passed Shannon out of the bathroom.

Shannon looked at herself in the mirror in silence. Hastily, she turned on the faucet and washed her face in cold water. It calmed the tension, not completely but enough to walk out into the living room with a calm composure.

Back in the living room, Colleen had taken the pizza boy's hat and wore it herself. "Boy, I ordered this here pizza three hours ago and now it's col'" she yelled in his face. "Who's gonna pay for that? I'm not! Not me!" One hand was on her hip and the other poked his chest every few words. "Now, how you gonna made this all better? Whatchu got, huh? Give it to me!" she said through clenched teeth, grabbing and pulling at his belt. She broke the act to look at the other two girls. "Is he tonight's entertainment?" she asked in a slow, sly draw, drawing circles around the back of his neck with her finger.

"I wouldn't try anything, I doubt he's fully functional right now," said Amanda.

Colleen exaggerated a pouty whine but laughed it off and went to make herself another drink.

"Shannon, grab the rope from that bag and meet us outside, please," said Amanda. She picked up the book, peered into the pizza boy's eyes and then jerked her head towards the door. The two of them left the cabin. Shannon found the bag on the sofa and pulled out brand new bright orange nylon rope neatly tied.

"Got it," she said. When she touched the rope, she felt intense heat and saw quick moving flames. *This doesn't feel good, this feels like last time...*

"Got it?" said Colleen. "Well let's go then, we're burning daylight!"

"It's already dark out, brainiac," Shannon sassed.

"It's an expression, smartass," Colleen teased. They both laughed nervously and left the cabin. Outside, they saw Amanda place the pizza boy against the tree as if she were lining him up for target practice. Shannon didn't like the piece she was putting together in her mind.

"Colleen, tie him to the tree," said Amanda. Colleen walked up, yanked the rope out of Shannon's loose hands and started to wrap it around the pizza boy. All the while she uttered sweet things to him that kept getting interrupted by drunken laughter.

"This feels familiar, this feels like Beth," said Shannon. "What are you doing?"

"Relax, I wanted to see if I could get him to come up here and bring the pizza like I told him." Amanda knelt on the ground with the book opened in front of her. "Now I want to see if I can break the trance." She paged through it under the light from a dark green flashlight from the cabin.

"Now," said Colleen satisfied with her binding. "Don't go anywhere." She snorted out another laugh and walked backwards to the other girls with a slithery grin on her face at the trapped pizza boy. "He's like a dumb dog, I probably coulda just told him to stay." She didn't so much coil him to the tree as much as simply run the rope around and around him with a lazy shoelace knot at the end to hold the rope in place.

"It's good enough, I think he just needs to stay still," said Amanda. "Ah, got it." She found the page she was looking for and told the other girls to sit down on either side of her about seven feet away from her in the center. The three girls and the pizza boy formed a connect-the-dots 3-D pyramid looking down from the sky.

"Hey, hey!" called Colleen through a handmade cone. "How's your German?"

"Better," said Amanda. She read the book at a more comfortable pace like a clergyman reading a verse that he'd grown all too familiar with over the years. *Better? Shannon* thought to herself. *Bullshit, this sounds spot on. What have you been up to?*

As Amanda continued to read the passage, the wind died down and the surround sound was muted out. It was as if an invisible hand placed an even more invisible glass dome over the plot of land they were on, cutting them off from their surroundings. Shannon found Amanda's voice strange, unlike her normal tone, and deep with echoes of other speakers. Even stranger was the overwhelming sensation that something watched them very closely from very far away.

In the dark night, there was a crack, then another crack, then a louder crack and then a long bend like a spring being unwound through an amplifier's distortion. Colleen and Shannon looked at the pizza boy tied to the tree. His steamy breath mouthed words along with Amanda while his limbs held locked in place. That was until the roots burst out of the ground and the tree stretched branches from its inside.

Swinging around like blind tentacles, the roots and branches lengthened and lengthened and then at the crack of a whip they locked into place around him and began to constrict like lumber anacondas.

Shannon spoke up, "I don't think this is what you meant to do! I don't think this is what it is supposed to happen!" The branches extended tinier limbs that looked like fingers. These began to take hold of his arms and legs and face, digging in until the broke the skin and the blood started to spill.

"No, stop it!" Shannon called. She got up and walked to the boy who was not bothered in the least by the tree. The only thing that came from him was a slow moaning in time with his breaths. She grabbed some of the branches and tried to pry them away with her hands. She yanked at the tree and didn't see another root reach around her right arm and twine itself around her. It squeezed tight, then ripped itself away with a hot friction burn that ripped the skin in a few places, cutting her in a spiral line. Another, larger root came from her left and knocked her back, pushing the wind out of her and popping stars into her vision.

"Stay back!" Amanda shouted. "Just stay back from it!"

Shannon rolled onto her side and yelled back, "Stop it, just stop it! Let him go!"

Amanda hurried to finish reading in that dark tone. When she did, all the air was sucked out from around them. A loud creak of wood was heard as the tree flexed and then all the little arms and fingers ripped apart at once tearing the pizza boy open at his stomach and legs and face and chest. His organs emptied out below him, and he flopped onto the ground right after. His blood soaked the ground in puddles. The puddles were sucked into the ground like a thirsty sponge. He never spoke or protested or moved a muscle, despite Colleen's shitty knots.

Without air, the girls couldn't breathe. After a few moments of chocking, the silence broke with a slow and then quickening decompression of a vacuum. Wind blew faster and faster and then without even as much as a stray spark, the eldritch tree ignited in large, bulbous red flames. It wasn't just the tree on fire, it was all around the tree that was on fire. And, even though the tree was on fire, it did not burn. The fire burned to the sound of a clan chanting and shouting in dance. It was deafening.

Just as fast as it came, it pulled away. The tree flexed, filled out and, even though it was fall and the leaves had already fallen, it grew new, vibrantly green leaves of abnormal girth right before their eyes.

"Wow," said Colleen. "Mind. Blown. Just wow!"

Amanda looked at Shannon and shrugged under a short smirk. "Well, I got 'im out of the trance."

"Jeez, I definitely didn't need to tie him," said Colleen. She gave a large hoot and danced with her arms outstretched.

Shannon pushed herself up from the ground ignoring the blood flowing out of her arm's length cut. "Are you crazy? Are you fucking crazy?!" she screamed. She raced right to Amanda and punched her in the face. Rage. There was only rage.

'Hey, it's a party! Watch it, now!" Colleen called as she continued to dance.

"What the fuck are you doing?!" shouted Shannon. Amanda barely even flinched when she struck her, she only rubbed her cheek a little. "Gimme that!" Shannon reached for the book with her blood coated arm, jerked it open and went to rip it apart. The book suddenly slammed itself on her like a trap and fell out of her arms, but not before slurping up a mouthful of her exposed blood. On the ground, it scuttled towards Amanda. The cover opened partway and let out a low grinding and crashing sound like a cave collapsing on itself.

"What the fuck? What the fuck?!" screamed Shannon. "Grrrrhaaaa!" She thundered back to the cabin, damn near kicked the door open and scoured the room looking for the Jeep's keys. Around the booze on the counter, nothing. In the grocery bags left on the table, nothing.

"Looking for something?" asked Amanda. She came into the cabin cradling the book with respect and care.

"I'm getting the fuck out of here. This is crazy. You two are crazy!" said Shannon. "Amanda, this isn't you. Please, this isn't you!"

Amanda simply smiled and, before she could answer, the scene was interrupted by the swing of the cat door at the other side of the cabin. Instead of the synchronized patter of paws and claws across the floor, the girls heard a drag and thump, drag and thump. Slowly, the fat cat pulled itself into the room. It looked different, warped. It looked like it had gone through the wash only to get thrown out to sea off a ship's deck into stormy waters, drowned, but came back from beyond to tell the tale. And did it have something to say.

"You've done it," said the cat in a raspy, tired, old man's voice. "You beat the demon's dare and now you will claim your prize. Quickly, though, your time is almost up. Give your blood to finish the deal." The cat's limbs locked up as it twisted its head with the strength of a devil. It broke its own neck and fell onto its side as a slow stream of dark current poured from its mouth.

Shannon struggled to keep balance on her sanity. "I gotta get outta here, this is all...I can't take it," she mumbled. All the anger flushed from her in place of cold disconnect. She shook and stumbled onto one of the sofas. She put her head into her hands and sobbed. "Please, just take me home."

"Ohhh, that can wait till morning," said Amanda, calm and content in the red dress. "Besides, we are all too drunk to drive and that would only be...dangerous. Right, Colleen?"

"Right."

The two girls sat next to each other on the opposite sofa, Colleen with her hands tucked under her legs and Amanda with the book held so dear. Shannon looked at them with blood-shot eyes. Wiping away some tears, she had never felt so helpless, clueless and forsaken.

"Don't you feel a little *too* drunk, Shannon?" Amanda asked looking deeply into Shannon's eyes. Shannon felt a pressure on her body and mind like someone had just pushed her. But, when she looked around, she saw that she hadn't moved an inch. Unable to remember how much she drank, she *did* feel drunk, *real* drunk. "Besides," Amanda continued. "You can't leave, you're in the book!" She lifted the book and patted it against her closed mouth.

"We are going to burn for this," Shannon slurred. "All of us."

"Hmmmmmm, maybe," Amanda replied. "But first, Colleen?" She opened the book to a random page and placed it on her lap.

"With pleasure," replied Colleen. She pulled a switchblade from her jacket and extended the 7-inch blade.

"Where'd you get tha...?" asked Shannon through a sleepy head.

"Oh, you know." Colleen pulled back her sleeve and put out her left arm. She motioned to Amanda and Shannon and said, "Sisters." She cut a long line down the top of her forearm and then pressed it down on the book.

Amanda took the knife and wiped it clean on the same page. She turned to another page while the sound of radio static filled the cabin. Her only word, "Lovers." Amanda opened her mouth, stuck out her tongue, sliced the blade along it and licked the full length of the page.

Shannon felt a dizziness take over her, but before she fell asleep, she caught an unusual, terrifying, otherworldly glimpse. In the empty air of the cabin, inner space unzipped in jagged lines to spill out an ancient, forbidden cosmos of purple and green and orange and blue constellations spinning like clockwork. Shannon passed out to the sound of girls laughing and evil howling at its awakening.

****

The next morning, Shannon woke up curled under a blanket on the sofa. Her skull pulsed as if a burrowed creature was ready to hatch out of it and the pain was akin to having it pinched in a vice. Once the pain made itself known, she tried to push it aside to think. "Ugggghhh," she moaned once the memory of last night came to her. She looked around expecting a mess but found nothing but the cabin in order. *I gotta get outta here, gotta get away from these people,* she thought.

"Morning, sunshine!" Colleen said from the kitchen. "Did somebody have too much to drink last night?" She spoke in a tone reserved for babies and excited dogs. At the stove, she cooked piles of eggs, bacon and a mix of vegetables in a large sauce pan. Occasionally, she dumped large dollops from the bottle of beer she drank. "Come, sit down, I'm just about done."

Shannon walked over to the counter and slumped down in a stool. She spotted Colleen's purse near her and fished around for a cigarette. She found the pack, plucked one out slowly and put it in her mouth, sucking on it without lighting it. Colleen slid a large plate stacked high with the steamy, cooked mess in front of her. "Eat this, it's part of the cure," she said. "And let me help you with that." She took the cigarette of out Shannon's mouth, walked over to the lit stovetop and leaned in to light it. After a few puffs, she went to hand it back to Shannon, but Shannon had started to dig in to the food like a starved, lost survivor.

Colleen watched with a small smirk as the food disappeared. "Here," she said reaching into the refrigerator. "The other part of the cure." She took a new bottle of beer, angled its top on the lip of the counter and slammed the cap off, marring the surface. Shannon stopped chewing for a moment and looked at the beer disdainfully. A moment or two of speculation passed, and then she took a large swig before setting it down and pushing it away.

"So, how ya feelin'?" asked Colleen.

Nothing.

"Don't want to talk about it?"

Nothing.

"Come on, what's done is done. We're all in this one together, remember?" She extended her bare arm across the countertop. Shannon wouldn't look at it. "Hey!" Colleen grabbed her arm and pulled it next to her own. The wounds had healed overnight. The scars looked clean and old like something that could have happened when they young children, definitely not less than 12 hours ago.

"Hmmphm," Shannon grunted.

"Okay, fine, be that way. But you'll feel it," said Colleen. She turned to put more food on plates. "You'll feel that super-awareness, that *early warnin'*" she sang.

"Yeah, maybe if I can get rid of this hangover."

"There she is! She's back!"

"I'm not *back*, we can never go *back*." Shannon cleared her plate in record time and washed it down with two large swigs of beer. "Now, will you take me home yet?"

"Ahhh soon, little dove, soon. But first, why so sour? Why not relish in this new skin we wear?" Colleen asked. She did a sloppy, but enthusiastic, pirouette with a little titter for accompaniment.

"Because I'm done. I'm out of this…this…*coven*. It's been…"

"Fun?" Colleen answered. She froze mid-ballerina position with eyes glowing up at Shannon.

"Maniacal," said Shannon sternly.

"You know, that's even better!"

Amanda came in through the front door wearing sunglasses and the pizza boy's hat. "Oh, honey, you made breakfast!" she said. She sat in the stool next to Shannon, neither looked at each other. "So, how's queenie this morning?" she asked Colleen.

"Oh, queenie is a little upset, but I think it's from last night's poison, right queenie?"

I won't let them get a rise out of me, I won't let them get a rise out of me. Shannon turned to Amanda, looked her right in the face and said, "I'm fine. In fact, I'm ready to go home now, can we leave?"

Colleen opened her eyes wide and looked at Amanda. Amanda breathed out of her mouth like she was blowing on a spoonful of piping hot soup. "Soon, soon, let me just get a few mouthfuls in first. Looks like you ate enough for the both of us anyway. Colleen, are you still hungry?"

"You know me, I can't cook without eating as I go." They spoke loud, louder than they should have. *I won't let them get a rise out of me, I won't let them get a rise out of me.*

They sat in silence for a few minutes as Amanda ate more than 'a few mouthfuls'. She colored every few bites with over-acted 'Mmm's and 'Ahhh's and smooth head nods to Colleen. Colleen nodded back and smiled a smile that pulled her face across her bony, sharp features that made her face look like a mask. This stretched out for eight minutes.

Amanda pushed her plate forward, leaned back and said, "Ahhh, well, let's hit the road, shall we? Things to do, ladies." She turned to Shannon, grabbed the bill of the pizza boy's cap and gave a short salute. Even through the sunglasses Shannon could tell she'd winked at her. She brushed it off and walked out of the cabin. *I'm not gonna let them get a rise out of me.*

Outside, the Jeep rumbled like a tied-up junkyard dog. It visibly shook every moment or so. "Shannon, don't you like what we did to the place? Did you even notice?" Amanda called out.

Shannon didn't turn around to look at her. She stood tall and flexed her back at her. "You cleaned up, nicely done," she said. Aside from the breakfast mess, there was no sign that anyone had even been at the cabin. There were no bottles lying around, none of the wrappers from last night's snacking and nothing to suggest that a young man spilled his insides out on the front lawn.

Amanda walked by Shannon with a slight brush on her arm, "But don't you want to know *how* we did it?" Colleen giggled and walked to the driver's door. All of them loaded into the Jeep; Colleen driving, Amanda in the passenger's seat and Shannon in the back, frothing. *I'm not gonna let them get a rise out of me!*

"Whadduya say, girly girl?" Colleen asked, excited. "It's such a nice day out, wanna put the top down?"

"You bet!" Amanda answered, matching the enthusiasm. Colleen ran around the Jeep to unhinge the cover top here and there until it was completely off. She chucked it behind the Jeep and Shannon was blinded by the bright, clear, cold fall morning. Colleen jumped back into the driver's seat, slammed the Jeep into gear and peeled out away from the cabin. She turned on the radio, but with the combination of the Jeep's sound and the rushing wind of their speed, nothing from the speakers could be made out. It was just more noise. *I'm not gonna let them get a rise out of me!*

The Jeep tore around the switchbacks down the mountain and into the outskirts of town. Colleen and Amanda shouted back and forth, really making a show of their laughter with intermittent glances back at Shannon.

Wilhelmina had people dotted here and there taking care of morning errands, setting up shop, walking dogs and jogging to start their day. Shannon made it about five blocks before she lost her patience. Most of what she said was lost in the loud volume of the Jeep. "That's it, let me out…" *interruption from noise* "Never should have…" *BANG, WHOOSH of the wind, SCREAMS from a live song on the radio.* "Fucking book!" *GRGLE GRGLE GRGLE of the Jeep.* "…ll crazy!" RU *RU RU RU, SHWOOOOO.* "…evil. EVIL!"

By this point, the girls in the front were laughing so hard that they were leaned over in their seats and waved their hands in surrender. Colleen pulled the car over to the side of the road and stopped. "I can't," she laughed out. "I can't drive laughing like this!" Amanda let loose more raucous laughter and stomped her feet down on the floor.

"Fuck you people," said Shannon. She climbed out of the back of the Jeep and started walking down the street away from them. She didn't turn back, and she didn't know where she was going, she needed to be somewhere without the two of them.

Colleen stood up and turned around as she wiped away a few tears from her face. "Hey, come on, come back!" she called.

"Let her go," said Amanda. She put her hand on Colleen's shoulder and pulled her back into the Jeep. "She'll be back. I know it."

"Oh yeah, what makes you so sure?"

"I've got something she wants more than she knows."

"What's that?"

Amanda put her hand on Colleen's leg, gently caressed it, moaned and then smacked her lips together in a loud kiss. Both girls laughed.

"Wait, seriously?" asked Colleen.

"Seriously, baby." They continued laughing and drove away in the loud, beat-up, stolen blue Jeep.

Chapter VII

Special Delivery

Ralph's weekend wasn't nearly as exciting. He noticed his breath steam in the air on his walk to the doctors' houses after school on Monday. It was a new sight to him and he enjoyed it. His stride was proud and strong on the leaf cluttered side walk. High spirits filled him because he had finally beaten *Cuazque* the night before. After persistent practice, late nights and patient planning in front of the TV, success was his. But, not total victory. Despite that bout of triumph, he was left with mixed feelings after the game ended. It was grim and the hero ended up dead anyway. At the game's closing, it told of undiscovered secrets that must be obtained in order to reach the proper ending. At first, it felt like a rip off, but now he was eager for the challenge, thirsty for it.

At the front door to the Jackson residence, he wiped his feet and reached in his pocket for the key. Since they had left the dog, Arty, he became more and more withdrawn and even a little crabby. At more than a few times, Arty full-on growled and barked at Ralph. He unlocked the door and entered the house.

Inside, he was immediately greeted by Arty barking angrily. "Come on, give me a break. I'm feeding you, aren't I?" Ralph complained. The dog back up in a corner in the kitchen when Ralph walked through to the laundry room, still barking. Ralph thought if he fed him, maybe he'd calm down. The barks didn't stop when he opened up the bag of food, something that once got Arty riled up. The barks didn't stop when he scooped the food into the dish, something Arty couldn't hold back excitement for. Instead, there was one high pitched yip that startled Ralph and caused him to drop a scoop of food on the floor. "Dammit," he said.

In a half-assed attempt to get it over with, Ralph grabbed the dog food pebbles from the floor with his hands and placed them in the bowl. At this, and even though he was in the other room out of sight, Arty went over the edge and his barks went from fearful to vicious and attacking.

Ralph walked into the kitchen and stared down the dog. Arty only grew angrier. "Fine, you little shit, I hope you choke on it!" Ralph left the house and slammed the door behind him. He fumed and cursed the dog for a block on the way to Dr. Capecci's. *Dumb mutt,* he thought. *I'm doing this out of the kindness of my heart, and you want to come at me like that? I oughta give you a good kick next time, yeah, right in the ribs, you stupid animal, you won't even see it coming.*

"Wham!" He punched his left fist into his right hand, lost in thought. Then, he felt a surge of pity. *Why would I do that? Why would I think I'd enjoy that? I wouldn't. He's just scared, is all.*

He shook off the feelings, both anger and shame, and walked up to Dr. Capecci's front door. Inside, the stack of mail was the usual bulk of catalogues and letters that looked like bills. He separated it on the kitchen table into already building piles, but then one stood out to him. It was a postcard. It was a pick and orange sunset postcard from Tuesday.

Ralph carried it over to the fish tank, transfixed by the colors. The hues were strong and the shapes of the palm trees were simple, but he couldn't tell if it was a photograph or painting. His eyes darted around the tiny image and looked for something, anything, to give it away, but found nothing. The longer he stared, the more it blurred and waved, making it too difficult to decipher.

He pinched out a portion of fish food and sprinkled it in the tank. The fish ate greedily. "At least you're grateful." He tapped the postcard against the fish tank's glass as he watched them eat, ripping the paper-thin particles with their jaws. After enough of the show, he placed the postcard back on the table apart from the rest of the mail. It never once crossed his mind to read it.

He left and headed for home. For the past few days, he'd been weighing a hunch he had about The Shop and decided today was just a good a time as any to call and ask questions.

After the short walk to his house, he dialed the phone number Kyle gave him and waited through four rings before the other line clicked as someone picked up the phone.

"Hey, this is Phil at The Shop. What can I do ya for?" asked Phil.

"Hi, Phil?" asked Ralph. He was nervous, didn't know how to word it, but pushed on. "This is Ralph. I'm friends with

Steven and Kyle, you know those guys, right?"

"Yes, I do". Crumbles of potato chips being eaten could be heard through the phone.

"Well, you remember that one game we talked about, *Cuazque*?"

"…Sure. Did you want to buy it? I think we have it in stock, if not, I could special order it." It sounded like he really wanted to have to special order it rather than simply having it in stock.

"Oh, no. I already have that, well, Steven's copy at least. Anyway, do you remember talking about that, uh, other game? The sequel?"

Chips crumbled a little slower then stopped. Phil was thinking. "Yeaaaah, I think I know what you're talking about. The pieces are coming back to me. In fact, yes, I know *exactly* what you're talking about." Ralph heard him slurp a drink and wipe the crumbs off his hands. "Tell you what, give me a day or so…yeah, come in on, say, Friday? I think you'll be ready for it then."

"Really? No shit?" Ralph was hoping for a lead, just a little information, but could this mean that Phil knew where to find it? He was sure it wasn't even real.

219

"Sure. Oh, and you have like fifty bucks?"

"Oh, uh, yeah, no problem!" He didn't care that his excitement carried over the phone. Was it that easy to get? Besides, fifty bucks wasn't going to break the bank.

"Cool, later," Phil said and hung up the phone.

The dial tone told him the line was dead, but Ralph said anyway, "Yeah, later." He walked out back to the treehouse, started up *Cuazque* and began to dig for that secret.

****

Two days later, Ralph walked to The Shop on an abandoned windy afternoon. The town's layout was simple to him now, familiar and clear. Walking everywhere really helped build his surroundings and he grew to enjoy the rich landscape so different from the desert. In fact, the desert hadn't much crossed his mind much these days, not since *Cuazque* called to him, needed his help.

On the walk through the park where he met the guys on the first trip to The Shop, he had to laugh a little. The way they talked to each other in a reverse-logic of appreciation and comradery was something he'd never thought he'd see much less fall in to so easily. On paper, it was terrible. But in practice, talking down on each other in down time, testing to see how they'd hit back showed a deeper friendship. They knew each other's brains and buttons and just how to get a reaction. It kept them in line, kept egos from getting too large from their heads, and kept everyone involved and, in a way, vulnerable.

So why didn't he tell them he was going to The Shop after school today? Steven might have some lame excuse that boiled down to not wanting to walk in the autumn chill. But, Kyle would have come along. None of that stuff, that shit-you-get-living-in-the-real-world stuff, really bothered him and any excuse to be with friends was good enough. Still, Ralph didn't want them involved, not right now. This was his mission. They'd hear all about it when the battle was won.

He walked through the alley to the back lot and up to The Shop's front door. The neon 'Open' sign was turned off. "Really?" he said. The parking lot only had a van in the back that was so banged up, bent and worn it looked like it'd had the life sucked out of it with large, industrial hypodermic needles. Not wanting to turn back now, he walked to The Shop's window and looked in. Phil sat behind the counter reading a magazine. Ralph knocked on the window with three hard hits from his back hand. Phil turned his head up, squinted behind his glasses and started to walk over. He put his face as close to the glass without touching it and stared for a few moments. Then, he put up one finger to say, 'wait a minute' and turned to unlock the door.

"Oh, it's just you," said Phil. "Come in, it's cold out there." Ralph walked through the open door into The Shop. It was changed afterhours. None of the TVs showcased new games, they were off. No music rolled out from well-placed speakers, it was quiet. And the color inside wasn't its usual neon overload. Instead, weak lamps at the front desk and the red glow from the exit sign above the door were the only source of light. The Shop felt both larger and empty. It felt off like an imitation of itself made in China for an eighth of the price. Ralph mentioned none of this.

"Alright, I think you're really gonna like this. Follow me." Phil lead him back to the counter and then through the beaded veil into the back office. This room didn't look like it belonged with the rest of The Shop, but with the old building before it was split up into different properties to lease. It had tacky flowery wallpaper, chipped paint on the wood sidings and a sinus-clearing odor of cleaning product that worked its way into the very being of the structure. The tang breathed out of the walls continually pumping the fragrance. The room housed a small cot bed, dresser and bathroom off to the side.

"Do you live here?" asked Ralph.

"For the moment," said Phil. "It helps with security." Phil went to the desk that was cluttered with papers and tiny boxes. There was no room to write or work on it, it'd been repurposed to be a shelf with drawers. He picked through the debris, "Where is it? Where is it? Oh, damn, I guess I didn't bring it up yet." He whirled around and pointed to the right of Ralph. Ralph followed his gaze to see a door he hadn't noticed.

Phil pulled a flashlight out of the messy desk and went to the door. He opened it up and Ralph felt the cool air linger at the top of the dark steps. Phil turned on the flashlight and beamed it down to reveal well-made steps that lead to a concrete basement.

"No lights down there?" asked Ralph.

"Scared?" was Phil's only reply before stepping down into the basement. Ralph followed. "I store a lot of extra stuff down here. I remember getting a copy as part of a lot sale. I don't think they knew what they had, otherwise I wouldn't have gotten it so cheap." Phil shined the light around a basement burdened with cardboard boxes, filled and tied garbage bags and plastic storage containers. Phil opened a box, fished through it and said, "Not that one," before closing it and moving on to another. This repeated for four more boxes until Ralph decided to look around himself.

With a small amount of light coming from Phil's flash light and the room upstairs, he poked around slowly looking for anything out of the ordinary. A small shoebox under the steps looked out of place enough. He knelt down and pulled it out. "What do you got?" asked Phil.

"A shoebox, does that sound right?" Ralph asked.

"Yep, I think you found it. Lemme see." Phil took the shoebox from Ralph, opened it to peek and said, "Yeah, this is it." He set the shoebox on a nearby box and took off the lid. Ralph looked inside to see a dozen game cartridges of different shapes, sizes and colors. One was large and red, another small and green and ovular. One was almost the length of the shoebox. What they all had in common was their labels. Labels that weren't official looking or appearing to be a copy of many. They were all scrawled by hand, words, titles, pictures, and adhered to the cartridge. Phil considered one after another and with each selection Ralph felt increasingly excited and anxious.

"This is it," said Phil. He handed Ralph a short cartridge that was bowed at the top rather than the traditional straight edges. It was heavier than usual too, weighing about five times the normal feel. In the flashlight's beam, Ralph read a title engraved on the front in jagged, sharp lettering; *Mazer*.

Phil closed the shoebox and put it back where it was. He started up the stairs and said, "That's it, well, that's what it *would* have been." Ralph followed him. "They didn't actually finish and release it. Word was that they died making it. *Killed* in a real mess. Butchered in their office and left to bleed to death."

"Jesus."

"I know, right? But, somehow, a few prototypes got spread around. It was supposed to be this great, complex puzzler that would always change and learn from the player. It could *think* and *plan*." They got back into Phil's 'temporary' living quarters.

"So you don't just play the game, you play against the game?"

"Exactly. *Exactly*, man!"

"So, you've played it?"

"Oh, uh, no. No. I don't know, I just forgot about it I guess. I mean, hell, it took me a while of you guys talking these games up before I remembered I might have one of these around."

Ralph thought about it a second. Something was off, something Phil wasn't telling him. "Screw it, fifty bucks, right?"

"You know what? For you, it's free."

Ralph laughed. "What?"

"Yeah, just take it. I went in on that lot with a bud of mine and this was in the mix. I can tell you're a solid dude, you'd pay when you pick up and keep it real, unlike the rest of those knuckle-draggers that roll through here."

Ralph inspected the cartridge in his hand. It was so heavy for a game, almost

226

too heavy. The exposed chip at the bottom was red colored and sharp to the touch with teeth instead of the usual green chip board. "Is this even gonna work?"

"This is it," Phil reached over to tap it a few times. "This is the game. Hey, I mean, if you don't want it..." His hand started to wrap around to take it back.

Ralph pulled it away. "No, I'll take it. It's just...it looks so fake."

"Ha! What'd you expect? It was never released, and they were working on a shoe string budget. There won't be any fireworks, just the bare bones. Functional game mechanics with no frills." There was a moment of silence. "Come on, I got places to go." Phil went into The Shop, grabbed a suitcase and turned around to wait for Ralph.

Ralph hesitated a moment, then walked by the front desk grabbing a bag along the way to put the game in. Phil turned off the lights as they walked out and locked the door behind them.

In the parking lot, Phil walked towards the large, exhausted brown van with the jumble of graffiti all over it.

"You might run into some bugs along the way...some problems. Relax, that's just because it's an unfinished product. I've played games like this before, sometimes you just gotta work with it."

"Unfinished product," said Ralph. "You know, they say that the Ouija board is unfinished and that's what opens the portal to, you know, *beyond*."

"Do they?" Phil asked without wanting a reply. He slid the door to van open and stepped up into a brown carpeted room on wheels with all sorts of knick-knacks to place the suitcase in the back. Ralph saw a boar's head mounted in a plaque, tape cassettes thrown about and cheap incense sticks burned to the base with their scent left behind.

"I'll tell you about it after I beat it," said Ralph. "See you next week?"

"Don't think it will happen, kiddo. I will be out for a while. Have to meet a friend for some work in the swamplands."

"Where are you off to? A big sale? A little romance?"

Phil laughed a little and shrugged. He sat himself in the driver's seat and turned on the van. "We'll see. Be a guy and close that door, will ya?" In one tug, Ralph slammed the door and thus completing the tasteless collage on the van's side. Phil rolled down the passenger's window and shouted out to him. "Don't tell the other guys I gave that to you. Next thing I know they will be linin' up with the gimme-gimme's."

"Yeah, I won't."

"Better yet, don't tell anyone about it at all."

"What?"

"A friend of yours?" Phil pointed behind Ralph. Ralph turned around and saw Lisa approaching him across the parking lot. Before he could reply to Phil, the window was already up and the van was backing up to leave.

"Hey," said Lisa. "Thought I'd find you here." She walked up to him in the now empty parking lot, cold wind blowing in her hair, her expression calm and controlled.

"You know about this place?" asked Ralph.

"Now I do." She smiled. "I followed you after school. Not where I thought we'd end up, but I like it." She stuck her hands in her oversized jacket's pockets. "Are you doing anything dangerous? Are you buying drugs?"

"Nope, nothing," said Ralph. "And I should be asking the questions. Why did you follow me?"

"Simple, we have work to do. Have you forgotten the group project? You

229

haven't come to see me in the library and Shannon has been M.I.A., shocker."

"Well, I've been a little busy, but we still have time, I'll get it done."

Lisa stepped to him until their feet nearly touched. She narrowed her eyes and looked around him invasively. "Not busy, more like distracted." Ralph stepped back to put space between them and laughed to cover up the maneuver. "What are you hiding?" she asked.

"Listen, don't worry about it," said Ralph. "I've already got some great research done for the project and we still have time. Don't worry about it." Ralph was walking backwards out of the parking lot step by step farther from Lisa.

"Time? It's due next week!"

"Right, I know that, but we can't get a lot done here in the parking lot. What do you say we meet this weekend, I'll call you?" The distance was so far that he had to shout to her. She didn't move towards him this time, just watched quizzically.

"You remember those demons you mentioned?" Lisa called out.

"Demons?"

"We're watching you, Ralph Marker. It wasn't hard to find you this time, it will be easier next time. Ciao." Lisa left in the opposite direction, leaving Ralph to head home as fast as he could.

Back in the treehouse, he swapped out *Cuazque* for *Mazer*. He flipped the switch, nothing. He took out the cartridge, blew in it, and tried it again. Nothing.

"Dammit," he said. He took Mazer out of the GRX to inspect the exposed chip at the bottom. *These sharp edges are probably gonna break my system,* he thought. Gently, he pinched and wiggled the chip to be sure it was secure. Right when he touched it, he felt a sting and a little blood dripped onto the chip from the tip of this finger. "Son of bitch!" he cursed at the game. "Fine, I'll get to you soon enough, you aren't going anywhere."

He put *Cuazque* back into the GRX and steadied in the game's rhythm.

That weekend was nothing but playing Cuazque. On Saturday night, he realized he hadn't stopped by the doctors' houses at all that day. He hurried in the dark hours to get the chores done as fast as possible.

At Dr. Jackson's house, Arty was in a particularly grumpy mood. He barked and barked at Ralph. Ralph tried to calm him down by offering his hand out for the dog to smell and make peace with. "Come on, buddy, you remember me," he said. The dog sniffed for one breath, and then chomped on Ralph's hand with a firm bite.

"Ouch! Stupid shit, that hurt!" Ralph shouted at the dog. Arty whimpered at the sudden temper change. "Fine, have it your way, you ungrateful bastard." Ralph stormed from the house irate at how uncool this run was starting to be.

On the way to Dr. Greenly's, he checked the dog bite in the light of a street lamp to find that it pierced the skin a little bit, but nothing too bad. He was still mad at Arty as he washed the hand thoroughly in the pink bathroom. *Great, that dumb pooch probably has rabies,* he thought.

En route to Dr. Capecci's, he felt his irritation start to simmer down. It was an odd day and he was getting tired. After a sprinkle of fish food, he checked to be sure that the mail on the table was correctly sorted. He wanted to have a positive note at the end of the night, something he could maybe do for the neurotic doctor.

That postcard from Tuesday still called out to him with its welcoming colors. He wanted that to be the first thing he saw when he returned so he set it out in tasteful display against the fish tank. The tank's blue light edged the card making it stand out, even in the dark.

Despite visiting three different doctors' houses, and even though they weren't medical doctors, it never occurred to Ralph to bandage the cut. After he washed it, it drifted to the back of his mind as he thought more and more about *Cuazque* and how to make *Mazer* work. It had to, it just had to, in his mind. That was how it would all make sense, *Mazer* was the key. So, without thinking, he didn't realize that his careful attention to detail placing the postcard in plain sight left a few drops of blood on the luscious paper portrait.

Chapter VIII

'A' Student

Shit! Dammit! Shiiiit! Ralph repeated in his head for the fiftieth time. In the back of Mr. O'Brian's class, Ralph watched the groups of students do their presentations one by one. Each time a group finished, O'Brian picked another at random out of a hat. It might as well have been Russian roulette because 'Mr. Marker' didn't finished the project and both 'Mzzz Kennedy' or Lisa were nowhere in sight. He had been too preoccupied with *Cuazque* to care that the bloodwork, so to speak, was due Monday with "No excuses" as Mr. O'Brian had claimed.

Ralph's only hope was to wait out the class period, find Lisa and *maybe* slap it all together that night. At five minutes a piece in a forty-five minutes time frame, they could squeeze in eight groups of twelve. Chances were that just about everyone but a few would present on Monday. With the seventh group wrapping up their bit on 'What Blood Types Mean and the Specifics of Blood Transfusion', Ralph sweat bullets down his face.

"Thank you, Stacy and Gunther," said O'Brian without even faked enthusiasm. "Let's see, who should be next?" He went to reach into the hat for another set of victims. Before he could grab one of the tiny squares of paper, his calculator watched beeped in alarm. "Ohhhh, I don't think we will have time to get to it today." Ralph let out a sigh of relief loud enough for all to hear. The students who'd already had to present glared at him. O'Brian just continued, "Thank you, everyone who presented today. To those who will now go tomorrow, I hope you watched for what did and didn't work and maybe you can take advantage of that. Class dismissed." Again, O'Brian's speech was lifeless, even a little mechanical. "Mr. Marker, please see me before you leave."

It's gonna be fine, thought Ralph. He's gonna see that Lisa and Shannon weren't here and he's not gonna say shit about me not having anything prepared, right? Wrong. Stupid, stupid game, I'm screwed with no backup! He lazily gathered his things and waited until the classroom emptied before approaching O'Brian. As he got closer to the large man seated in the swivel desk chair, Ralph felt a difference in the tyrant's attitude as if all the hellfire inside had been extinguished.

O'Brian stroked an impressively sewn, deep red tie with a cloudy expression. "Ahhh, Mr. Marker. Excellent work on the project! I really appreciate you and your partners' initiative to present all your great work personally! A+ for all of you! Especially that Mzzz Kennedy, she's weathered so well after all that scary stuff she's been through."

"What?" asked Ralph. He was completely bewildered and afraid that this was a trap, some sort of scheme to get him kicked out of school.

"Strong-willed girl, a real go-getter going and getting, if you ask me!" O'Brian's words were so kind and excited that Ralph thought he'd gone crazy. "Now, run along. I bet you have more heads to turn and *killer* work to do!"

Traversing from nearly shitting his pants to being exonerated was not what Ralph would call 'thrilling'. But, after a confused climb from a fearful expression to a large inspiring smile, Ralph would say that it was worth the trip. "Thank you, sir!"

he said. He turned on a heel, asked no questions and left the class in the best mood he'd had all semester. He was not going to wait around for O'Brian to take it all back. *Holy shit, that was awesome! Maybe this game is good luck!*

The rest of the day breezed by without any sign of trouble, or Shannon or Lisa. On his walk home, Ralph decided to call Lisa and see what'd happened. That girl never missed school and today was too coincidental for her to just be sick.

Coincidence went right out the window when he saw her sitting on his porch waiting for him. Even though she was there to see him, she didn't look happy.

"Hey!" said Ralph. "You won't believe what happened today."

"Damn right I won't believe you, because you're a liar!" said Lisa. "You said we'd meet up to work. You never called. I waited and waited all weekend, but nothing!"

"It's all fine, it's all taken care of."

"What, you took care of it yourself? Bullshit."

Ralph thought about lying and taking the credit, but as he was still in the dark about the whole thing, he figured it best to tell the truth. "No, I didn't. But

Shannon did, somehow. She musta really worked her charm on O'Brian because he gave us an A+." Lisa stared at him and said nothing. "I was freaking out in class until he told me. Where were you today?"

Her expression changed, lost its anger and replaced it with shame as she looked down to her feet and said, "I skipped school today. I didn't want to go in unprepared and I was mad that you tried to trick me into doing the whole thing alone. Just because I've done that shit in the past doesn't mean I like it." She looked up at him. "I just didn't want to believe that you'd be the type to bail on me. I thought you were an outsider like me." She walked passed him to leave.

"But it all worked out." Ralph said after her.

"Yeah, lucky for that," she said and kept walking.

****

Tuesday was not so lucky. "Ralph Marker, please report to the Principal's Office," the PA wailed. "Ralph Marker to the Principal's Office immediately."

"Dammit," Ralph said to himself. The call came in between changing periods and he was headed for lunch. "It's taco boat today." He rerouted to the principal's office. He hadn't been there since his first day, but he easily remembered it was near the front entrance of the school. Inside, the white-tiled floor speckled with random black dots contrasted with the red walls and faded purple chairs. He never got used to the odd mix of school colors and they were turned all the way up in this office. The only things out of that color scheme were a plain-clothes man he did not recognize and a uniformed police officer.

"Ralph?" the secretary asked. She squeezed and rubbed her hands nervously in her red and purple sweater.

"Yes?" Ralph questioned back. Suddenly, he was flush with the fear that O'Brian's group project was too good to be true.

"These two men would like to talk to you about some things. I don't think you're in trouble or anything..." she glanced at them with hopeful eyes, but the look was not returned. The secretary gave Ralph an apologetic expression. "They just want to ask you some questions, okay? The principal thought that in your...situation it would be best if you just took the rest of the week off." She chuckled, threw her arms up in an 'I don't know' gesture and then sat back down in her chair to get busy at looking busy.

"Come with us, son," said the plain-clothes officer. "We need to talk." Ralph's eyes opened wide and, although he was conscious, he felt himself pulled through the motions without his help. He followed them without any resistance in hopes that this cooperation would make him seem innocent instantaneously thus nullifying the whole shake down. Instead of the officers turning the shit around and saying, "Well, you just can't be the guy we're looking for!", they preferred Ralph's response to 'play dead' and just go with it. Only meant less work for them.

The black and white police car was parked outside of school and right in view of the long windows that walled one side of the cafeteria. Inside the orange room with imitation grain wood tables say about 250 kids. One-third of the school watched Ralph get into the back of a police car. He looked over at the windows for a moment, but the feeling of his guts falling through his shoes forced his head to ignore it. Still labeled as 'The New Kid', just about all of them knew who Ralph was. Ralph hoped that Steven, Kyle and Lisa just happened to be distracted at that moment. The two officers didn't handcuff him or even read him his rights. Without hesitation, they loaded him in the back and drove to the station.

Ralph asked, "Am I under arrest?"

"Not yet," answered the plain-clothes officer. He added a short inclination at the end of his tone to show it was something he wanted to happen. There was hope in it the way a game show host talks about prizes for lucky contestants. The rest of the drive was silent except for the police chatter over the radio. Number codes and quick messages relayed back and forth, encrypted to Ralph. He swore the driver talked about him once or twice through the radio, but tried to ignore it and keep his composure. He'd been in the back of a cop car before and he knew that giving them as little as possible was the best move, even if he didn't know exactly what they wanted. Albeit, that time was for lighting off fireworks alone in the desert.

They led Ralph into the police station were angry, suspicious faces stared him down. Passed the front lobby and down a hall, a door waited open for them to a dark room with a table and chairs. Another time, Ralph asked the plain-clothes officer, "Am I under arrest?"

"Not yet," the officer repeated with even more excitement. "Come on, we just want to ask some questions." Ralph obliged and sat in a chair. After closing the door, the officers say opposite him and sized him up for a moment, waiting to see how he'd react. He held. The uniformed cop set an opened file on the table and stood back. Again, they waited for him to make a move. They waited like this whole thing was his idea.

"School says you're new around here Ralph. That true?" asked the uniformed officer.

"Sort of. I would spend summers here with my dad, but I'm new to the school."

"So, you know some people in Wilhelmina? Friends, neighbors?"

"Yeah, I guess."

"Right," the officer reaffirmed. "So how do you know doctors Greenly, Jackson and Capecci?"

"Dad's colleagues. They asked me to do some favors for them around their houses while they were away. Simple stuff, really. In fact, they should be back by now, haven't heard anything from 'em though. Did they call to tell you I did a bad job?" Ralph teased.

242

"We'll get to that. Ralph, what do you like to do for fun?"

Confused, Ralph answered, "You know, I'm just an average kid. I like to spend time with friends and play video games, no harm in that, right? Public school isn't what I expected, but I'm growing in to it. You know, it really isn't all book learning. There's so much to learn about people you can't get anywhere else."

The plain-clothes officer wrote notes while Ralph spoke. All in the room noticed it, but no one said anything. "You were homeschooled, right? That musta been something else. That musta sucked. Trapped inside like that must really bite, huh?"

Ralph sensed this was an indirect way of getting to the center, but with nothing to hide he decided to play along. He didn't know how Shannon took care of the project, but he knew he had nothing to do with it. "It wasn't too bad. I wasn't trapped. In fact, I was outside whenever I could be. My mom, she loved the outdoors." Ralph's mood changed at the mention of her.

"Your mom was the teacher? Just you and her in a classroom. Kinda makes you a momma's boy then, don't it?" The officers looked at each other and over acted their laughs. They were bullying him, but he didn't know why.

"No, I wouldn't say any more than you two," he said in a flat tone. "But I would say *this* feels like total bullshit. What do you want? Why am I here?"

The officers cut the laughter. "We went by your house today, but no one was home. Dad was at work?"

"Out of town, actually. He and those other professors left for some sort of academic conferencing. They didn't tell me much about it, but I guessed it was just boring detail."

"Uhuh," said the plain-clothes officer writing notes down quickly. He fixed his tie, looked at the other officer and stood up. "Give us a minute, will ya, kid?" They left and closed the door behind them. Ralph sat alone in the grey, dimly-lighted interrogation room.

He tapped his left-hand fingers on the table to drift off in thought. *Could they have been looking for something at the house? What is even there? They could have planted something, but for what?* While these questions floated around in his mind, another voice, unfamiliar, faraway but still mentally audible, answered clearly and confidently. *They know nothing. Stabs in the dark that will get them nowhere. This is a joke, bringing you here. Soon, it will be alright. Very soon.* And just like that, a soothing wave washed over him refreshing his senses in a jolt of wakefulness. Along with it, confidence and collection. The folder on the table was left open and Ralph pulled it over for a peek. On top was a photograph of a car submerged in water. A convertible with a figure in the front seat. The same sea-foam green convertible that belonged to Dr. Capecci.

The door swung open and the two officers sat in front of Ralph with a unison sigh. The plain-clothes officer took the folder back and closed it. "Ralph, you were the only person to enter Dr. Greenly's house in the past few weeks. That's opportunity. That makes you the lead suspect. Do you know what that means?" he asked the uniformed officer.

"It means he knows what he did," he answered.

"What'd you put in the soap, Ralph? How'd you do it? You're a smart kid, you read books, did you add acid to it?" Ralph's eyebrows raised higher and higher at this accusation. None of it made sense, so he said nothing. "Yeah, that's what I thought," continued the officer. "And then you enjoyed beating that dog, didn't you? You were the only one there, too, and dogs can't speak, right Frankie?"

"None that I know, Georgie."

"So, you rough up the pooch and starve 'im until he was so angry and hungry that the next thing that walked through that door got the business! You *knew* that would be Dr. Jackson!" Ralph held the wide-eyed stare and didn't crack. He didn't know what the officer was talking about, so he didn't know what to say. His silence irked them and he saw them readjust ever so much to regain superior footing in the conversation.

"What, Frankie, you see that? He didn't barely move. That's the problem with you know-it-all-kids. You think you are so much smarted than everybody else that you get surprised when you see any other intelligent life. Well, I got news, kid, you ain't as smart as you think. In fact, you are pretty dumb, and you are making yourself very obvious right now."

Again, Ralph said nothing When the cops saw this, they turned their internal intimidation dials up a few notches.

"Alright wise guy, you think you're bad? Well, we know about that trick you did on Capecci's car. You had access to the

246

garage so you snipped the brake lines! I bet you thought it was clever, didn't you, putting distance between you and the victims. Thought it would throw us off the trail. But, you were the only one with opportunity. You had access to all three murder weapons. Make it easier on yourself and just tell us how you did it."

Snip the brake lines? Ralph doubted he could even find the brake lines. He was more in the dark than the cops. That calm control held him as he took a deep breath, stretched his arms back behind his head and sat in a relaxed position. Fire ignited in the officers' eyes.

"All three of these fine college professors are in the hospital right now! They are doing their best, but it doesn't look like they are gonna make it! They are fallin' fast and you killed 'em, didn't you? Your name is all over this mess!" Frankie screamed.

Ralph studied them. The two officers were caught practically midair about to bounce. They needed his word to attack, but Ralph wasn't going to give it to them. Rather, he leaned forward, unfolded his onto the table and spoke slowly, "You know he doesn't even drive, right? Hasn't since his wife died in a car accident." They said nothing. "You got three victims with three different means of attack that clearly make no sense to you, so your *best* idea was to bring in a teenager?" They backed down a few inches. "Just so I got it straight, you think that I somehow messed with Dr. Greenly's soap landing him in the IC unit. Soap. Antagonized and brainwashed Arty, a dog, so intensely that he attacked Dr. Jackson, his own family. Brainwash a dog? I've had three goldfish die on me in as many weeks. And, and, *then* I cut the brake lines in *doctor* Capecci's car to top it all off with a bonus?" Officers Frankie and Georgie pulled back from their poise, eyes lowered, teeth put away. Ralph heard that far off voice whisper help that was winning the fight. "Your faith in this case is so strong that you brought a minor into questioning without his parent's consent. I mean, you obviously didn't talk to my dad today, *you* told *me* he wasn't home." They gripped the back of the chairs, but they weren't ready to sit down and admit defeat just yet.

"Right," said Ralph. He got up and walked to the door. The plain-clothes officer grabbed his arm, but Ralph swiped it away and said, "I'm innocent, but what you're doing is illegal. So, I am gonna ask one more time. Am I under arrest?"

"No," said Frankie embarrassed. But he wasn't going down without the last word. "But don't think you're off the hook just yet, punk. We know where to find you and next time will be the last time and they are gonna throw the book at you but good."

"Welp, I'll be at home, playin' video games for my five-day weekend. I'm awfully sorry about what happened to the doctors, I really am. Good luck with your investigation."

Ralph opened the door and walked out of the station. This time, the faces looked confused. They aimed at him and then at officers Frankie and Georgie who stood by and let him go. Head held high, he had seen a clarity that he had dreamed of since puberty. He had total control of the situation and they had bupkis.

Damn, that was smooth, he thought. The unfamiliar voice that guided him hushed to a low hum no more invasive than the high-pitched tone of electrics. *I was the only one to go to those houses and I know I locked them up. Something is definitely very off here, I need to find out more.*

****

249

"What do you mean, like an instructional tape?" asked the video store clerk. He sat with his legs propped up on the counter in a relaxed lounge while a movie with girls with guns on the hunt for some creature in the jungle played on a small TV to his left. It was a good thing that there was a sign behind him along with the message, "How can I help you?" on his shirt because he clearly was not going to make the effort. "Cuz that's over there in the 'Instructional Videos' section." While the movie played, he'd been reading a magazine catalog of musical instruments way out of his paygrade and looking at the TV in intervals.

"No," said Ralph. "I mean like a regular *movie* movie, you know with a story and characters and stuff that hypnotizes the viewer."

The guy behind the counter leaned back further and rested the magazine on his chest in contemplation. He looked unkempt, but proud of it like he had lived in this store since it opened, sleeping in the back, showering in the rain and living on a steady diet of slurpies, beef jerky and the smelliest cheap cigarettes loose change could buy. His eyes held a distant gaze as he tried to remember something that may or

250

may not have happened. "Well," he said after some time. "There was this one movie this music...it was like the same melody through the whole flick. Eerie and electronic, something really far out, you know? I can't remember the name, but it was about these girls at a dance school run by witches...Yeah, that one pulled me in."

"Really? Did it make you do anything unusual? Something that you, or maybe anybody, wouldn't think themselves to do?"

"I couldn't sleep well if that's what you mean."

"I mean, like, uhhh..." Ralph looked around the store at the other customers perusing the aisles of assorted genres and 'picks of the week'. He leaned in closer to the clerk and in a hushed tone asked, "Did you go into a trance and do bad things you would regret?"

The clerk leaned forward and let the magazine slip from his chest. His face contorted into a shocked expression and then quickly turned quizzical. He nodded his head back and forth calculating an answer in his mind. "You mean like masturbate?"

"What?" Ralph scrunched his face at the surprise answer. "No, not like that."

251

"Oh, well, then no. Not really."

"Lemme be sure, you have never seen any movie that got into your head and implanted secret instructions you were defenseless to act on, right?"

"Kid, I been from one side of the video store to the other, seen a lot of strange things, but I ain't never seen a movie that caused me to sleepwalk and piss on my neighbor's yard, if that's what you mean."

"Yes, that's exactly what I mean."

"No," the clerk answered defiantly. "Look, do you wanna rent something? I'm kind of busy here." At this, he motioned his arms to display the amount of hard labor he had in front of him.

"No doubt," said Ralph rolling his eyes. He didn't want to talk to the guys about it, they wouldn't take his word seriously. But, Lisa might want to help, if she wasn't still mad at him. "Ok, well, I might have a girl coming over later. What would you say? And nothing girly, she's more into weird stuff, science fiction, you know?"

"Sounds like a cool chick. Here, take this." The clerk popped out the jungle girls tape from the VCR and handed it to Ralph. "It's a good one."

"I'll pass. Thanks for the offer though."

"Suit yourself. Hey, you want me to come by? We could talk more about your movies filmed in Hypno-Vision!" He coned his hands and amplified the last few words to give it theatrical flair. Then, he grinned a stained smile and gave a creepy, gropey twinkle from his eyes. Ralph wasn't interested or amused.

"Nah, that's cool. Maybe some other time."

"Fine. I'll see you back here." The clerk waved one arm slowly over his view of the store as if it were a grand, sprawling landscape. "They always find their way back."

Ralph didn't give it a second thought before he left. Well, that was a bust. I should play more Cuazque and think on it some more.

Chapter IX

Show & Tell

After the events in the woods, Shannon needed to isolate herself, regroup and find her balance. Everything from how the world appeared to how her body felt internally was distorted and warped. She wandered the neighborhoods and reached out with her mind to find an empty house. People noticed her easily, but didn't stare much more than a minute. She hadn't even changed her clothes from the previous night. A few glimpses of her reflection in car windows revealed her to herself. Roughed up, strung out. Miles of trial and error on an unplanned route that led in circles more than once. And then, she found it.

It wasn't abandoned, but she could feel that it was vacant for the time being and she was so worn down that anything would do so long as it was safe and she could be alone. It was a squat brick house with a low awning over the porch and dark windows all around. Her first thought was to wait until dark, but she tossed that idea right out the window. Her head was in agony and a day of stretching it out did no help. She walked to the end of the block, turned and proceeded to walk behind the houses. *Act natural, act like this is a normal shortcut.* A man on a riding mower spotted her. He waved, lifted the beer can from between his thighs for a sip and kept on cutting without a care.

In the backyard of the empty brick house, she looked for an easy point of entry. First, she tried the back door on the off-chance that they had simply been forgetful. She turned the knob and it gave, but the bolt lock above it caught the door. *That's okay, it would have been too easy anyway. Come on, just a little push to find another way before I break a window.* She closed her eyes to concentrate and feel out the house. Windows and doors, all of them locked. But then, a group of flowerpots in the back yard came in to view of her mind's eye. Bingo. A spare key hidden beneath. She wouldn't even have to use force.

She let herself in through the back of the house. The first thing she did was take a long, hot shower in the stained bathroom. It took the water about ten minutes to warm up and the pipes groaned like geriatric joints. With only the clothes on her back, Shannon opted to 'borrow' the robe that hung in the bathroom. She walked into the living room and passed out on the sofa.

Sleep was her only activity that weekend. Her headaches lessened at the first relief of shelter and rest, but then grew to the sensation of closed bear trap on her brain. Dreams were populated with scenes of sacrificial offerings of humans strapped to wooden planks in the forest, on a stone tabernacle in a dank dungeon, even in an office conference room with men and women in expensive suits eager to spill the blood of beggars and runaways.

Shannon was a fly on the wall to these unspeakable acts unable to turn away, unable to wake up. All the while, that damned cat from the cabin roamed around participants with that same twisted figure. It would gaze at the display of barbarity and then stare at Shannon with an aroused appetite.

Each time the setting changed, jumping through eras and locations, the cat took on more and more of a humanoid figure. First, it stood on its hind legs and walked up right. Then, it grew to the size of a teenager. Finally, it was taller than a grown man with long, crooked teeth jutting out of its gaping mouth, nine eyes glowing emerald green and black fur that moved on its own like scores of worms writhing over its body. At this stage, in a dark cave behind a waterfall as the moonlight poured in, the cat approached her, caressing her face delicately, and lightly dragged its two-inch claws down the front of her. She was helpless to strike back.

The nightmares played again and again, on a loop starting from kitten and ending at caressing creature, all through different occurrences of murderous deeds. Shannon, mute and immobile, prayed for escape. Then, there was an interruption. A phone rang and rang until it materialized in the dream. A bright red phone rang off its cradle *ring, ring, ring, ring*. It snapped her awake.

In the empty brick house, a beige phone rang on the table at the end of the sofa. Happy to just be awake and out of that hell, she picked it up.

"Hi, pumpkin," said an unwelcome, familiar voice.

"Amanda? How did you...?"

"Really?" Amanda interrupted. "This far in the game and you still ask questions? You are supposed to be the smart one, Shannon."

"Leave me alone!" Shannon sat in darkness. It was night, but she didn't know what time or even what *day* it was.

"That isn't really an option now, is it?" Amanda continued. "Whether you like it or not, you are part of this. You made a blood pact with Colleen and me and the book and only way out is, well, death!" Amanda didn't hide her thrill on this last word. "I think you should come back to us. Come on, it'll be great! We'll hang out, maybe do a little light reading from the book and then I can hold you in my arms, close, safe with me. I'd be so gentle with you..." Amanda giggled on the other end. Shannon was scared, pissed off, and her heart stung. "By the way, I helped you on your biology project for O'Brian. Even those dorks, Marker and Meadows, got a freebie on that one. Next time you see them, tell them to be thankful, and if they aren't, well, I'll have to kill them, too." This time, she cackled.

"I'm hanging up now."

"Wait, wait, wait!" Amanda cried out. "One more thing. Have you had your period this month? Any flow?"

Silence.

"Didn't think so. Us neither. Welp, bye!" Amanda hung up first and left Shannon with the dial tone. It never crossed her mind and now it seemed like something she should have noticed. She was late. She was way late. For a virgin, that was a red flag.

The empty brick house wasn't safe. She put her only clothes back on and left.

****

Ralph woke up earlier than usual on Wednesday. His 'involuntary vacation' offered him gobs of time for video games and waking up for that was so much better than waking up for school. Pieces slowly formed and slight connective tissue formed. Something was wicked about *Cuazque*, but even he couldn't prove it, much less those nitwit cops. He had to stay ahead of them, keep a tight lid on things and then he could crack it. Then he could fix things.

He'd kept his strange suspicions surrounding the game a secret. He hadn't told much of anything to Steven and Kyle. His dad was still out of town. Lisa might figure things out if she kept showing up unannounced. The only other person who might know anything about the game was the last person he thought he'd have to deal with, the last person who'd even be interested.

Ralph walked into the treehouse and noticed something off immediately. The heater glowed a slow red and a figure was curled in a sleeping bag on the floor. There was a stranger sleeping in his treehouse. His nerves froze, he wasn't ready to find that in his home. But, he had to do something. He looked around for a weapon and decided on a folded metal chair that rested against the wall.

Making the first move to it was the hardest part for fear that that would be when they noticed him and sprung in to action after lying in wait for the perfect moment to strike him down. He took a few, slow, deep breaths and forced himself to move for it. His energy became wild and unleashed. He couldn't maintain confidence as he lifted the chair, banged it on the ceiling and shouted, "Hey! Who there!"

A girl moaned from the sleeping bag, unphased by his intimidation. Ralph hesitated out of fear more than caution. Pale white hands pulled the sleeping bag away down to reveal Shannon Kennedy, hair frazzled as the bare limbs of an old tree in fall, eyes sunken and bloodshot and a face that looked seven years older than the girl Ralph met in biology.

"It's so cold in here," she said. "Can you heat it up at all?"

"What the hell happened to you?"

"I'll tell you about it, but first, please, I'm so cold." Ralph checked the space heater and saw that it was turned all the way up. He couldn't tell if this was a good or bad sign that she snuck into his treehouse, again, but she definitely looked like she needed help.

"This one's at max. I think there is another in the house," said Ralph. He set the metal folding chair back against the wall and walked into the house for the heater. Shannon could have cried. He was the first friendly face she'd seen in days and it wasn't until then that she really knew she wasn't dreaming. She wanted to cry and tell him everything that had happened and let it out. The weight of it crushed her. But, she knew that she couldn't bust the floodgates just yet, she needed him calm first.

Shannon brushed the hair out of her face, wiped the back of her sleeve across her mouth and waited for him to return. The heater he brought back was larger and the difference was felt within seconds of turning it on. Ralph sat down in a chair in between Shannon and the doorway and gave her a blank expression. "What was it, out drinkin' late with the girls? Met a couple of older boys and had one hell of a time?" he asked in a snarky tone.

"Something like that. Look, can I stay here for a bit? Things got out of control, this seemed like a safe place and I need to collect myself before I..." she didn't finish that thought.

Ralph weighed what she said. He was happy that she didn't turn out to be some stranger or someone dangerous. "How about a hot cup, then you can tell me allllll about it," he said with sarcastic enthusiasm.

"You seem to be in a good mood."

"School gave me a special vacation, I've been playing video games, trying to beat the 'rap' and O'Brian gave us a clean one-hundred on the project, thanks to you. This is the least I can do. You must have really impressed him because even though I had nothing and Lisa bailed on us, we still aced it. So yeah, I'm feelin' alright." He left her to go fix some warm drinks.

The room started to warm up as the day brightened. Shannon looked around the room to get a better look at the assorted electronics and gizmos lying about. For the most part, they looked used and forgotten. All except for the GRX that sat next to the TV with a sheen of glory around it. Perched atop high ground, it looked like a trophy.

Ralph came back, still in a cheery mood to contrast her raggedness, with two steaming mugs. "Here, I have choices for ya; cream and sugar or," he held that mug closer to him and stretched out the other. "Freshly brewed black coffee, mmmmmm!" His emphasis was clearly on the latter.

"I'll take it black. Feels more appropriate," said Shannon. "And turn that up high as it goes, it needs to be hotter." She took the mug, drank a piping hot sip and enjoyed the burn a little. All that recent shit whirled around in her head restlessly, but that one sip broke the sequence enough to breathe. It was all so alien, so bizarre, but so strong it resonated in her bones.

At the highest setting, the heater began to make a low rumbling, the sound of a lawn mower in the distance. It called back memories of the summer that only just slipped away to vanish faster and faster into the past. The heater wafted bad smelling air, *burnt* smelling air, through the treehouse. She didn't want to check to see if it was real or her brain was trying to show her something. She felt friend, burned-out, like a drained battery. She doubted her vision was 20/20 right then, much less prescient.

"So, what's up? You wanna hang out or something?" Ralph's question brought her back. "I'm very interested in how you ended up in my backyard."

"Can I sit here for a little while, compose myself? Do whatever you were gonna do, I just want to shrink away, you know?"

"Cool." He hadn't attempted to play *Mazer* since that first day when it just screamed at him. Instead, *Cuazque* still held secrets. He beat the game once already with all the PUZZLE PIECES and that took long enough that blowing through it now was like riding a bike. It was all that ending that sounded ominous and bleak, a foreboding, cartridge fortune teller.

For a good thirty minutes, the kids said nothing as Ralph mechanically and methodically worked through the game. Shannon watched with unfocused, glazed zombie's eyes and finished her coffee by the second level. At first, she watched to unplug, like a metronome for meditation, a buoy to hold a hand onto so she could zone out and think about nothing with the rest of her concentration. But, as fate always has a cruel sense of dark human, she caught something that made her take notice and pulled her back into the reality that had been quickly, sickeningly become a *sur*reality.

"What are those pages you are collecting?" she asked at the fourth secret Ralph obtained.

"Amox Tzin." he asked after a sip from the now tepid coffee cup without looking away from the screen.

"Yeah, that, what is it?"

Ralph maneuvered the character over a large gap while dodging an axe in the air, then ducked under an attacking enemy, hit him until he froze in pain and bled out before collapsing down on the stone floor. He paused the game. "Well, it's for the hidden ending, the *real* ending. You see, when I beat it the first time, I got a bad ending where I was killed as a sacrifice. I got all the items, build the raft out of broken plane parts, but still, got the shaft in the end. It even gave me the 'Game Over' screen. Damn, that pissed me off. But, it tells you that if you had the ancient magic scrolls of Amox Tzin you would arrive at the true ending and that one was just a split reality where I didn't. You follow?"

"Uhhh, yeah, I got it," said Shannon. "I don't play video games, so…"

"Shocker," said Ralph. "Anyway, I went back and played it again. This time, I needed to find all the pages which, boy, I tell ya, that was a doozy." He wiped his brow and rolled his eyes. "It took me days to figure out that the music worked with the pace of the level and that the parts where the music skipped meant that the secret room was nearby. Used that, got all the pages, and then the ending was different. The pages had the power to bring people back from the dead. I used them to revive the other passengers from the plane that were captured by the villagers.

"Big mistake. They turned on me. But, as they held me down on the sacrificial altar I got sucked up into this…tear, I think."

Shannon got a jolt at that end part. She'd been listening mostly out of ingrained politeness, but that was too much of a coincidence. "This tear, did it look like outer space?" she asked. "Did it look like it ripped through the air out of nowhere and just sucked up into darkness?"

"Yes!" said Ralph. "Exactly like that!" He laughed with excitement. "Man, it was crazy, but so cool, I never saw it coming and the colors on this thing really out did themselves, it actually looked like it was *in* the TV and ripped from somewhere beyond. Hahaha, I even touched the screen, but all I got was a nasty static-shock bite!"

Ralph looked at Shannon's face and saw that she shared none of that enthusiasm. In fact, she looked like she thought he was being stupid. Or, she had to be the one to deliver terrible news he hadn't heard yet. She would have said it was both.

"What's wrong? Better yet, how did you know how it looked?"

"Because I saw it the other night?"

"What, the game? It isn't really popular, and, you know, you don't play video games, so…"

"No," she cut him off. "I saw it real, in person. I was there. I hoped it was a dream, but the longer I think about it, the more it haunts me. I'm gonna tell you something," she said. "But you better swear to Christ that you won't think I'm lying, freak out, call the cops, *nothing*, got it?"

"What is this?" Ralph pinched his face. "Are you trying to scare me? Prank me? Knock it off."

267

"I'm serious."

"Dead serious?" he asked sarcastically.

Nothing.

"No way."

Nothing.

He looked from the TV, and then back to Shannon. With a deep sigh and a whistle, he said, "Screw it, what do you have?"

Shannon told him everything starting from the top with Beth's demonic burning. Then, the fate of the convenience store clerk and the dismemberment of the pizza boy. Finally rounding out the store with the phone call at the empty brick house. She fought tears and shook the whole time. Ralph just listened with the game controller held in his hand.

When it was over, she looked at him for a reaction; judgement, advice, laughter. Anything. He looked back to the game, almost resumed it, but stopped himself. Breathing in short, forced pulls and pushes, he went back and forth between the girl and the TV. He gave up. "What the shit, man?! Are you for real? Serious. Are you for real?! This is fucking scary stuff! Goddammit, get out! Get out of my treehouse!"

268

"Can I just stay here for a few days while I make a plan? I want to end this. I *need* to end this."

Ralph shook his head at her, breathing like a bull through his nostrils. "Why did you come here?"

"Something was calling to me. I thought it might have just be for safety, but I think it was those games. I think, somehow, you are involved."

"Bullshit."

"Try the one that wasn't working. If this is playing by the rules I *think* it's playing, it'll work now."

"Fine." Ralph turned off the GRX and switched out the *Cuazque* cartridge for *Mazer*. He doubted it would work, he figured it for a bust. But, something felt different. The air inside the treehouse seemed to permeate his skin when he grabbed that odd, plastic computer part. Deep down, he wanted the game to work. He wanted to know more about this power to bring the dead back to life.

He jammed it into the console and flipped the switch. No screams. This time, bright, luminescent colors blasted from the screen in descending sheets in red, blue and green. Choppy, eerie music came through

269

with crystal clear sharpness and the screen simply flashed, *Ready?*

"Just like I thought," said Shannon. "You're neck deep in this shit, too."

"No, this is different, you got people killed."

"And why are you suspended from school right now?" Ralph said nothing. "You don't even see it yet. I've got a feeling we're going to need each other's help." She got up to leave the treehouse.

"Where are you going?"

"I want to grab some things from home. I don't feel like myself and I think it will help. I'll be back." She looked at the screen gushing out colors and said, "I know telling you not to play the game won't stop you, so, just, be careful. Try to figure out how it works and maybe we can make a plan. Or at least stop things from getting any worse."

After she closed the door behind her, Ralph pressed Start on the controller to begin the game. He did want to pay attention, he did want to find out what power this game had. But, his mind quickly slipped in the TV's wondrous light show that whisked him away to a blank slate Zen game-scape running through *Mazer*.

Chapter X

Instant Replay

When Shannon went home, she realized she hadn't eaten anything for days. Her mind was in so many different places and her body was in pain all over, food hadn't been a high priority. But, when she walked into the house, the familiar comfort put her at ease and she practically ransacked the kitchen. On the refrigerator, he father had placed a sticky note that read, "I will be gone for a few days on business. Amanda's father is taking some potential clients out on a trip and he wants me along. Stay out of trouble, I'll see you this week, Love, Dad." At the top of the note, he'd written the date. It was that past Saturday. *Well, at least he left a note,* she thought.

She showered, packed a bag of clothes and toiletries and left the house. She had walked back through yards using the street as little as possible in case Amanda and Colleen were out on patrol for her. Now, with a full stomach and a bit calmer, she could feel around with her mind. *They didn't come here, not yet. They must still be feeling weak like me. If I take my car, I'll have it in case I need to get somewhere quick. Shit, what if they see it? I'll have to hide it. Ralph has a garage, I'll park it there out of sight. Is there anything I need before I go back to the hideout?* She paced her bedroom in thought. *Help is what I need. Some clue as to how to get the hell out of this mess. Information! Books.*

She grabbed the bag, locked up the house and drove away in her green Volvo sedan.

It was dusk when she returned to the treehouse and when she opened the door, she walked in to a room coated in electric blue light playing that same short melody. Ralph sat in front of the TV slumped, drooling and asleep. Shannon briskly turned off the GRX and TV. This woke him up.

"What? Why'd you do that? I was in the middle of game,"

"You were asleep."

"No, I wasn't. It's been like ten minutes since you left, I didn't get in any game time."

"I've been gone for half the day. It took me hours to walk home from here the way I did to stay off the streets. Look outside, it's almost night out there." Ralph looked through the doorway and saw the sky burn as the sun set. "See?"

"But, you were just here. I pressed Start and started running, running through a maze of passages and colors. I was just getting my bearings with it and you turned it off."

"I told you to be careful."

"It's just a video game."

"This is black magic."

"We'll see. Maybe I fell asleep and lost track of time."

"Maybe. But when I turned it off, nothing was happening in the game. It looked like it was watching you. It looked like it was singing to you."

"I'll be more careful next time."

"You should have somebody with you while you play, just as a lifeguard. I won't do it. I know this feeling, there is definitely something wicked going on with this. That is why I'll be inside doing," she pulled out two books from her bag. "Research." The two books she held were titled; *Germanic Folklore: Myths of the Deutschen* and *Occult Practices: The Unseen and Beyond.*

Ralph eyed the books and said, "I'm still waiting for this all to be a trick, some elaborate prank." He rubbed his eyes. They didn't feel like he'd been asleep for hours. They felt dry and burned like he'd been staring at a light without blinking while a fan blew in his face. He was so tired, too.

"A joke? You're in denial. I was there, too, longer than I should have and I paid for it. People are dead and more will die if we keep playing stupid. Admit it, nothing about any of this feels normal or rational or like something you can just explain away. Dark shit is working hard while we let it into our lives ignorantly. We need to be ready."

"Sure, fine, I'll do that," said Ralph with a yawn. "Tomorrow. Dammit, I'm tired." He turned everything off in the treehouse and headed back to the house. "Do what you need to do, I'll be sleeping inside. Wake me up if anything happens."

Shannon had slept enough, now she was ready to work. She was about to follow him in the house, but thought it might be a good idea to keep an ear out for anything around them. The yard was well covered and she'd parked the car in the garage and locked it in. Ralph had left the door unlocked.

She sat down on the ground, took out a box of cigarettes from her bag, lit one and started to read. It took her two hours after the sun went down to realize that her vision in the dark was even better than during the day.

****

Shannon was still awake reading when Ralph walked outside in the late morning. "Sleep well?" she asked as she exhaled cigarette smoke. "Feels like you had some bad dreams, about big snakes. They had something to tell you, something to show you, didn't they? And you still think this is plain ole boring reality." She didn't look at him as she spoke or expect a reply, she only turned the page of *Germanic Folklore*. "Before you go in there, why don't you get that lifeguard we talked about?"

"Why don't you join me?" Ralph asked. His mood was sour from the night before. He *had* had some bad dreams, dreams like never before. Dreams of feathered and scaled flying creatures descending from the sky starting as small dots in the desert horizon that grew larger and larger until they were the size of ocean liners circling him under a black sun, whispering his name in smoky tones. The eyes, blinding white, shot light out from within that pierced his skin and tickled his insides.

Their lisp-filled voices made promises of power, inhuman power. The power to raise the dead. None of this comforted him, he only wished for the power to rise from this sleep. And when he did, he was flushed with relief, but only for a moment. The promise of the serpent tempted him. He could erase all the damage he'd done in Wilhelmina and, most importantly, out in the desert.

"I'm not going in there while you play that game. That's your hoodoo to catch, if I get anymore I might burst and I've still got a mission. Get one of your friends. Lisa would probably do it for you."

I don't want to involve Lisa, she's already pissed and she's too, too fragile for this, he thought. "One of the guys will do it. Kyle is solid. I better grab any recording equipment my dad has. I can't remember anything from yesterday, but I know something came through the TV."

"Good idea," said Shannon.

Ralph went back in the house and headed for his dad's office. Locked. Of course it would be locked. Where was he, anyway? All the other professors had come back but he was still gone. He left Ralph alone in this house where all of them once lived. They brought him into this world and now they left him in it all alone. He turned the handle again hard. Still locked. "Dammit!" Ralph kicked the door open, surprising himself.

He saw the cases of cameras and tape recorders on the shelf behind the desk and went to collect them. He gave a brief glance at the desk and saw why his father hadn't returned yet. Photographed in black and white, the large oval stone Ralph found not six months passed but still so long ago. It stood isolated in some unknown warehouse. Next to it was a telefax requesting his presence. *He's looking for answers, too.*

"Here," said Ralph back in the yard. "Add this to the collection." He handed Shannon a book titled *Gods and Monsters of Mesoamerica*. He went to the treehouse to set up the equipment and wait for Kyle to get out of school.

****

"Damn, took you long enough!" said Ralph. He opened the door to the treehouse and let Kyle in. "What, did you have to do your hair?"

"Yeah, nice to see you, too," said Kyle. "It might help you to be a little nicer to your friends, you know, probably the only people that think you are innocent of whatever the police picked you up for." He walked in, passed Ralph and looked around. "Speaking of, what the hell is all this…this whole setup looks elaborate to say the least. Where did you get all of this?"

Kyle sized up the array of cameras and sound recording devices around the room. He even spied a contraption with knobs and a monitor showing green waves grow and shrink on a graph. For whatever Ralph was trying to 'study', this all seemed to be overkill.

"Yeah, this is what I want you here for," said Ralph. "My dad keeps all this in his office, so I repurposed it, temporarily. Look, this game is really messing with me, in a bad way, a *personal* way, alright? And, I want you to see it, well, more so watch me. Don't look at the game at all, just watch me, got it?"

"You want me to watch you play video games? The hell with that! I'm outta here, man."

"No, wait," said Ralph as he moved to block the doorway. "I am serious. I need, no I would like your help, please, as a friend." He held his hands up in a submissive pose and loosed at Kyle in the eye. Kyle was unsure. *What is all this,* he thought, *is this some shitty prank?*

"Look," said Ralph. "All I want you to do is watch me play this game without looking at the TV. One hour, twenty bucks. Whaddya say?" At this, Ralph reached into his pocket, pulled out a twenty-dollar bill and held it out for Kyle.

"Shit, man, fine," said Kyle. "I'll do it for the money, but damn, don't act like an addict so much. We're still friends, right?"

"Right. Now, what I want you to do is…"

"Yeah, yeah, I got it," Kyle interrupted. "Watch you and not the TV. Roger." He pulled a chair up next to the TV, put the back rest forward and saddled it with his arms crossed along the top. "Cool?"

"Yes, cool. Stay there and watch, okay?" Ralph walked around the treehouse and turned on the various pieces of equipment one by one. It was quite a ridiculous setup, like kids making a mock-up news report with too much access to legit paraphernalia. There were five different cameras around the TV aimed at different angles. Two sat on either side of Ralph's chair pointed at the TV. One rested on top of the TV pointed at Ralph when in the chair. The last two were placed on opposite sides of the treehouse facing each other in an attempt to capture the whole room. After he pushed all the tapes in and pressed record, he walked up to the stereo system that was plugged directly into the pyramid shaped GRX. He turned that one, waited for the feedback to kick in and adjusted the volume so a low electronic hum was heard over the static snowstorm. He moved the recliner and walked backwards looking around the room with a finger in the air to count off all the difference pieces and make sure they were all 'ON'. Clumsily, he fell back into the torn up old lounge chair and grabbed a tape recorder small enough to fit into a pocket. He pressed record and said, "This is Ralph testing *Mazer* with Kyle Lauder as witness. The date is October 15th, 1995."

Kyle could no longer hold it back and started to laugh bent over the back of the chair. "What is this, dude? 'Testing the *Mazer*'," Kyle mocked. "Star date 1179!"

He laughed at his own joke. "Why so serious about this? Are you going for a world record or some shit? Because if you are, I would actually use a more popular game, you know, one people actually care about more than *'Mazer'*." At this last part, he raised his fingers to put invisible quotation marks in the air with raised eyebrows and widened eyes. "What the fuck is this shit, man?"

"Hey, listen," said Ralph. "Just go with it, alright? I am paying you twenty bucks, can you keep it together for 45 minutes, you troglodyte?"

"Okay, okay, sure. I think I can handle this...I'll try."

"Fine. Just do yourself a favor and don't look at the TV."

"Fine."

Ralph leaned forward and switched the GRX power switch to 'ON'. Immediately, without any sort of credits or intro, the game began. Coming from the TV, a green screen coated Ralph in the chair and reflected brightness in his eyes. Simultaneously, a tune started to come from the game. *Sounds like a lullaby,* Kyle thought. It was slow and simple, but dark and repetitive. Drops into minor keys with a tone that sounded like it kept misstepping at unpredictable intervals.

From Kyle's perspective, the game seemed to lock on Ralph directly. Only a moment's delay before the game was in play and Ralph was quickly moving something around the screen using mostly the D-Pad and only occasionally pushing the buttons. Without looking at the TV, Kyle was forced to imagine what was happening on the screen. What struck him as odd was how the sounds were about one generation too old. With this system, there was stereo sound that pumped out nice chippy melodies with cool sound effects like laser beams or fiery explosions but now it was rudimentary. It was an old computer sound and the game didn't really have any sound effects aside from a dull thud that Kyle guessed occurred when Ralph ran into a wall or fell. All the while, it was that tune, that melody that once he thought he got the hang of it changed ever so slightly or a note would come out sour and throw it off.

The awkward silence that fell on them like the solid neon colors coming from the TV onto Ralph was broken when after about five minutes a loud announcement from the game said,

"Ikuha". It stood out like the way an announcer on the subway stands out from all the crowd chatter to say, "Make way for the closing doors, please." It was canned and sounded like it was spoken through a tube with grating in it. The rest of the audio sounded different. That seemed to come from the game itself, the foreign word had a presence in the room...like a voice in the treehouse said it.

"What the hell?" asked Kyle to no response. There wasn't even a flinch on Ralph's part. He stayed glued, glassy-eyed to the TV and continued the quick motions on the controller. *Shit, he must really be into it, Kyle thought.* He wanted to peer around the corner of the TV, but felt hairs on the back on his neck tell him to stay put.

They say in silence with nothing but the game echoing around the room. It kept calling out words periodically and after an attempt to piece them together, Kyle realized that they were nonsense and didn't amount to anything. They didn't combine to make a larger word, but what if they were just jumbled? He looked around the treehouse for something to write with and saw a notebook with a pen in it next to Ralph. He slowly leaned forward while trying to stick to his objective. Magnetic static from the TV made his arm hair stand up on end. He got it after about the third or fourth swing and flipped to a blank page without looking at much else. *Shit, I've already missed some,* he thought. Without much care for the lost words, he started to jot them down as they came.

Kyle looked at his watch a while ago when only ten minutes had gone by. Now that he was engaged in the game as well as keeping track of the words called out, he wasn't watching the clock anymore. It was only when he had filled the page with words and when to flip it with his left hand that his watch caught his attention. "Shit, dude stop!" he said. "Time's up! Time's up!" Kyle waved his hands and made the 'Time-Out' gesture at Ralph, but the only reaction was a bit of drool drip out of his mouth. "Hey!" he said as he got up from his chair. Still nothing. Finally, he walked around in front of the TV and reached for the power button. He paused for a moment to look at the TV thought. *What the hell?* It looked blocky and plain like and old game. An *old* old game. All that was on the screen was multiple doorways that Ralph chose. After choosing, the screen flashed two colors along the frame of the door and zoomed through it. Then, at the next crossroads, the colors switched from muddy browns and reds to minty greens and blues. His attention was interrupted when Ralph began to claw, kick and snarl at him from behind.

"Shit, man!" said Kyle. His hand rested on the power switch and he turned it 'OFF'. He turned around and looked at Ralph break from his attack to a relaxed, almost defeated, collapse. "Goddamn, man, must be some game. You were catatonic, you didn't say anything when I asked you questions. Then you threw a fit when I blocked your view!"

"Shiiiiiit, I was afraid there was something off."

"To have you locked like that, hell yeah!" Kyle thought for a moment. "Tell you what, how 'bout we switch? I'll play and you watch, here, take the money back, no worries man."

"No!"

"Yo, come on, don't be so greedy, lemme try it."

"No." Ralph got up from the chair, walked around the room and turned off the cameras, stereo and tape recorder.

"What is it, like a secret or something?" Kyle felt a little dejected. "Why you gotta be like that? Did something happen while you were doing time?"

"Sorry, it's just…" Ralph started. "It's just an experiment, from my dad's school. You know, they want things to be accurate."

"Ahh, whatever. I guess twenty bucks is twenty bucks, right? But you gotta give me a try later, you make it look, I don't know…*hypnotizing*. Anyway, what was with the words? Does it all mean something collectively?"

"Words? What words?" He returned to the beat-up recliner with everything off and started to rub his temples.

"The words, dude, you know, the ones that that robot voice says. Here, I wrote 'em down." He handed Ralph the notebook and he looked at it for a minute.

"What is this? It looks like gibberish. *Reylar, Kuji, Nevka…*"

"I know, I was thinking maybe it's like a jumble or something, you gotta move the letters around to spell it out. A puzzle."

"Maybe…Listen man, I'm gonna tell you something, but it doesn't leave the treehouse, got it?"

"Go for it."

"My dad told a couple neighbors that I would help them out while they were out of town on academic business, right?"

"Right, you told us about that. Easy money, if you ask me. Hell, I would like something like that instead of my dumbass sandwich job. It's like people feel that they have the right to treat you like shit when you wear a lame uniform, ugly hat and name tag. Why?"

Ralph swiped this away with his hands. "Yeah, anyway, listen, you know the professor that lives alone over on Vine Street?"

"Uh,"

"Well, anyway, Dr. Greenly was going to conferences with my dad and the other professors. At least I *think* my dad was with them, but that's not the story right now. Now, when I went there last week to get the mail, I had to wash my hands. I, uh, had an accident and I was bleeding."

"An accident?"

"A dog bit me."

"Why did he bite you? Were you being naughty with peanut butter?"

"No, gross! I was just trying to stretch out my hand so he'd know it was me and he bit me, I didn't stop to ask questions!"

287

"Okay, fine."

"Right, so I went into Greenly's house to wash my hands. He has this dorky bathroom, but it's clean. I'd been using the bar of soap from the shower because I couldn't find any more. Soap is soap. I washed my hands and put the soap back in the shower, cool?"

"Uh, cool?"

"That's why I thought. Few days later, the guy comes home. Then, I hear that he had this terrible acid burning accident in the shower."

"Oh, shit, that Greenly? My mom's been talking about him. She's a nurse over at the hospital. That guy's in the ICU right now! Burns and boils all over his body, they have him on so many painkillers he can't even talk, much less describe what happened!"

"So, what if I had something to do with this? I mean, what if that's why…"

"Dude, what are you saying? You, like, poisoned his soap with your bloody hands? Come on, it could have been anything. Unless there is something you aren't telling me, do you really think you had a hand in this?"

"No…yes?" Ralph quickly, harshly scratched at the scars on his hand. The

288

bleeding had stopped pretty quickly and the skin scabbed and healed fast. The dog's bite hadn't been deep, just a lot of sudden pressure. "I don't know, Kyle, it's all messed up. Maybe I'm just paranoid…again."

"Come on, you know science. Try it again. I mean, buy that soap, use it and then I'll try it. If I burn, then you're cursed. Get it?"

"Yeah, maybe you're right. The scientific approach…"

"Yeah, I'm right! What kind of soap was it?"

"The bar kind."

"Can you be more specific? What did it smell like?"

Ralph slowly pulled his hands down his face from the sides of his head. His features stretched and warped for a second. "I don't know, clean skin?"

"Nice one, inspector."

"Shut up!"

"I'm just trying to help, duder."

"I know."

"Well, you know what we need to do?"

"What?"

"We need to watch that tape."

Ralph walked over to one camera in particular. "That is an excellent idea. Here," he said and pulled out a VHS tape from the camera. "This is the only one that records right onto VHS, the rest have to be developed."

"So, what is it, are you trying to catch something that happens fast on the screen or something?"

Ralph paused for a moment before pushing the tape into the VCR. "Would you believe me if I told you that I don't ever really remember what happens in the game while I'm playing it? I mean, it's like I know I am playing the game, but my memory doesn't retain everything so it's all just this blurry image of a bright screen. Oddly enough, I feel *different* after I play. Not stronger, really, but fuller, as if the blood in my veins pumped thicker and faster." The VCR took in the tape and Ralph hit the 'Rewind' button. The VCR whirred as the machine worked and Ralph sat down next to Kyle.

"I can't believe that. It just wouldn't make any sense. But, then again, you didn't let me see the game and then you lashed out for a second when I got in the way. Thanks for that, by the way. But that music was sort of eerie. Sounded like a broken, demonic siren call."

Ralph gave a quick chuckle at this. "That's specific. I can hear it, but I can't focus on it." The VCR came to an abrupt halt and started to spin the gears in a slower forward motion as it automatically played the cassette. "Anyway, let's go to the tapes."

The boys watched themselves sit around the TV and exchange some words. "Man, that's what I look like on TV? My forehead is huuuuge, dog!" said Kyle. They both laughed nervously, but said nothing about it. The video showed Ralph start the game and the light that poured out of the TV was visibly viscous. It brimmed over the edges of the screen in vibrant green covering Ralph as if he stood in front of the Sun. The simple graphics depicted sets of doorways that the player moved through into new rooms with more doorways. With every few rooms, the color would change, but the effect was the same unusual glow.

In one room, an object like a letter caught in between two languages hovered in one single doorway. Lines like something Arabic with Russian stamped over it. Either way, it was noticeably archaic. When Ralph advanced on the symbol, a rectangular faced white animal flashed on the screen for a brief moment. It had large eyes squeezed by pulsing, bleeding socket muscles. The mouth riddled with knife-life teeth opened in a silent scream. The game announced in that voice, *'Ikuha'* and the face vanished.

"What?" asked Ralph.

"Yeah, that's what I'm talking about," answered Kyle. They didn't look at each other while they spoke, their voices tired and slow. Their mouths hung open and their eyes stayed fixed on the TV screen. Now that the one word was collected, the screen's color began to fluctuate in a very slow rhythm growing brighter and the fading back down.

As Ralph continued through the maze and collected more of these alien words, that pattern grew stronger. The brightness would build and descend at a faster pace with each word and the face returned periodically at different angles and pained expressions. Faint, off in the distance, as if it were from somewhere outside the treehouse, the boys heard light chanting.

The more symbols collected, the more the sequence would crescendo until there was a point of blatant absurdity. The

292

chanting entered the treehouse and the luminescence level changed so rapidly it was like a propeller blade spun away in front of it. Ralph felt cold sweat perspire on his brow and he saw something unreal. On the TV, the recorded image appeared to distort, but only part of it. Only the GRX started to stretch and heave…it started to breath. Pulling then constraining, the GRX glowed from the inside peeking out light from three ports. This formed a face on the console that held malice and purpose. Sinister desire caught on camera.

The GRX inflated and deflated and started to exhaust a cloud from its vents. The cloud built and built filling the treehouse. Chanting with hoots and howls was undeniable. The energy of it intensified the boys' uneasiness, but they were stuck to their chairs by an invisible force that pried their eyes and mouths open. Kyle's insides had the sensation of hanging at the moment at of the first drop of a rollercoaster, but instead of being quick and over, it held in sickening anticipation. A combination of colors erupted from the screen in a thick mist of light that bled around the surroundings, engulfing the boys.

Finally, with one large whoosh and hush, the cloud sucked itself back into the

GRX. On the screen, the boys saw Kyle turn the GRX 'OFF' and Ralph walk around the room stopping the cameras. The tape ended and the screen was a sea-blue blankness of an idle VCR. They had no memory being in the fog or anything else from that tape. Kyle and Ralph were speechless.

After a solid minute of silence, except for the high pitched electric whistle of the TV and VCR, Ralph stuttered out, "Wha…What? What the fuck was that? What the fuck just happened!?"

****

Lisa felt guilty for ditching the group at the last moment. It was very unlike her, but she was frustrated at the lack of communication, but also, in her own way, she wanted Ralph to surprise her. Everyone else was so boring and typical, but then this kid from the desert comes out of nowhere talking and acting differently.

When she saw him picked up in the squad car, she figured it for a shake down immediately. She needed to know what the deal was and when he didn't show up to school that Wednesday or Thursday, she decided it would be best to go to the source.

She called him after school. He sounded confused, even a little paranoid. "At least they didn't arrest you," she'd said.

"They couldn't do anything. They, uh, made weak connections and jumped to conclusions," said Ralph.

"I heard you were in those people's houses before they died, is that true? What were you doing in there?" Her fingers twined the phone cord as she spoke.

"Yeah, but it wasn't as bad as that sounds. Those people paid me to housesit, but that's the only connection, I mean it. Look, I don't want to talk about it on the phone, why don't you come over and I'll explain the whole thing?"

"Really? Sure, I could be there soon. This is all so bizarre!"

She headed right for Ralph's and it never occurred to her, despite her teasing, that Ralph could actually be dangerous. Lisa felt like she stumbled onto a mystery, something exciting and special. But, when she got to his house and saw Shannon there, Lisa was no longer amused. "What is she doing here? Why would you let these people in your house, Ralph?" She didn't wait for a reply. "Jeezus, she's just loafing off you because her parents kicked her out, and after they burned Beth Gardner at

Amanda Klein's house, she wasn't welcome there either. She's a vampire, a parasite. She's using you and you don't even see it!" Surprising even herself, she shoved his shoulders. She was pretty strong for a scrawny girl.

"That is not how it is all," said Shannon. "Listen, I think you should know what's going on and that I have not, will not, do anything with your 'boyfriend'."

Messy black bangs spilled over Lisa's face and glasses. The heat from her body sent out waves of sour negativity directed at both Ralph and Shannon. It was starting to feel like a long con prank, and she wouldn't have it. "Fine," she said. She pulled out a kitchen chair and plopped herself down in it. She adjusted her hair, pushed her glasses up the bridge of her nose, and said, "Spill it, bitch," in a taunting manner.

Shannon went through the steps of explaining everything start to finish, from Beth up to her arrival at Ralph's. She wasn't as shaky and exhausted as she'd been when she told Ralph the same story. The fact that it didn't scare and upset her as much on this revisit in turn scared and upset her. On the bright side, it had become a cleansing process, momentarily absolving her of her sins by spelling it out. Secretly, it gave her hope for redemption. But, again, only momentarily.

After an hour or so of recounting, the climate in the room calmed from earthquake tremors to that chilling empty peace after a heavy storm. Lisa had grown even paler, but still held her stiff upper lip in protest. She drummed her fingers on crossed arms in calculation, and then made a single, "hmph," before she took off her glasses and placed them gently on the table.

"Prove it," she said to Shannon.

"Uhh…okay…with those?"

Lisa nodded.

"It's been sorta touch-and-go since, well, the cabin…"

Lisa tilted her head forward and glared. "What did I say? Bullshit."

Shannon glared back and picked up the glasses. She sized them up in hands like she was pricing them out for an auction. She sat up straight and put them on. After a deep breath and sigh, she took them off, folded them neatly on the table and slid them back to Lisa.

"They were your grandmother's."

"Lucky guess, give me more."

Shannon sat on the request for a moment. Looked at Ralph annoyed, and then said, "They are the only thing you have of hers. You took them from the old house that you used to stay at whenever your parents had to leave town or just wanted some 'alone time'."

Lisa said nothing.

"Your selfish uncles stopped taking her to the doctor, let her suffer and sold everything else after she died and threw away what they couldn't, lock, stock and barrel. You only have them because when you were crying alone up in her room at the funeral, they were left out on her dresser...like they were put there for you special. They aren't even your prescription, they help you just enough, but you wouldn't dare drive with them. You wouldn't dare drive anyway, you're too afraid of it. It doesn't make sense to you. How can all those people rely on each other to drive safely all the time when they are all so stupid *all the time*? And, deep down, you're afraid that you're just as dumb and your fear is the only thing that pushes you hard enough to..."

"Okay, stop it, that's enough." Lisa's mood had changed. It wasn't accusatory anymore, but not mellow either. Still resentful that she was left out, she turned her attention to Ralph. "Where do you fit in all of this?" she asked with a deep, piercing stare.

"Oh, I, ugh…follow me. Grab your jacket."

Ralph led the girls back to his treehouse and turned on the lights and heaters. "Okay," he said rubbing his hands really quick. "This is what we have so far." He pointed to the chalk board that he started to write scattered data on after Kyle left. There were bad drawings of a book, scenes from video games and listed names in two distinct writing styles.

"Wait," said Lisa before Ralph could even start. "You let her in here before me? Unbelievable…"

****

"Whoa, now, I was trying to keep it away from you. Plus, she let herself in. So far, seems like anyone who gets involved with this shit, you know, gets *involved* with this shit and bad thing happen…I was looking out for you." This didn't cool her down as much as he hoped, but it did silence her for a moment.

"This is what we have so far," he repeated himself. "Amanda got the book, some book from family in Germany, and brought it back here. Now, whether or not she actually knew what she was doing is anyone's guess. I think she knew *exactly* what she was doing, but Shannon wants to give her the benefit of the doubt. I wasn't there, I don't know, but I still think she is sinister and I wouldn't put it passed her to plan something like this out. She's been using the book with better and better skill to do her demonic deeds around town. Shannon says that she loosely remembers a possessed cat claiming that the pact was sealed and the three girls' powers will only grow, that this is just the beginning. What does Amanda want? What does she need? Can't tell ya."

"Before you start pointing fingers, understand that I fell into this whole thing...sort of by accident...I swear!" Lisa's face had started to tense up again like a batter right before cracking the ball passed the back wall. "I was just putzin' around, playing video games when this shit started to reach out from the television. Before I knew it, it was working through me, *using* me." He pointed at *Cuazque* sitting near the TV and GRX. "That is where the trouble started. It was unlike anything I'd played before with new levels of detail and immersion. It became an obsession, not only to beat it, but mostly to unlock the secrets. I thought it knew how to…I wanted more. More of the same, but different."

"Phil, at the game shop, told me about a sequel, a follow-up." He pointed to the black semi-circle jammed into the top of the GRX. "*Mazer* really got into my head…we think. I couldn't even tell until I caught it on camera when I had Kyle come check it out. I blacked out for periods of time, felt drained and heavy afterwards. I didn't lose total control, but it was like someone else stepped in to take it from me. When I got pulled out, I couldn't remember what happened. I can't fully explain it, I don't know which details are important and which are just, well, coincidence, but I am really starting to think that these two games, me giving them what they want, are what burned Dr. Greenly, made Arty attack Dr. Jackson…even sunk that car in the lake."

There was a thick silence in the room. It held them in place, mute, for a few minutes.

"And?" Lisa asked.

"And that's all we have," said Ralph. "That and whatever Shannon got from her reading which has been almost too much to sift through. We know something bad is here, with us, but we don't understand it."

Lisa looked back and forth from the board to the games and then turned around to give Shannon one long stare trying to dig into her mind. "It's not gonna work, it only goes one way," said Shannon.

"How do you think it is linked?" Lisa asked.

Ralph and Shannon looked at each other. Shannon started to say something, but Ralph cut her off. "There are signs of the book in the games. The way about the black magic, but that's about it." He swayed his hands up and down in balancing gesture searching for the right term.

****

"Shared behavior of the beast. Besides, with all this gnarly, eldritch shit going on, coincidence doesn't seem likely."

"And I was just about to say," said Shannon. "That in some of my reading, it seems like demons don't like the power of other demons, black magic has to be pure to be effective and if other influences come into play it causes conflict."

Lisa pointed at Shannon. "I can work with that. That's good. Do you still have those books?" Again, no wait for a reply. "We need to start from scratch and get a handle on this. You two are my sources, I'll be the brains. Let's start with basics; people, dates, malicious items, etcetera." Ralph took a deep breath and looked at Shannon for back up. "Let's go, people are dying!" said Lisa without turning around.

Shannon went to collect her books and Ralph went to play the *Mazer* tape.

****

Curses, demons, and black magic? Sure, fine, Ralph was on board at this point. Anything and everything and why not some more while they were at it. Terrifying dangers bent on ripping souls from mortal flesh. But, in his gut, in this moment, he was annoyed and tired. Lisa had grilled them in the treehouse for hours and it still didn't make sense.

The chalkboard had been erased and then filled with connected ideas, people, places and items. Then, once things were crossed out or signified, Lisa erased it again and reorganized the 'pertinent' information neatly. The words 'Blood Pact', 'Sacrificial', and 'Dark Forces' boxed up nicely in white juxtaposed their intended purpose.

Shannon, having been up for almost two days, was finally starting to get sleepy after all the brainstorming. Lisa was more invigorated than ever. "We're still missing somethings about this," she said staring at the board. "I know there's gotta be a secret somewhere. If we throw out coincidence, we are left with only significance. There must be a weak point. Some sort of leverage…"

"Maybe it's just chaotic, like an animal trying to survive?" Shannon suggested. "Consuming as much as possible for nourishment and growth?"

Lisa ignored her. "Ralph, it doesn't seem like you have any powers like Shannon or even control over the influence. It seems to be using you like a conduit, a throughway. Could it be stopped? Collected and channeled?" she wrote these questions with several others on the board including: 'Can the evil be stopped without killing the people cursed?' 'Can we protect against it?' and 'Has Amanda always enjoyed being a murderous bitch or is this a new thing?'.

"Listen," said Shannon. "I felt weak for days after the last accident. I am guessing the same thing happened for Amanda and Colleen. We should do something quick before she gets any stronger. I don't think we have time for theory, and besides, it isn't helping us."

"Isn't helping us? It is telling us everything," said Lisa. "We know that there is a number system to it that both you and Ralph share in common. It needed three offerings to be fully activated. We can't tell if Amanda is temporarily weak like you said because of what she did to O'Brian. What we don't know is what you're really doing here. How do we know you aren't just a spy sent here by the ghoulish girls' club to seduce Ralph into joining, or worse, killing him and claiming more black magic?"

"I'm here because I want to stop this. I can't take it anymore. I thought that things would change, I thought that she would stop. I had to run away from it, but I can't quite give up on her yet. I think if I just talk to her, maybe even get in her head, I can calm her down. This isn't her. I can find her and bring her back to herself."

"What makes you say that, huh? I think that's just more lies."

"Because I love her! She...I know she loves me too. That's our leverage."

"Lotta good it's done so far," said Lisa. Shannon glared at her. "But that does give me a plan. We could use you as a diversion and then bag her. She knows more about this than anyone and she has the

305

book. We need that book if we want to find a way out. And if your love is like you think it is, then we won't need to anything like that, fair?"

Shannon thought for a moment. She really did believe that Amanda loved her too, but what if that Amanda was long gone? She had to know for herself, but she couldn't do it alone. "Fine," she said. "But you have to let me talk to her first."

"Agreed," said Lisa. "Ralph, think you could get your friends to help us out? Just as back up."

"I don't want to get anyone else hurt," said Ralph. "I've done too much damage already."

"They'll be fine. I'll come up with a plan and we'll make moves tomorrow. It's too late now to get everything in motion, besides, I want to think this over, don't want to just jump in like you two 'winners'". Shannon and Ralph made a glance at each other that was both annoyed and shameful.

"I'm not sure how these forces will interact when they meet, but you guys are getting along fine. Hey, maybe that's the secret, evil just needs friends." She laughed at her own joke alone. "Let's wait till tomorrow after school. No, I have piano

306

lessons, after that. Piano always helps me think, it will be good for a clear mind. Stay out of trouble, Ralph, and don't play anymore video games."

The group dispersed for the night, Lisa going home while Ralph and Shannon stayed at the Marker house. Exhausted, Shannon fell into a deep sleep that was thankfully dreamless. Ralph, on the other hand, was alternately terrified and hysterical all through the night until he vomited on the floor and passed out in his bed.

Chapter XI

Witch Hunt

Knowing that Kyle had at least seen some proof of all the batshit craziness, Ralph thought it would be best to have him talk to Steven as a go-between. Kyle agreed instantly. His phone call with Steven was a debate with bargaining, reasoning and explaining similar to taking a child to the dentist's office.

"I really think you should hear him out," Kyle said on the phone. "I mean, he was always a little weird, but come on, we're friends, right? Why can't you give him the benefit of the doubt?"

"Because he got arrested at school the other day!" Steven shouted. The volume used would have been reasonable if he was actually trying to call out to Kyle, four blocks away, with nothing but his vocal strength and will power. "I heard that he put three people in the hospital and killed a dog with his bare hands! You heard what they're saying at school. Latest I heard, he kidnapped Shannon Kennedy! Something is way off here, man, I can smell it."

"Yeah? Really? Smell it? If he had done any of that for real, why would the cops let him go?" Heaving breathing was Steven's only reply. "Exactly. I saw him yesterday, he needs our help and I plan on giving it to him. If you get butterflies in your tummy and want to leave, fine, but at least hear him out, deal?"

"And you give me *Space Pirate*, no bitching, no discussion?"

"What?!"

"Don't worry," said Steven. "That's only *if* this whole thing is as bad as I know it is. If it is nothing, then you keep it. Those are my conditions, deal?"

Kyle went mute for a few moments. Only the sound of Steven's mother vacuuming down the hall broke the silence. "Is that your mom workin' in the house? What's she wearing?" Kyle asked.

"Shut up, asshole! Deal?"

"Deal."

"Now, you have to meet me down the street from his house. We go in together. I don't want any tricks."

****

Guarded escort was crucial to Steven's conditions. "I don't want to end up tied to a chair and made to watch some sort of creepy nude, blood-soaked dance before he kills us right then and there," he said.

"I doubt that will happen," said Kyle.

"You don't sound so sure!"

"Come on, don't be a baby." Steven shook his head and said nothing more on the way to Ralph's treehouse. They let themselves in through the door and saw Ralph at a chalkboard littered with small phrases, names, number and squiggly lines to connect them. He held a notebook and stared deeply into, almost through, the board. He turned around with a jolt when they entered, but calmed down when he saw it was them.

"Nope, I'm done," said Steven. He crossed his arms and wouldn't make eye contact with Ralph. But, he didn't leave the treehouse.

"Dude, shut up," Kyle said to Steven. Steven made a stupid face with high eyebrows in response. "Show him the tape."

"You got it," said Ralph. He set the notebook on the TV and plugged the power strip back into the outlet. "I didn't want to leave it plugged in when we weren't using it. I don't understand it, but I thought it might be a good idea. Now, I don't think watching the tape has any effect, but let me know if you start to, well, lose your head."

"What the hell are you talking about, man?" Steven asked.

"Just, please, for the next twenty minutes don't ask any questions. I want your help and it's best if I just show you first, cool?"

"I guess," said Steven as he threw his arms up in an 'I don't know' gesture.

"Cool," said Ralph. He pushed play and they watched the tape start up. This time, Ralph watched them watch the tape from the side. He'd seen it too many times already. So now, those eerie sounds were the only accompaniment to the light show pouring from the television. His stomach turned at the memory of that show.

About ten minutes in, Kyle and Steven were still silent. "You guys still here?" asked Ralph.

"Yeah," said Kyle in a voice deeper than usual.

"Yes," said Steven. He sounded like someone had their hands on his throat. His preconceptions aside, this was quickly becoming highly unusual and that demanded his attention.

Ralph looked back and forth between them as they continued to watch in silence. The announcer called out the words and the now familiar WHOOSH of the room changing played out. Ralph didn't like how glued they were to the TV, how eager to soak up the colors. "I think that's enough, I'm gonna stop it."

"Nah, dude, let it go a little longer," Steven said in that slow, amazed voice. "So bizarre…"

"Nope," said Ralph. "I think you get the picture." He stopped the VCR, turned off the TV and unplugged the power strip.

"Dude, holy shit!" said Steven. He stretched his jaw out and widened his eyes at Ralph. "What was that? Where did you get that?"

"From The Shop. From Phil. For free," said Ralph. He stood in front of the now blank, black, but still buzzing TV. "Here's the deal, Steven, that game you lent me, *Cuazque*, I beat it a couple times."

"Really? Three times? Damn, I never beat that one. It cheats!"

"I knew you lied when you said you beat it." Ralph shook his head. "Anyway, the first time I beat it, the game said I finished the levels, but didn't totally complete it, there were secrets to collect. So, I went back and looked for them. After a while, I got good, *real* good. It's a lot of patterns, but if you listen to the music, there is a rhythm to the game. You have to know what's coming and keep up with the tempo. I didn't get it for a while because I would mess up at parts even going with the music. That is how I found the secrets to find out what the game was really about."

"The whole games mission isn't for you to just get the parts to fix a boat and leave the village down river. It's really about collecting the eight pages for the Amox Tzin scattered around the levels in hidden rooms. You have to stand at a specific part against the wall, jump, and then attack in the air and it takes you there. Cryptic shit. After you get in, solve the room puzzle, and grab the page, it takes you back out into the game and the music restarts."

"Typical, I got ya," said Steven.

"Yeah, same old same old. Now you get back into the swing of the rhythm and whoop on it but good."

"Did you beat it with the secrets?" asked Kyle.

"Yeah," said Ralph. "But it wasn't what I expected. The ending was very different. Instead of the first time where I see the guy going down river in the boat with warriors hiding in the bushes at sunset, this time it was night, and this time he used the pages to bring the rest of his crew back to life, but it didn't go so well. I thought they'd help me escape and we'd all be saved. No. Not at all. They started to attack him and hold him down atop one of the temples sacrificial tables. They turned on him and ate him alive. Game over."

"Shit," said Steven.

"'Shit' is right. It was pretty harsh, too. They took a knife, stabbed him at the bottom of the neck and dragged it down below his belly button. He spilled out all over!"

"So, I played it again, made sure I got all the secrets and this time, ending was different. The guy used the ancient magic to revive everyone and they *did* help him. They gathered around him and protected each other as we marched through the treacherous city. The warriors couldn't touch us, the spells of the priestesses did nothing. We were unstoppable with those pages."

"What does that mean?" asked Kyle.

Ralph shrugged his shoulders. "That this magic can be good *and* bad? I can't tell."

"So, what does it have to do with what you just showed us?" asked Steven.

"As far as I can tell, *Mazer* is my way to that magic. It's giving me the words and showing me the way. But I'm scared to try to use it."

"Because of what happened with those doctors? Why the police picked you up?" asked Steven.

"Exactly. I've gone beyond disbelief. I know there's something going on."

Steven's composure changed. "I don't know, man, it seems farfetched. You better let me have a go at it."

"No. Kyle, you saw what it was like for me. I was out. Hell, I can't remember even playing it. *Every* time I'd black out! That's why I had all the recording equipment and you to babysit me. I had to see what happened. At first, I couldn't believe the tape. The games are working *through* me, you guys. It knows what I want…"

"What do you want?" asked Kyle.

"To help them. To bring them back…all of them."

"And what do you need from us?"

"I'm not sure yet, the girls know better than me."

"What girls?" asked Steven.

"Lisa and Shannon."

"Bullshit."

"Nope. Totally true. They'll be here soon. Lisa ought to be on her way and Shannon has been meditating, trying to collect herself. And if you think my shit's weird, you ain't even heard the half of it."

The two-way phone in the treehouse rang. Ralph picked it up. "Hey," he said. "Yeah, we're all here...yeah, sort of, you'd better add your side to it." He hung up the phone.

"Who was that?" asked Steven.

"Shannon. Like I said, she was inside meditating. She says it helps with, well, she'll have to explain it."

"Bullshit."

"Just wait."

After a few moments, Shannon opened the door. "I knew you had secret club meetings in here." Her joke didn't break the ice like she hoped. All she got was Kyle and Steven's dumbstruck expressions. She got the idea for meditation in the *Occult* book. It claimed that it strengthened mental abilities and calmed the spirit into better cooperation with the body. It was right. She felt better than she had in days and stronger than she had in her entire life. The deeper she went into her mind, the more certain she was that its stretch outward was boundless. She could feel out the areas around her with a mental touch far superior to the physical touch.

In contrast, Steven was pissed. He sat with crossed arms and a pouty lip that stuck out in a swollen fashion. He didn't like that there were so many oddities and goings on without his knowledge. It had to be a prank. Ruling out the impossible, it was the only remaining solution. But he'd play dumb just a little while longer, at least until he saw the trap coming. He wasn't going to let them get him that easy.

"Do you wanna tell them?" Ralph asked Shannon.

Before she could speak, Steven volunteered a solution. "How about you just let me play the game, it'll give me a better idea if I get at it firsthand."

"Ohhh, no, not gonna happen, pal. Not even a drop, sorry, you're gonna have to trust me on this, okay?"

"Maybe you are just weak, you think of that? Let me take a whack at it, I bet I'll exorcise it right up, come on!"

317

"You shut up with that, people are dying, we know this is connected. I can't let you open that can of worms anymore that I already did."

"Right," said Kyle. "What do you need from us? I mean, this whole thing is fubar, but that doesn't mean I'm running away. Hell, if I'm gonna be honest with y'all, I feel a little excited."

"I think it's stupid!" said Steven. "It's a crock of shit, you are just scared kids trying to get others to believe you because in your messed up little idiot brains that will validate all of your fantasy, right?!"

"Look, it's really not like that," said Shannon.

"Oh bullshit! You're trying to trick me! You just want me to do something stupid like, like, like follow you into some dumbass 'haunted' house where someone's gonna come out from behind a corner in mask and scare me because that's how the human body reacts to sudden surprises. You're just like those lame ass 'horror' movies that pop things on the screen! It isn't dangerous, it's just a reflex!"

"You say that now," said Shannon with a cold interjection. "But you haven't seen what these girls can do. You haven't been there when they are laughing like hyenas as they spill blood. You haven't seen the near narcotic high they get right after a 'girl's night'. You don't know how every time after, the space in and around my head stretches out and digs deeper with a penetrating cloud of thunder and lightning giving me hallucinations clearer than yesterday's memories more detailed than what your normal senses can pick up. This…hidden knowledge feels like a curse!" She had their attention. "I know what it's like to get to the edge, look back at everything you knew and thought, and then have something push you across an intangible fence. And once you are on the other side, that old world is gone, dead forever. I now exist outside the rest of humanity…"

There was a long pause. Even the hands on the clock mounted on the wall waited in anticipation. "I'll show you," said Shannon. She walked to Kyle and Steven and placed a hand on each of their heads.

"Whaaaaaaaat?" asked Steven.

"Go with it," said Kyle.

Shannon closed her eyes, took a deep breath and as she exhaled, the boys spoke secrets to each other. Secrets they didn't know themselves.

"I play games that I don't like just so we have stuff to do together," said Kyle.

"I am jealous of how calm and collected you are because I think smart people are only cold and calculated like me, but I know you're smarter than me," said Steven.

"I wish I had a family like yours where your parents are around and attentive and you aren't an only child. I feel like they had me to try to save their marriage, but it didn't go the way they expected."

"I cheat on tests and lie in school."

"One time, I was taking a shower at your house and decided to jerk one out in the shower. Your mom came in on accident and saw me doing it. She didn't say anything she just stared at me. She's been uncomfortably nice ever since."

"She asks about you all the time, now I know why!"

Shannon released them. Kyle's eyes welled up as he looked at his friend. Steven made a face like he was about to vomit. "How did you do that?" he asked Shannon.

"That's what I'm trying to show you, and that was me being nice," she answered.

"Being nice? You damned witch, I'll show you *nice!*" Steven jumped out of the chair and threw a wild punch at Shannon. She dodged it, but wouldn't let him take another chance. She punched him square in the jaw and he fell to the floor.

"Daaaamn," said Kyle. "One of the hottest girls in school, and you fight like a man! Shit that looked like it hurt." He laughed a little, but he was shaking from what he just shared with Steven. Steven moaned on the ground and started to lift himself up.

Then, the phone on the wall lit up and rang. Ralph picked it up. "Lisa, what took you so long? Why are you calling from in the house? Doesn't matter, you should come on back here, you just missed…"

"Ohhhh, wrong guess, loser," said a voice that was not Lisa's.

"Ummmm…"

"I'll give you a hint, if you look at Lady Kennedy's face, I bet it's all spelled out for you." Ralph looked to Shannon and saw that her face paled, her expression tightened.

"…Amanda." Ralph felt his insides sink below his waist line.

"Ding! Now, let's see if you can guess who I have here with me." Pause. "Oh, what's that, you don't want to talk to him? Not ever again? You want to see him rip his own eyes out from his puny little skull out of pure terror?"

"Shut up. She isn't part of this." Ralph gripped the phone with white knuckles.

"Anyone's a part of this if I say and I say tiny Lisa just got a lead role. You got my note, you know the drill…"

"What note?" Ralph interrupted.

"What? The note I left on the damn…" Amanda made an aggravated growl. "You're ruining it!" She howled. She took a deep breath and then continued. "Let's do a trade. Your girl for my girl. What do you say?"

He looked to Shannon who shook her head.

"Meet me at the old Witch's House. Tonight. One hour. I know you'll be there." Ralph heard a click on the other end and the line went dead.

"She's got Lisa."

"She's gonna use your feelings against you. We could lose everything. Don't fall for her trap," said Shannon.

"You guys know that place, right? Maybe we can get the jump on her."

"What place?" asked Kyle.

"The Witch's House," said Shannon.

"Yeah, in a way."

"Alright, that's it! I'm outta here!" shouted Steven. "You drag me over here after getting arrested! You lie up all this bullshit about voodoo and kiddie superstitions! You put on a lame rehearsed phone call from a treehouse! And now you want me to go to that shit heap shack in the woods?! It's shit! I'm not buyin' it!"

Very calmly, Shannon countered his argument by saying, "You still don't believe it? Steven Young, the boy with so much to prove has no spine in the end. Fine, we don't need you, run home to your video games and escape the problems in front of you. You already will never be respected like your brother, so what's the use in trying, right?"

"Shut up," said Steven.

"Momma's little baby boy, no wonder you are so nasty to her, deep down, you like being coddled and sweet talked…"

"Shut up!" Shannon was trying to embarrass him into action, but she was unsure if it was working. Steven keyed in on some point right behind everyone's head as he looked at them individually. "It's a joke. I'm not afraid of jokes. I'll go with you and I'll see for myself, and in the end, *I'll* get the last laugh, just watch." He cleared his throat with determination and a dash of spite, got up and walked right out of the treehouse.

"Yo! Let's go!" Steven called from the yard.

"This is no joke. We need to be careful. These girls have killed people for less," Shannon said to Kyle and Ralph before leaving the treehouse.

"Keep an eye on Steven, he's got a crazy look in his eye," Ralph said to Kyle.

"You're one to talk," said Kyle. The boys laughed nervously, more out of habit than humor, and left the treehouse.

Out in front of the house, Shannon and Steven argued. "Let's just take my car, we can all fit in it. I hid it in the garage," she said.

"No, that's just what you want me to do, you fuckin' gypsy palm reader! Let's go on bikes, I want to sneak up on them," Steven replied.

"He's got a point," agreed Ralph.

"But I don't have a bike here," said Shannon.

324

"Well, then I guess you'll have to walk, bitch!" Steven said with pride. No one acknowledged it and Shannon just shrugged it off.

"You can use one of my dad's bikes, it might be a little big for a girl, though," said Ralph.

"I'll manage."

"Alright then, let's go. Oh, and I'm callin' the shots now!" said Steven. He jabbed his pointer finger at them each to accent this. Rather than it seeming confident and intimidating, it just made him look more unstable.

No one answered him, but they obliged all the same. They rode in silence to the Witch's House in the autumn afternoon.

****

The sun dipped behind the horizon and hung right on the precipice when they arrived. From the hilltop vantage point in town, the surrounding trees covered up the house. Now, after they dumped their bikes here and there, it revealed itself and looked like it needed life support. The house hunched on itself and moved with a lifeless sway back and forth in the wind like a limp corpse dangling from a noose. Ralph could swear he had seen structures made of cards that were sounder.

For Shannon, the quiet was the first thing she noticed. No birds in the trees and wind didn't blow so much as push things back and forth like they were tied to fishing wire somewhere off stage. Their steaming breaths were amplified and the leaves cracked and echoed around them, even in their stealthy approach.

Steven said he knew this place, but he still looked scare. *I guess it's really sinking in now*, Ralph thought. On the ride up, Steven went from angry determination to ruin the 'joke' to oh-shit-I-might-actually-die-if-this-black-magic-is-real. He was quiet and his eyes darted in all directions. Kyle, on the other hand, oddly enough looked happy just to be there. Always a positive attitude. The calm could be felt through the group, except for Steven.

"Okay, man, how do you want to do this?" Ralph asked Steven.

"Well, she knows you two are coming, but she doesn't know that we're here," Steven said with a nod to Kyle. "Let's split up, we'll go in the side and you guys take the front or back, this way, we can sneak up and get her."

"Get her?" Shannon asked, making the plan sound stupid and childish. "I can't believe it, you haven't listened to a word I've said. These girls aren't like other girls. Just...don't try anything foolish...don't give her a reason. And *don't* look her in the eyes."

"A reason to what? What can she possibly do, *really*?" He shook a bit, but he kept talking to build courage. "We got this in the bag, the only thing to look out for is the house. Speaking of, do go all the way upstairs...that's where the place is really busted up."

Shannon and Ralph locked eyes for a moment but said nothing. Steven shrugged, walked passed them and into the house with Kyle. "Whaddya think, whiz kid?" Ralph asked. "You getting any signals?"

Shannon focused for a moment, tried to force it. Nothing came out. It was quiet. White noise. There was nothing here, and if there was, it was all forgotten. She shook her head. "Nothing..." But it wasn't nothing, it felt like a trap.

"We should be sure, though," said Ralph. They walked around the front of the house, peaked through dusty windows into empty rooms with furniture organized

327

sparsely. On the front porch, Ralph had to admit that despite all the rumors, this place did look pretty cool all broken and old. Like it had a firm grasp on the time of its relevancy, but then the rest of the body flailed in the wind as time blew on in its violent storm.

"Did you even try to find her? I mean, did you call her?" asked Shannon.

Ralph froze at the door. *Shit*. He got so caught up in it all that he didn't even think to at least check to see if Amanda was lying. She *did* make a phone call to his treehouse. But, then again, she could have figured it out through the house phones somehow. For a moment, in a small place at the back of his mind, he wanted her to have captured Lisa and hold her in this house right now just to be right and not made a fool. He hated himself for that.

No chickening out now, not after coming this far. Ralph pulled the front door open with his torso clenched in case of any sudden jolt that might be on the other side of the doorway waiting for him. Nothing popped out, nothing was waiting.

"Not yet," said Shannon. She walked passed him into the house, stepping like she would on broken glass with bare feet. Nimble, but it still made noise. Once

328

inside, Ralph saw that it didn't look like anything he had imagined. Instead of holes in the floor, cobwebs, broken or missing stairs and the echo of a far-off faucet that still leaked, there was nothing. Well, practically nothing. It was an old house that was left behind, no one came back to pick up the pieces. Some graffiti was on the walls, but that wasn't shocking. There had been no skinned animals out front to greet them, no deep set red stains on the floor surrounded by melted candles and hand-drawn enchantments. All in all, this didn't feel like a witch's house, it was just old, forgotten Wilhelmina.

They walked through the empty front room into a cramped, but still empty, hallway into a kitchen that looked cut up and torn down and then into a room with a sofa facing a dusty outline where a sizable portrait used to be. On the sofa, gazing at the outline, sat a tiny, thinly-framed, dark-haired girl.

"Lisa!" said Ralph. He ran around the sofa to her and saw a lifeless expression in her eyes. Not glazed over like a dead person, but clear and sharp and empty like a doll's eyes.

Through her mouth, though not using it, her voice trickled out the slow way a drop of water seeps through ice only to freeze in its path. "You came! I am so happy you made it! Miss Kennedy, you are looking simply *wicked* these days, you have a certain darkness around you that is simply delectable. I say, if looks could kill..."

"Oh, that's right, *mine* can," Amanda finished. She had been in the corner of the room, leaned up against the wall wearing a letterman's jacket and cheerleader's skirt. "And you, Ralph Marker," she continued in disgust. "You thought you could hide her from me? You and your feathery friends have some neat tricks, but you decided to come in the game too late to stand a chance. But, out of respect for the powers that be, we can make this easy." She pointed to Lisa. "Do you like my party trick? We practiced that routine all afternoon, she struggled at first, but I knew she'd come around. What about the setting? I had Shannon in mind when I picked it." She put her hands in Lisa's hair slowly at first, and then grabbed a handful and jerked her head around with a giggle that was painfully unnerving.

"Bitch! What did you do to her?" asked Ralph. He started towards Lisa, but stopped four feet away. Like a cheap, run-of-the-mill magician, Amanda slid a switch blade out from her sleeve and extended the knife near Lisa's throat. She didn't touch the skin. Instead, he held it and let it shine in her hand as if to show it off.

"And I didn't even have to say anything that time," said Amanda with a smile that cut across her face, glistening with red lipstick. "You catch on quick."

"They aren't part of this, come on, we can talk it out, what do you want from me?" said Shannon.

"From you? Nothing," Amanda answered. "I want *you* completely. You are coming with me and Colleen because we are all part of this. That's the deal. You failed to notice that you are in over your head, there is no going back. There will never be anything else for us now. Baby girl, we started this thing together and that's the way we're gonna play it."

"It doesn't have to be like this...we can use it for something else."

"We can have anything we want."

"Fine. I want none of this."

"That's not what I mean and you know it!"

Amanda's attention was solely on Shannon. Out of the corner of his eyes, Ralph caught glimpses of Steven and Kyle coming into the room from two different doors. They waited for Ralph's signal. Amanda wasn't holding the knife to Lisa's throat anymore. She felt it was a better idea to point and jab it at Shannon while they argued.

"People die all the time. It happens. It's the only thing we can *really* count on. Why not take a little capital in something so natural and let the living live? I mean *really* live? We can go anywhere, be anybody. The book is the answer to any question and problem."

Ralph looked at Kyle, then to Lisa, and then back to Kyle. Kyle understood and began to creep slowly up to the couch.

"That book is nothing but problems. Nothing is like it was and we are not the same. I felt so close to you once. You got under my skin and I loved it. But you aren't that girl anymore and honestly, I never want to use those powers again." Shannon trembled in her truth.

The room froze. Amanda's eyes bulged and seemed to give off light in rage. "I will make you eat those words, but first!" She took the knife and slammed it point down into wood backing of the sofa. Without any breathing space in between, Lisa snapped up, whirled around, climbed over the couch and took the knife in one fluid motion to face Kyle.

Kyle, shocked, started to back up with his hands raised. "Whoa, whoa, whoa, Lisa!" Kyle said in a raising crescendo. Lisa swung her arm up and in one swish, a spray of blood shot out of Kyle's arm. "Whoa, shit!" Lisa dropped the knife, reached up with her hands, grabbed hold of Kyle's head with both hands and brought down with a loud thud on her raised knee.

Now limp, Kyle was thrown against the wall like he was made of straw and slumped there, bleeding from his face. Dumped, broken and beaten, but still breathing. Without saying anything or even gasping for air, Lisa ran out of the house and into the surrounding woods, crashing through the trees like a rabid bear.

With a battle cry and the broken off leg of a table, Steven roared into the room looking only at Amanda. All that humiliation and embarrassment and revenge fantasy culminated into one boiling wild swing. His teeth looked sharpened. His brow was cocked up in a savage expression eager for the hunt.

Amanda coned her hands around her mouth and shouted, "Colleen! Now!"

Two floors up, Colleen yelled, "Cannonball!" and then she was heard crashing down through the ceiling. With a force that shook the house, she landed, feet spread, in a cloud of debris five feet in front of Steven. He kept charging ahead. Colleen opened her arms and said, "Yeah!" before jumping directly toward him. Her strength was greater and she tackled him to the ground.

Straddled on top of Steven, Colleen dug neon green polished, claw pointed nails into his chest. He screamed out in pain. "Come on, don't you like a little foreplay?" she laughed and cut gashes along his face with her right hand.

"Fuck with me again! I dare you!" said Amanda. "Now, take some time, think it over and get your shit together. You're having a party tonight at your house, come find me. And you," she said to Ralph. "Stay away from my girls while you still have people to lose and *maybe* I'll spare them."

Just then, the roar of the stolen blue Jeep stormed through the brush outside. "Colleen, that's our ride, time to go," said Amanda. She ran out of the front door without waiting.

"Aww, just when I was getting warmed up," said Colleen. She bent

334

forward and licked the cuts on Steven's face. Immediately, they started to burn and bubble a sickly yellow while he screamed with tears. Colleen dove head first through a window to join Shannon and Lisa in the Jeep. The car sped around the house once, the horn beeped and beeped, and then it was gone. Just gone.

****

The sun was below the horizon, but it was still early evening and so much had happened already. Watching Amanda and Colleen move with such malice and seeing Lisa play along without hesitation was pushing him over the edge. It was real, and he was up to his neck in the malevolence.

After the girls left, Ralph and Shannon carried Kyle and Steven to the road. They were hurt, but not enough so they couldn't move their feet and carry most of their weight.

"We got lucky, they could have just killed us all," said Shannon.

"Did you hear what she said? She talked about my 'feathery friends'. She's talking about the creatures from my dreams. She knows something is up," said Ralph.

"When I went to your house, I felt covered, hidden from her, especially in the treehouse. It was just a feeling, but she said she had a hard time finding me."

They reached the road and continued walking. Most cars passed by without care, some slowed down to look at them. Finally, one pulled over. A middle-aged woman wearing a cable-knit turtle neck sweater called through the rolled down window, "You kids weren't playing in that old house, were you? It's dangerous. I keep telling them to tear it down, but they never listen."

"Yeah, my friends had a dare, but it ended in an accident. Can you help us?" asked Ralph.

The woman sighed and made a face that said, *well, I've come this far, haven't I?* "Throw 'em in the back, I'll take 'em into town. You kids oughta know better, especially you, Shannon Kennedy, boys are trouble."

Kyle and Steven winced as they got into the back, but then relaxed into the seat cushions. "You all got lucky. I'll be seeing you," said the woman. She drove away with the boys.

"Do you know her? She knows you," said Ralph.

"No, but I think they'll be safe. I felt her out and she did mean to take them

336

to the hospital. She probably knows my dad. He and Amanda's dad are well-known around town and mentioning his daughter to clients wouldn't be a surprise…Oh, no, I didn't even think about it."

"What?"

"A party at my house, my dad will probably be back by now! What if they got to him? We need to go, now!" She turned and ran back to grab the bike. Ralph ran with her.

They raced back as fast as they could, but it was still a long ride. "Wait a minute," called Ralph in the rushing wind. "I think Amanda might be afraid of me, well, whatever *power* is working through me. She didn't touch me at all and just said stay away. They doesn't sound like her, right?"

"Right," Shannon called back. "Maybe that's why she just attacked those two and then ran away. But, can you use it? Can you control it?"

"I got an idea, we need to go to my treehouse." They detoured and made it to Ralph's house ten minutes later.

When they returned, Ralph found the note that Amanda mentioned nailed to the front door of his house. She knew they were there and they had no clue she got so close. It was a Polaroid photo with a message writing on a small piece of notepad paper. It read:

I got your girlfriend, she never did make it to piano lessons. If you want her, you can find her at the Witch's House. Don't try anything stupid, just you and Shannon come see if we can make a deal.

XOXO

Amanda & Colleen

Lisa was photographed in the back of the Jeep with her eyes closed sitting erect and blank faced.

Ralph carried it to the treehouse and set it down on the table. "I have to do something," he said. "But I think the only way is to use the game." He went to the GRX.

"I thought you said you were done with video games," said Shannon.

"I am. I think the power is *in* the game. I just have to get it out and wear it, or something." He fought with the GRX to get the *Mazer* cartridge out, but it wouldn't budge. It was as if it was welded to the system.

"Give me that," said Shannon. She took the white and purple GRX from him, lifted it above her head and smashed it on the floor. Ralph felt a twinge of pain to see it destroyed so quickly. Pieces of plastic and microchips scattered on the floor, but *Mazer* remained intact. Shannon scooped it off the floor and noticed the jagged tooth cartridge input on the bottom. Holding it started to burn her hands. She smiled despite the heat. "Too easy. Do you trust me?"

"No."

"You're gonna have to." She took his hand, placed it on the table palm up and raised the smoking cartridge above her head. She looked at Ralph who whistled at what was about to happen before nodding her on.

She slammed the game down hard into his hand and he screamed in pain instantly. Blood poured up and out of his hand as the cartridge dug into the flesh of its own volition. As his arm turned red, it crawled its bits and pieces through his veins like venom, jutting out and contorting the hand unnaturally. There was a sound of fresh cabbage leaves being ripped and light bulbs popping as his skin from the elbow down moved like boiling pasta sauce and neon orange, pink and blue lights flashed from within. In one loud snap Ralph was curled up on the floor. He breathed heavy, but stood up and didn't seem to be injured too badly.

Shannon, impressed by her quick solution, found she no longer had the strength to be surprised by these scenes anymore. Honestly, it was about par for the course. Ralph cradled his left arm. The scabbed flesh smoldered and sparks flew up in purple smoke, but it held and he did not feel pain. He stretched out his fingers and counted a few too many. Thumbs were now on both sides of a palm nearly twice the size with five long, strong fingers in between.

"Ralph, are you still in there?"

"Yes," he answered in a deeper, wider voice while his arm crackled. He held out the arm and flexed it a few times. The forearm could move at the elbow and the hand would open and close at his command. He looked around for something in the room, anything that would fit in his palm. A large book on the shelf caught his eye. He reached for it and when he held it, it started to burn instantly. He crushed it in a flash of fire and ash.

"Any pain?"

"No. In fact, I feel kinda good," said Ralph. His eye color had changed in one eye to a piercing gold with a dangerous gleam. Just the edge they needed. "Now, didn't Amanda say something about a party? Let's crash it! Let's grab that bitch by the throat and end this! All or nothin'!"

Without waiting for a reply, Ralph walked to the treehouse door and, instead of turning the handle, he blasted the door off the hinges in one open handed thrust. Shannon followed him out into the chilly night and without any words, they got into Shannon's dark green Volvo they'd stowed in the garage and headed for the party.

****

They parked the Volvo behind a line of cars that led up to the large, three-storied house in Shannon's well-manicured private neighborhood. Nearly all the lights were on and music could be heard out in the street.

"She has my dad tied up in his bedroom!" said Shannon. "I can feel him in there. We need to be careful. She's expecting us, but I doubt she'll make a scene right when we get in. If we can blend in, we might be able to grab my dad's gun without her noticing."

"Do you know where it is?" asked Ralph.

"Yeah, he showed me in case I ever needed to use it. Why don't you grab it?"

341

"Great, where is it?"

"Inside," Shannon said impatiently, quickening her pace up the walkway.

"Dumbass, I've never been here before. Use your words!"

Shannon stopped, stretched her fingers out, balled them into a fist and repeated to clench as she spoke. "I wanna try something I've been kicking around. I don't know if it will work, but I have a good feeling about it." She took a deep breath and thought to herself, Upstairs, down the hall, last door, first door on the left, blue shoebox. Upstairs, down the hall, last door, first door on the left, blue shoebox. Upstairs, down the hall, last door, first door on the left, blue shoebox. Keeping it on loop, she held Ralph's head on either side with a tight grip.

"Watch it, man-hands."

Upstairs, down the hall, last door, first door on the left, blue shoebox.

Her mind made the jump, but this time it was like she was carrying a triple locked briefcase. Her third eye opened within Ralph's headspace. She stood at an encampment in an endless desert holding the briefcase. The people, almost all of them looking like some version of Ralph's features, stared at her, but were not

342

alarmed. A small child that looked how Ralph must have appeared at five or six pointed towards the sky. Against a black sun, a large serpent flew with grace as if it were submerged in the clearest of waters.

It screamed at her as the shape in the sky grew larger, closer. She dropped the briefcase which flung open when it fell to the ground. Upstairs, down the hall, last door, first door on the left, blue shoebox. She closed her third eye.

"...first door on the left, blue shoebox. Upstairs, down the hall, last door, first door on the left, blue shoebox. What, what the hell?!" Ralph said as he pulled his head back from her grip. "Damn. Yeah! This is some really cool shit, I can actually *see* it!"

"Alright, in case we get separated somehow, you need to get my dad out," she said. Ralph nodded, still a little giddy after what just happened, and they headed for the front door. "Try to hide among the people and don't make a scene with that...thing."

"Got it." He took off his jacket and hung it from his crossed arms. It didn't burn his own skin, but anything it touched started to singe so he had to place the molten appendage under his other arm or the jacket might catch too fast. It made him look a bit dorky, but it was better than the alternative.

The front door opened not to pretty girls, well-dressed guys, jazzy colored lights and flashy dancing, but instead onto a high school shit show. Kids who overestimated their ability to hold their booze. Girls cried to each other and then cursed each other out without warning. Boys flexed unnecessarily, eager to fight anyone just to prove they had it in them.

Colleen was talking to a boy only slightly taller than her with wavy auburn hair, square shoulders and a tucked in white polo shirt. She was talking to Mikey, the boy who still hadn't let Shannon go. She twirled her hair and drank up the attention until she spotted Shannon.

"Shit, go," said Shannon. "Just go." She pushed Ralph towards the stairs, but it was too late for her. Mikey caught her arm and said, "Shannon? God, it feels like it's been so long. You look great! I, I've wanted to see you, to talk to you, but you're so hard to get ahold of these days. Amanda and Colleen, they said you'd be here, I was just about the leave, but Colleen keep talking and talking." He laughed, she did not. "What has been keeping you so busy, not another man, I hope!" He laughed again, and again she did not. "Come on, talk to me. Don't you miss me? Don't you miss *us*?"

"There never was 'us', Mikey. I wasn't yours just because you picked me and told other people we were dating," said Shannon. She could see he was hurt, but she didn't have time. "Look, I gotta go. You're a great guy, really, but trust me, I am *not* the girl for you. Just, leave me alone, okay?"

Without anything to say, he just watched her go up the stairs and out of view. Soon after though, a slender arm hooked itself around his elbow and whispered, "Come on, sugar, I'll give you someone to love."

Shannon saw Ralph had found his way into the master bedroom as the door was open for her. Inside, she let out a little yelp when she saw her father. Mr. Kennedy, tied up to the bed at the ankles and wrists, held a half-lidded stare and moved with drunken mannerisms. From what she could see, he was naked under the disheveled sheets.

"Shannon!" he said with exhausted excitement. "You have the breast," he hiccupped. "I mean, best friends! So kind and gentle to an old man like me." He laughed a little and hiccupped again. Shannon started to untie him.

Ralph returned to the room with the revolver in hand. It was loaded, so he carefully pointed it at the floor with his right hand. "I think he'll live. Are you good?"

Shannon's father fell back onto his bed and gave that same goofy laughter. "Yeah, I think he's okay. I don't know exactly what she did to him, but it looks like he'll be fine." He fell asleep and started to snore. "You know how to use that thing?"

"...Sure."

Shannon gave Ralph a look and said, "All we need to do now is..."

A blood-curdling scream erupted through the music and voices. The party held its breath for a moment, and then chaos ensued. Leaving her father still asleep in bed, Shannon and Ralph made their way through the mess of people, half leaving, half crowded around the source. The monstrosity they found in the kitchen made Ralph's hand look like a paper cut.

Mikey, alive and breathing not five minutes ago, was stretched out on the floor with his chest broken open. Sitting with his head on her lap, Colleen held a large

346

kitchen knife in her shaking hand. Blood coated her skin from her finger tips down to her elbows and splashed across her chest. Red covered hands ripped a no longer beating heart out of the gaping hole in Mikey's chest. It was attached with the necessary tubing of arteries but she kept crying out and pulling at it, pumping more blood onto the floor and filling out a deep red abyss that pushed people farther out of the room. The toxic smell of newly spilled blood and vomit rushed up Shannon's nose to her brain and adrenaline fueled her instantly.

Acting like a school of fish, the party crowd attempted to flee the scene as one. It didn't work. People were shoved against walls, tackled down and tripped over. Clothing was torn and bone smacked flesh in their mad dash. When Ralph thought they were all gone, he heard the soft cries of a girl stuck on the floor claiming her legs were broken.

Shannon lunged for Colleen, but was stopped by Ralph's grip on her arm. He redirected her attention. Coming from the adjoining room to the left, a pair of fiery red heels stepped onto the blood and walked across the spill. Amanda was calm as a Buddhist monk as she walked to

Colleen and caressed her head in her hands, giving her a little peck on her blood-spattered forehead.

"You don't deserve him, you never did!" said Colleen, coughing up tears. "It didn't matter if you ignored him, he only wanted you and you only wanted to run away with *her*. Look what she made me do! You don't deserve anything you're given!" She touched her and his foreheads together for a moment, and then looked back up. "She said she knew how I could have his heart. I didn't mean…I didn't want…"

"He had nothing to do with this and you know it!" Shannon shouted at Amanda.

"I know it," Amanda said smugly. "He had nothing to do with this. But, she thought different. What a girl wants is what a girl needs."

Colleen let out a low, guttural sob hearing this from Amanda. In that wretched, infantile cry, Ralph could tell that on some level she knew how far she'd gone. She knew, then, she could never go back. None of this could go back. He looked to Shannon and saw that she was crying. Slowly and silently, tears trickled down her cheeks.

"So, have you considered my offer? Ohhhh, we will make such a good pair."

Amanda's voice had changed. It had become deeper and filled listeners' ears with a smooth, velvety touch. She reached down between Colleen's arms towards Mikey's heart and plucked it out with a juicy snap. Without breaking eye contact with Shannon, she raised the heart in cheers and then drank from it spilling blood down her chin. The room was silent. Ralph could only think, just like the game.

"Colleen, cutie pie, can you hear me?" she spoke softly into her ear. Between sobs, Colleen manager to let out a puny, defeated, 'uh-huh'. "Good," Amanda hushed. She snaked her hand down to Colleen's and took the knife from it. "Now, you will feel *nothing*." Amanda pulled the knife above Colleen's chest. With a brutish strength in a hasty downward motion, Amanda forced the knife right through Colleen's chest. Inside, she twisted the knife forty-five degrees. With her pain erased and her life slipping quickly, Colleen's mouth opened in surprise but not even a single breath escape. She knew wat was coming and welcomed it. Amanda pulled out the knife with a forceful jerk, veins bulging unnaturally out of her pale white arm, and Colleen went limp. A dead corpse held by a dead corpse held by a would-be prom queen.

"Mmmmmmm," said Amanda. She let a slow sly smile spread onto her face. "You have no idea how this feels…it's like an orgasm that starts at your toes and steadily sends electric tremors up your legs and body till it hits the top of your head and blows your brains out." She closed her eyes and shivered a little. "Every time it gets louder and makes me stronger!"

"Colleen was too reckless to keep around, too unstable. It's best that we kill her and take her power now before things really get movin'. You see Shannon, baby, I'm not a horrible person, I just know what people want."

Ralph didn't even take the time to aim. He lifted the gun and pulled the trigger in Amanda's direction. Wood cracked on the cabinets behind her from the bullet that caught her flesh near the middle of her neck to shoulder. She didn't even flinch. She locked eyes with him, walked forward slowly and said, "You missed. Now dropped the gun."

At first, he hesitated. But then, his left arm snatched the gun out of his right and threw it to the floor. That arm reached out to Amanda and in a voice of flames and tribal howls and sacred power, Ralph began chanting unknown incantations in short, sharp syllables not heard in hundreds of years. At once, both the girls fell to the ground and writhed in pain. Covering their ears was useless and their skin began to shift and burn from below the surface.

Ralph was shocked at the result and pulled himself out of the trance momentarily. Amanda saw her opportunity and in a red flash, she dove towards him. His left arm pushed against the wall and forced him to the ground out of the way. Amanda missed and then disappeared. They didn't hear or see any more than a scream before she vanished in a cloud of red mist. In her speed, the spilled blood leapt from the floor and splattered the entire kitchen.

Shannon, her ears ringing, called out, "We have to stop her!" Her eyes were blood shot and she looked like she had aged ten years in thirty days. "I got a glimpse of her plan. She's going home to complete something, something bad, something she needs Lisa's body for."

"Then we need to go now," said Ralph.

Again, in silence, the pair got in to Shannon's Volvo and drove to destroy Amanda Klein. The radio was still on, but neither complained. They listened to help them focus for the coming fight. Monica, the music maven, spoke, "...warm up to a chilly forty-two degrees tomorrow. And that's not all, no way. I want all you listeners out there to look out your windows into the sky and see what I'm seein'. Here's a hint with a classic, a personal favorite…"

In a slow, solemn ballad, Ella Fitzgerald sang of lonely heartbreak under a blue moon.

****

Bloodied, betrayed and bewitched, Shannon and Ralph parked the car down the road a little ways from Amanda's mansion of a home. It was brightly lit and, like the siren's call of a bug lamp, it beckoned them. "Okay," said Shannon when she turned the car off. "I'm through with trying to reach her. She's a wrecking ball and I can't let anyone else get hurt. I'll try to distract her so you can get Lisa out of there. That's all you need to do, just get her out of there," she spoke into her lap. She looked like she had been dragged out of a fashion show and thrown onto the street, but she wasn't giving up the fight yet.

"She's *your* girlfriend," said Ralph. Shannon turned her big eyes to him. Instead of retorting angrily or physically, she stayed silent. Black eyes on the precipice of tears engrossed him. "Sorry. You would know best."

"What was with that *voice*?" she asked.

"It came out of nowhere right when she tried to control me. I felt cold hands go through my eyeballs and into my brain, but then everything inside ignited and before I knew what was happening, I had her on the floor screaming. When I realized it is when it stopped."

"It's a good thing you did. I was in just as much pain. Use that only when we have no other option or, you know, she *gets* me." She didn't like the idea of that, so she changed up the question. "What about that hand?"

Ralph held up the hand. Inflamed lumps cluttered the still smoldering limb. "It protected me when I didn't react fast enough. I can trust it...I think. What's your plan?"

"I'm not sure yet, but let's try to get the two forces close to each other. I think if you grab her with that hand and talk her into submission, we'll have a chance."

"I like that. I feel...excited? My body is burning, thirsty for the fight." Shannon noticed then that both of his eyes had turned that piercing gold and even his facial features seemed sharper and far from his old, boyish looks. He turned away from her stare and looked out into the night. "Ha, that's what she was talking about. Wasn't the full moon the other day? Has it changed at all?" he asked. Shannon looked through the windshield and saw that the moon was indeed full, defiantly so, stuck in the cycle. "That doesn't surprise me. Anyway, we ready for this?"

"Yeah, fuck it," said Shannon gravely. "Things can only get worse, right?"

"That's all they've been doing." Ralph got out of the car and shut the door slowly behind him. Shannon did the same. They edged along the side of the yard cautiously, staying in the shadows. "So how do you wanna go about this, right through the front door again?"

"No, that's just foolish. Maybe there's a way to surround her. When we snuck out of the house, we would climb out of her window and down the side on vine gratings, but...ah, shit, she would think of that. There has to be another way in."

"Can't you fish around in her head? Find a weakness or something?"

She tried. "I, I can't do it here. It's like this whole area is blocking me." She looked directly at the house and had to shade her eyes against the glaring lights. "It's like there is all this white noise coming out from it...come on, let's look around a bit. But be careful, alright? I don't want you blowing this for us."

"You and yours got us into this, sister, so don't point the finger at me."

"Me and mine didn't get your neighbors killed and your friends attacked, *you* did."

"You and yours did exactly that! They captured Lisa for bait and lured us into that trap, so you can just shut your little wench mouth and..."

BARK!

"Shit, the dog! How did I forget the dog?" Shannon grabbed Ralph's good arm and bolted to the back yard away from the barking. They tried to stay in the shadows, but in a sprint they were exposed sporadically. They made their way around the house, but not fast enough. A large, dark shape that didn't reflect but absorbed the light growled at them before they heard a shift and push as the dog leapt into the air at them. Shannon saw the black shape was no longer just a dog but a creature that had a jaw that stretched double the normal length and its paws…it's furry *hands*…had thumbs that reached around with fingers long enough to grab hold of something.

Its sharp teeth caught her defending arm and she felt rows of ragged teeth rip at the skin before it was tackled to the side. Ralph snatched him out of the air with his left arm and held him high above his head. In the moonlight, the dog kicked and clawed at Ralph, but the engorged, burning arm extended it out of reach and squeezed the neck with sizzling pressure. The neck broke with a loud CRUNCH and the dog fell to the ground to lay still and lifeless on the lawn.

Shannon moved around Ralph to get a look at the crumpled beast. This was not Brinley, the family dog. This was not something to play fetch with. This was something that killed and devoured and belonged at Hades' gates. She turned her attention to Ralph and was startled at his face. He breathed heavily thought a slight smirk looking down at the dead animal.

With no comment, she got closer to the dog. "I'm gonna see what I can find." She didn't even have to try this time. It was like whistling. She just opened her mind and moved it into the dead dog to search for clues. She got flashes and slow-moving memories like a camera filming in a storm, but she could piece it together. Amanda did this. She used the book that they swore never to use again after the first time to turn the once lovable Saint Bernard into a hound from hell. She killed the cats for a blood sacrifice and then fed the enchanted remains to the animal. She knew they were coming…she always knew.

"Will that work?" Ralph asked pointing to the basement storm doors.

"Those doors lead into the basement, I wanted to get around the house to get her from both sides."

"You're using logic and strategy right now? This shit is insane, right now! I wouldn't be surprised if caskets rose out of the ground and the dead started attacking us!" He went for the doors.

"Keep it together! We can do this! We *have* to do this! She's powerful, but she isn't bullet proof. You already shot her once." She went after him. "Maybe this is a good idea. It wasn't what I would have thought of, so maybe she didn't think about it and if we keep winging it she won't see us coming, right?"

Ralph stopped at the doors and said, "We are gonna die here. Tonight." He grabbed the door handle with his left hand and ripped it right off the hinges. "It's too bad I jerk off with my left hand. Damn I'm strong, but this shit is not cool." Ralph smiled lightly at her before descending into the basement. She shook her head and went down after him.

It was dark, dank and the linoleum floor stuck at each step. It smelled of gasoline and laundry detergent. "I can feel her," Shannon whispered. "She's upstairs in the living room. Okay, I think I have a plan. When we get up there, I want you to sneak around while I distract her."

"What am I, bait? What are you gonna do?"

"I'm gonna talk to her, make it look like I'm giving her what she wants."

"Yeah, great idea. Just talk to her. Why didn't I think of that?" Even in the dark, Shannon could pick up on his rolling eyes. "Whatever, you want the gun?"

"No, she'll know if I have it. Anyway, I have one more trick I want to try." She took his right hand and placed it on her forehead. Vibrations went up his arm and into his skull. Pressure increased pulse by pulse until he thought he could take no more. At one instance, he felt his head ring and ring like a madman hammering a bell, and he thought it would crack open from the inside like a bird hatching. The fire grew inside him. But, the moment passed when Shannon pulled her head back and broke the physical connection.

She broke the physical connection, but a psychic thoroughfare took its place. Instead of his skull erupting, a harmonic voice replaced the pain and the two were consciously conjoined. It wasn't disorienting, but it was terrifyingly liberating and empowering to be both in one's and the other's shoes in separated symbiosis.

It was a hormonal cascade akin to the highest of criminal or sexual rushes. "I know the whole house! I can see everything!" Ralph said a few decibels above a whisper. Silently she agreed, and he felt it.

They crept up the stairs with Ralph in the lead. He was sure of himself in their collective security. He opened the door slowly and edged along the wall to the left, heading towards the far side of the house. She took a right, going straight for the lair of the witch. It was silent on the main floor except for the crackling of a large fire in the living area. Then, the silence got broken by a deep, buttery voice, "Helloooo,

Shannon!" That last word cut through her like a knife and she froze with one leg in the air. "I know you're there, why don't you come in, make yourself at home, grab a drink…Let's talk, shall we?"

Shannon didn't have to look over her shoulder to know that Ralph was quickly moving undetected. *Fuckin' winging it,* she thought to herself. She relaxed a little and walked down the hall, around the corner and stepped down into the living room to face Amanda.

Amanda Klein sat in the middle of a large white sofa that faced the open doorway. She was still dressed as she was for the party, but there was not a speck of blood on her and her hair was marvelous. On the coffee table in front of her, little Lisa Meadows was laid out, breathing unnaturally fast. Her shirt was torn open and her chest adorned with finger painted hexes in blood.

Shannon walked towards her slowly, making eye contact but also taking in her surroundings with her peripheral vision. *Fire pokers, end table, ash-tray, high heels…dammit, there nothing here,* she thought.

Still moving forward, still wingin' it, she sat down on the opposite sofa and noticed the wound on Amanda's shoulder. Pink, gooey flesh like freshly spit bubblegum covered the recently ripped open gash on her shoulder. Amanda drank a luminescent purple liquid out of a bulbous wine glass, poured some in Lisa's open mouth and then offered it to Shannon.

"Wanna party?"

"No thanks."

"Don't worry, it isn't alcohol, but *damn* if it isn't still intoxicating on a whole new dimension of sensations!" She took another healthy gulp from the glass. "Found it in the book and decided to whip it up. It's a home remedy to help me with the damage from our little scuffle." She pointed to her pink scar. "You really out to try it, it is quite something."

Shannon stared at Lisa for a solid minute, saddened at the sight before Amanda interrupted her. "Like the new issue of the book?" she asked proudly. Shannon looked around the sofa she sat on and found something utterly breathtaking. Among a small pile of magazines to her right, Amanda had in her possession an issue of Cosmopolitan with her on the cover. Dressed in the very red dress that she was wearing, Amanda struck a sexy, smiley pose with headlines surrounding her.

'Eternal Beauty Can Be Yours In These 5 Easy Steps!' and '7 Ways To Get Him To Do Exactly What You Say!' and last but not least, 'The Perfect Murder: A How To Guide From Amanda Klein'.

'You're not yourself," said Shannon trying to keep a cool temper. "Ever since that book...no, ever since you got back from Germany, you..."

"What?" Amanda interrupted. "Change from the girl that you fell in love with to something devious, twisted and utterly vile?" Shannon said nothing. "I know why you're here, Mzzz Kennedy. You want to kill me for what I've don't, right? So immoral I've become that I am comparable to a dog that needs to be put down, *right*? For what, so you can stop the spread of evil or something as noble and contrived? Ahhh, no. You just want revenge. Plain and simple." Shannon let the breath out of her mouth in surprise. "Took the words right out of your mouth, didn't I? Ahh, the book *never* lies!"

Shannon was puzzled for a moment, but then she started to put the pieces together. "Now you're getting it," Amanda said with sparkling eyes. She took another swig from the glass and feed some more to Lisa, it was about a quarter full now. "Colleen didn't see it coming, but she played right into my hand, although it wouldn't have been hard for me. Colleen was stupid, Shannon, we both knew it. She took a little umph, though, needed to be softened up a little. But, hell, two kills for the price of one, that ain't bad! To tell you the truth, I wasn't sure if it was gonna to work. I wasn't sure if we were even mortal anymore."

Shannon was starting to see a larger picture unfold and it was gruesome. Being this close to Amanda, she could feel her more. She pressed against the intangible walls rotating around her brain and in one instant she felt an opening and took it. WHOOSH! She jumped through to the other side, saw one breadth, and then, like she was never there, she was kicked out.

"Hey now, can't have you seeing everything just yet, but I think you get the drift."

"It couldn't all fit into one person, not one *human*," said Shannon as if she were reciting a passage from memory. "That's why there were three…and now this girl…" She sorrowfully looked down on Lisa.

Amanda made a gun out of her left pointer and thumb, slowly lowered the aim down to Shannon and pulled the imaginary trigger. She set the nearly empty glass on the table and stretched her arms across the back of the sofa in a lounging position. "We've attracted too much attention to ourselves lately, we need to change things up, and this little nobody here is our ticket out. No Colleen, just you and me sharing one body as one person, bound in complete harmony. And then we take it on the road and honey, we are gonna show them some shit they ain't never seen before! Now, hubba hubba hubba, who do you love?"

"No."

"What do you mean, 'No'? You're gonna do this."

"No."

Amanda put her head down and signed. "I would be lying if I told you I didn't want you to see this. It was such a gas to put together!" She lifted a remote control and started a tape on the widescreen TV across the room. It was the security tape from the convenience store that they took.

Shannon couldn't believe it. "This tape was broken. I remember I…" Amanda hushed her so they could watch the events unfold. They watched in black and white as Shannon Kennedy walked up to the store clerk and pulled a gun out of a hooded sweatshirt pocket. The clerk hesitated and started to hand the money over. He finished, and the tape jumped. The Shannon Kennedy on the tape was laughing and laughing as she shot him again and again at point blank range decimating his body against the back counter in bullets. Ignoring the money on the counter, this imposter emptied the gun on him. The body of the clerk slumped in a mess of blood and flesh and then this Shannon Kennedy faced directly into the camera and grinned a painfully large grin. The tape skipped and then proceeded to repeat itself.

Amanda clapped enthusiastically. "Ohhhh, you go girl!" She whistled at the TV. "You come with me or the police get this tape and I promise your father will suffer for this too, why do you think we left him alive?" Amanda's grin mirrored the ghost Shannon Kennedy's from the tape. Feeling the opening from the level of distraction, Ralph came into the room from behind her and aimed the gun's barrel at her head. Shannon looked over at him and in an instant their element of surprise was lost. Without turning around and without breaking composure, Amanda said, "I wouldn't bother, it isn't loaded."

Ralph stopped at this. Amanda stretched it out a moment longer. "Don't believe me? Pull the trigger."

In their psychic connection, Shannon could feel that Ralph was still in control but just playing dumb. He switched the gun to his left hand and crushed it in a fiery explosion he was impervious to.

Enraged, Amanda slid back and over the couch in a crimson slither and was on him in an instant. With her speed, she toppled him down and cackled as she pulled his arms away from his face despite the burning his left arm caused her. Long sharp teeth came out of a smile sliced into her face as she inched towards his neck. Her eyes burned with a wickedness so passionate, so focused, it was palpable. He felt her teeth begin to puncture his neck and that was when the fire ignited.

His whole body took on the texture of his left arm as the ancient, eldritch words boomed from his throat. Amanda let her grip go to cover her ears in futile hope as she wailed with the sound of glass shattering. He persisted and watched her face take on a severe, disfigured visage as it bubbled and dropped and tore open.

Shannon covered her ears the instant she heard Ralph's voice, but she felt no pain. Their connection. It protected her! She looked to Lisa and found that she was not so lucky.

Lisa jerked awake on the table and flailed her limbs in agony. She jumped up, ran across the room and leapt through the window. Shannon saw he run off into the woods away from the house.

In the horrendous roar of forbidden magic and witchy caterwauling, Shannon grabbed the wine glass from the table, rushed over to Amanda and slammed the base of it through the side of her. The broken glass went more than two inches into her throat and she stopped moving. Ralph stopped the chanting and shoved Amanda off him, tossing her like a doll through the air to plop on the floor with a hard thud.

He got to his feet and walked over to her glowing with the fire that had spread throughout his body, emitting a cloud of black smoke around him. "She's not dead," he said.

"Listen, she isn't breathing. There's no way she could survive that," said Shannon.

"I'm telling you, she isn't dead!"

"I killed her! She's not brea…"

A low, husky cough like a cat hacking up a fur ball came from Amanda. She spit out shards of glass in a puddle of blood and shouted through eviscerated vocal chords, "Burn! Burn! Burn!"

Shannon and Ralph felt the whole house take a deep breath and when it exhaled, flames spread around the room like napalm in waiting.

"I told you!" Ralph shouted over the spreading fire and Amanda's cursing. "She's not fucking dead!" He gripped his hands together and started to slam his fist down on her like raining boulders of fire. After five crushes, Ralph stopped. Shannon looked at the crumbled body and saw the head was demolished.

The house was now heaving like an accordion. "Leave! Now!" Ralph shouted.

Shannon went to leave, but turned back to call to him, "Ralph, come on!" He was unable to get up and his hands stretched towards the large puddle of blood Amanda's body swam in. Like mosquito-sponges, his arms began to sop up the blood and fill his body. Soon, his arms doubled in size and the rest of the body grew as well. His rough, burnt flesh began to darken and the cloud around him turned darker and denser. Shannon could feel their telepathic link dwindling and that was when she knew. They were doomed, they both knew it, but going together granted an unexpected peace.

At the limit, Ralph's body took no more and burst like a watermelon with an air hose jammed into it. Burning bits of flesh went everywhere in the thriving fire.

Shannon hobbled to the front door, ripped it open and, for one instant, saw the full moon framed in the doorway. In the next, the fire caught hold of the fresh air flow and explosion kicked her out the front door with such force that it broke nearly half the bones in her body. Before she crashed to the ground, killed by the impact, she felt her mind drift away to the memory of a certain sweaty spring afternoon.

****

The house burned down faster and faster in vibrant red flames. The closest neighbor wouldn't see the fire for another two hours and by then it was far gone, just a smoldering ruin cloaked in fire. But in that time, a very short girl with jet black hair, ragged clothes and blood on her came out from the woods behind the house. Did the heat simply draw her in? Was there a spiritual tugging that brought her here? Nobody knows. And nobody knows that in the backyard, well away from the burning house, she found a sparkling red dress and shoes to match laid out waiting for her.

Without question, she put them on. "Like a glove," she said in a voice she had never spoken before. She was refreshed by the dress, cleaned of any injuries or blood on her body. She breathed in the cool night and watched the house fire with indifference through piercing gold eyes, and then, she turned around and disappeared back into the woods.

About the Author

Christopher finds some of his best, most impactful conversations are with books. Raised in the Pennsylvania woodlands, the outdoors call to him in sacred whispers to contemplate the stories he's read and tales he's spinning. He works to fill his writing with high-energy, comedic fun, human insight, and deep, dark imagination.

When he's not writing, he enjoys practicing and producing music, watching horror films with a fervent, academic eye and getting lost in a crowd while traveling alone. Make sure to visit Christopher online at www.ink-smith.com and don't forget to leave a review on Goodreads and Amazon!

Want more? Listen to the Suburban Legend EP soundtrack for free at youtube.com and bandcamp.com!